To Brian.

from G

(Gary M-......)

GW00546571

By the same author:

Belfast Girls

Danger Danger

Angel in Flight:
the first Angel Murphy thriller

Angel in Belfast:
the 2nd Angel Murphy thriller

Cover main photo & design: Raymond McCullough

WWI photo: Wikipedia: Public domain image resources

Johnny McClintock's War

*One man's struggle against
the hammer blows of life*

Gerry McCullough

Published by

Precious Oil
PUBLICATIONS
www.preciousoil.com/publications

ISBN 13: 978-0 9929432 0 2

ISBN 10:   09929432 0 5

First published **2014**

10a Listooder Road, Crossgar,
Downpatrick, Northern Ireland BT30 9JE

'He who would valiant be,
'Gainst all disaster ...'
John Bunyan, *The Pilgrim's Progress*

'I was at peace and He broke me asunder ...'
Job 16 v.13

Thanks to my husband, Raymond, for cover design, editing, proof-reading and general encouragement.

Chapter One

John Henry McClintock met Rose Flanagan when she was sixteen, and he a year or so older.

They met at a tent mission, which is a gospel meeting in a large tent. It was in a field miles from anywhere, in County Down, in the depths of Ireland.

It was a soft, warm summer night. Music poured from the lighted tent as John Henry drew nearer to it. He was one of a large crowd of people, stepping cautiously through the long grass at the field's edge – soon to be trampled flat by the hordes of visitors – and trying, not always successfully, to avoid the still wet sticky cow pats laid down that day, and the big purple thistles which grew everywhere.

The huge dirty beige tent, which looked dull by daylight but now, in the gathering darkness, shone out as a bright focus of warmth and good fellowship, had no ribbons or other decorations. There was only a cardboard placard set up at the entrance giving the times and the dates of other meetings, in bright red against a whitey-yellow background, with the name of the speaker in a bold dark green. There was a similar placard attached to the gate at the entrance to the field, where a blossoming hawthorn hedge spread its white, sweet-smelling flowers close enough almost, but not quite, to obliterate the writing.

John Henry hadn't seen Rose yet. He had gone along to the tent with friends of his own age, just as she had done a few minutes earlier. A tent mission was one of the free entertainments on offer in Ireland, in these days just before the First World War. You could be sure of meeting a large crowd of young people, who would seldom be gathered together in one place otherwise.

They pushed into the tent, nudging each other and whispering.

'There's Annie Kilpatrick! She's a whizzer!'

'Get off my toe, you great lump!'

'Aw – sorry, Tommy! Hey, there's Sadie Wilson with Geordie Milligan! Didn't know they were walking out!'

'Pity – she's a lovely girl!'

John Henry listened in amusement, but didn't contribute much. He liked his friends, Tommy, Willie and wee Artie, but he sometimes wondered how much he had in common with them. They had all left school early and had shown no reluctance to do so. John Henry himself had done the same, but not by his own choice.

When John Henry had left school at the age of fourteen, a few years before, it had been at his father's insistence, in spite of his evident ability. And in spite of the desire of his teacher that he should stay on, even try for teacher training eventually (the idea of university an impossible dream in the minds of most).

The master of the local Church of Ireland school in the village, Michael Patrick Fyfe, was a descendent of the French Huguenots who had come to those parts a couple of centuries ago, driven out from their homeland by persecution, and had brought their linen making skills with them. Fyfe was a clever man who deserved to be doing more than teaching in a village school. He felt this particularly when a pupil who should have achieved much more was forced to leave by his family's desire that he should go out and earn his living.

In John Henry's case he had felt it so strongly that he'd called round with the boy's father to make his protest.

Fyfe rehearsed in his mind what he would say as he knocked on the door of the three storied house beside the church grounds. He could see that the house had once been an impressive building. Tall, built in grey stone, it was covered nearly up to its second story in sweet smelling rambling roses. And the garden spread around it on all sides, neglected and overgrown with nettles and thistles now, had clearly at one time been a pleasure to see. The owners had obviously gone downhill, and the house with them. He knew that Douglas McClintock, John Henry's father, was a widower, and had heard that he drank. Maybe that was where the money for house repairs went to.

Fyfe, who was a small, thin man, still young and unsure of himself, wondered again if he was doing the right thing. Would his intervention make any difference? He took in the scent of the pink roses growing beside the door as he waited apprehensively, listening for the sound of approaching footsteps inside.

The door opened at last in response to his repeated knocks, and a tall dark haired man with a craggy face peered out at him.

'Mr McClintock?' Fyfe said nervously. 'I'm Michael Fyfe, the village school-master. I'd like a word with you about your son John Henry.'

'What's the wee skitter been up to now?' roared McClintock. He made no effort to open the door wider or to invite Michael in.

'No, no, it's not that he's in any trouble,' the schoolmaster said hastily. 'Far from it. He's a first rate scholar. That's why I'd like to suggest that you allow him to stay on for another year or two and eventually take his teaching certificate. I know you've said you want him to leave at the end of the school year, next month, but I really think it'd be a crying shame. A waste of the boy's ability. He could do so much more with his life.'

McClintock's face, which had been growing red with anger as he listened to his visitor, began to swell up alarmingly. Fyfe noticed in apprehension that he carried a strong blackthorn stick in his right hand. As he stopped leaning on this stick and raised it threateningly, Fyfe took a hasty step back. McClintock advanced on him.

'I'll be the one who says what my son should do with his life!' McClintock roared. He pushed his red swollen face so close to Fyfe that the schoolmaster could smell his rotten breath, an unpleasant reek of onions and alcohol. 'Don't come round here again telling me what to do with my own! I say it's time the lad got out and earned his living, and that's the end of it!'

The young schoolmaster jumped back out of reach of the blackthorn stick, just managing not to trip over the crumbling front doorstep, and the heavy wooden door slammed in his face. He tottered away down the village street, thankful to have escaped unmolested. He was very sorry for John Henry. But he was quite clear that there was nothing more he could do for him.

So John Henry had taken a low-skilled, and low paid, job in a linen factory, and was now contributing to the family income, like his older brother and sister, and helping to support his younger sister. To his father's great satisfaction.

John Henry was philosophical about it, but he wanted quite fiercely to get out of the linen factory, to do something that mattered with his life. He knew his abilities – his quickness to learn and to understand. He had been top of his class by a mile every year since he first started in the small local school. He wanted to make use of the intelligence he had been given.

Rose Flanagan was also working, as nearly everybody of their age and social class was; helping, mainly in the kitchen, at a nearby farm, fortunate in that she had been able to find work near her home and could return to her father's cottage most nights.

She'd got the job through the good offices of her parish priest, Father Donnelly, who knew her father well and who still thought of Rose as a sweet, innocent child, one he was glad to help. Her new employers, the Reillys, owned a small farm and were currently looking for more assistance, since their former kitchen girl had moved away to the

3

other side of County Down when she married recently. By recommending Rose, Father Donnelly knew he was helping the Reillys, also parishioners of his, as well as helping Rose's father who could do with the extra income Rose would bring in. And, of course, he was earning the gratitude of the pretty wee girl herself. All good, Father Donnelly told himself.

'You'll work hard for these good people, won't you, my dear?' he said to Rose, giving her a toothy smile.

'Oh, certainly, Father,' Rose answered. She wished Father Donnelly would stop stroking her arm. However, her father was there, so it was safe enough. Rose wouldn't have liked to be on her own with Father Donnelly. She'd heard stories.

Annie Reilly was a kind, motherly woman, and although the work was hard, Rose enjoyed it well enough. She was used to working hard. Her mother had been a bit of an invalid in the years before she died, and since her death Rose had carried the burden of the household work at home. The work at the Reillys' farm wasn't much worse.

It was her friend Mary McCartney who'd suggested going to the tent meeting.

'There'll be lots of talent, Rose. I heard Frankie Murphy and his pals are going. They think it'll be a laugh, see? I really fancy Frankie, Rose! And you know rightly that his pal Peter O'Rouke fancies you, girl! Peter was asking me if you and me might be going. Let's tell them we'll join in and go with them!'

'I don't think we should go just for a laugh, Mary. And what if we get into trouble? They might not like people from our church going.'

'Not at all! The poster says, "All Welcome!" So they want us, see?'

'I think it might be interesting, Rose,' put in Maggie Kilmore. 'I've never been to a Protestant meeting. I'd like to know what they say that's so different. And I heard the preacher was a Jesuit before he left it. I was wondering if he'd tell us why he left. That would be interesting, too.'

And Peggy McCracken, a schoolmate of Rose's since early childhood, had also been eager to go, and said, shaking back her red hair, 'Ach, come on, Rose! It won't be any fun without you!'

'Oh, all right, then,' Rose agreed at last. But not without a lingering worry.

The girls met up with Frankie Murphy and a few other boys by arrangement at the field gate, and made their way across the rough grass, avoiding the cow pats and the stinging nettles until they reached the tent door.

They and the boys went in together, greeted at the flapping doorway of the tent by a beaming, friendly man, with a red, wrinkled face, who had lost most of his hair. This man was holding out sheets with the words of the choruses, and the huge crowd had already begun to sing, as a warm-up to the meeting proper.

A group of boys whom Rose had never seen before were entering at the same time as Rose and her friends. As the two groups stood near to each other at the door of the tent, taking the sheets in turn from the friendly man, John Henry and Rose each noticed the other. Rose saw a tall, well built boy with dark hair falling over his pale face, and a sweet smile which switched on, as if instinctively, as he caught her eye.

John Henry saw a small, slim, and very pretty girl, with light brown hair, blue grey eyes, and a perfect complexion. Roses and cream, he thought, thinking of one of his favourite songs, *The Mountains of Mourne*. There was a bright intelligence in her eye as she glanced in his direction which attracted him even more than her looks. They were strangers, but through the mind of each went the fleeting thought, *Perhaps – not for long?*

Chapter Two

They went on in, and found places with their own friends, in different parts of the tent.

'This is daft, Johnny!' hissed John Henry's closest friend Tommy Maguire. Tommy was tall for his age with an attractive boyish face, smooth sandy hair and very bright blue eyes. He never had any problem getting off with girls. 'What the heck are we doing here?'

'Well, it wasn't my idea!' said Willie Morgan on Tommy's other side. His freckled face was one large grin at the idea, as he wriggled his fat, overweight body in the hard seat, trying to get more comfortable.

'Or mine!' retorted John Henry.

'It must have been yours, then, Artie!' said Tommy, nudging the small, dark haired boy beside him. Artie, the usual butt of the group, flushed bright red.

'I just thought it might be fun, Tommy!' he protested. ' See, just look round you. What about that for talent?'

Tommy looked round. Yeah, there were lots of girls, some of them quite pretty.

'Got a point there, Artie,' he admitted grudgingly, sweeping his hand back over his smooth, sandy coloured hair, as always held down by hair pomade. 'Not a bad idea, old man.'

Artie flushed again, but this time in delight at being praised by Tommy and addressed as 'old man'. The youngest of the group, he was constantly running to catch up with the others, and trying hard to seem as sophisticated as his idol Tommy.

Gradually the singing drew to a close, and the meeting opened.

The speaker was a gifted orator.

'Friends,' he began, in a soft, gentle voice, 'you all know that there's someone out there. Someone who made you. Someone who loves you.'

A collective sigh went round the tent. John Henry stirred uncomfortably. He didn't much want to be moved by this man, to respond. He was only here for a bit of fun, for company.

The speaker went on, 'Yes, friends, it was St Patrick who first opened our eyes, as Irishmen and women, to the presence of God in all nature. But St Paul said it before him, and David said it in his psalms, the songs he wrote from his shepherd's heart, "The Heavens declare the glory of God!" '

The speaker's voice grew louder, more emphatic. John Henry's attention wandered.

For a few moments he was back in his very early teens, experiencing again the wonder of the beauty of the earth in springtime. The freshness of early morning. The pink and white of the apple blossom all around. The still nights. The feeling of something – something. A presence that was trying to speak to him – which he longed, but was afraid, to listen to.

When he came back to the here and now, the speaker was quoting the Irish poet Joseph Plunkett, the young Christian Brother who had recently joined the republican movement.

> *'I see his blood upon the rose*
> *And in the stars the glory of his eyes.*
> *His body gleams amid eternal snows,*
> *His tears fall from the skies.*
>
> *I see his face in every flower;*
> *The thunder and the singing of the birds*
> *Are but his voice – and carven by his power*
> *Rocks are his written words.'*

The speaker dropped his voice, which had been soaring to the skies a moment before, and went on, speaking quietly.

> *'All pathways by his feet are worn,*
> *His strong heart stirs the ever-beating sea.*
> *His crown of thorns is twined with every thorn.*
> *His cross is every tree.'*

Something caught at John Henry's heart, stirring and exalting him. He no longer wanted to resist; to fight whatever it was that was drawing him, reaching out to take him captive.

The speaker went on. He was quoting from the Bible now, referring with all his eloquence to the death of Christ, to the need for surrender to him. All at once, John Henry knew what he was going to do.

In another part of the tent, tears streamed down Rose's face as she listened with her whole heart to the speaker's emotional words. She was miles away from that place, wandering in a bright garden, hand in hand with someone who loved her so much. The pain and the joy were intermixed to an unbearable extent. The need for action, for response, overwhelmed her.

The speaker, dropping his voice to its initial softness, drew to the end of his message.

For a moment there was silence.

Then came the final prayer, and the appeal.

At its close, when the speaker called for people to come forward, as a sign that they wanted to give their lives to the Lord, Rose Flanagan stood up and walked to the front.

While she was waiting afterwards for her turn to pray with one of the counsellors, she noticed someone standing next to her, also waiting. It was the young man she remembered seeing as she came into the tent before the meeting started. It was John Henry McClintock, although as yet she didn't know his name.

Coming out of the tent, John Henry spoke to her. 'Marvellous evening, isn't it?'

'Yes, it's lovely,' Rose agreed. The clear starry night of early May, with its dark navy blue sky studded with distant silver stones, was very beautiful.

'Come from round these parts?'

'Dromore,' she said. This was a village some five or six miles away.

'A fair distance,' said John Henry. 'If you'd like some company for the walk home, I'd be glad to go along with you.'

Rose had plenty of friends who had come with her and would have kept her company on the way back.

But for all that, she accepted the offer.

Over the next months, they saw each other regularly. John Henry made a point on the first Sunday of going to the church that had organised the tent mission where they had met. But he found that Rose, like himself, didn't belong there, and had come only for the mission. The following week, having found out which was Rose's own church, he went there.

It was then that he realised that Rose was a Catholic by upbringing.

Chapter Three

It didn't matter, John Henry thought. Rose was Rose, and he knew from their conversations that what she believed was the same as what he believed. And that was what mattered. He remembered the first walk they'd taken together. He'd arranged it before they separated on that first night.

'Come for a walk with me on Saturday, Rosie?'

'Well, Johnny, I'd love to. But I'll be working all Saturday for the Reillys, see?'

'When do you get off?'

'Around eight – depending on what comes up.'

'Okay, I'll pick you up outside the farm kitchen at about eight – that is, if you'd like me to?'

Rosie's beaming smile left him in no doubt of her opinion. 'Yes, Johnny, I'd like that.'

That Saturday evening they had walked slowly through the deepening dusk, arm in arm, talking about themselves. Rose was quite forthcoming. John Henry had for some reason expected her to be shy, but he soon found that she was happy to tell him all about her life, her dreams, her beliefs, her ambitions.

He, in turn, told her how much he longed to make something of his life. 'Especially now, Rosie. I don't know about you – but I feel as if my life's been turned around by that preacher and what he said. I want to do something worthwhile, not just work in the linen factory until I'm seventy and then die!'

'Me too, Johnny. I don't mind working for the Reillys. But sometimes I think I'd like to go to India like Amy Carmichael or Francis Xavier or somebody like that and do something worthwhile.'

John Henry was slightly alarmed. 'Hey, don't go disappearing off to India just yet, Rosie!' he protested. 'Not until I have a chance to get to know you better!'

Rose laughed. 'All right, Johnny, I'll not go just yet.'

11

When they'd been going out together for a couple of months, John Henry decided that he should bring Rose home and introduce her to his family. And he would like to meet her people, too.

'Would you like to come to tea at our house next week, Rosie?' he asked her. 'Meet my family.'

'Yes, I'd like to, Johnny.' Rose blushed. This was a clear sign that John Henry wanted to be serious about her. 'But. Well.'

'What, Rosie?'

'What'll they think about me being a Catholic, Johnny?'

John Henry paused for thought. 'I don't know, Rosie,' he said at last. 'I don't know. But they'll have to find out sometime, won't they?'

'I suppose so.'

Next morning, over breakfast, John Henry said, 'I've been walking out with Rose Flanagan for a couple of months now. I met her at the Tent Mission. I'm asking her round for tea this Sunday so's you can all meet her.'

His younger sister Peggy gave a squeal of delight. 'Oh, Johnny, you've got a girlfriend! I can't wait to see her! What's she like?'

Martha, his older sister, smiled but said nothing.

His brother Dougie grunted and pushed back his chair. 'I'm away out to work before I'm late, Johnny. I suppose we'll see what she's like at the time.'

'Who is this wee girl?' Big Douglas asked sharply. 'Flanagan? I don't know any Flanagans.'

'She comes from over Dromore direction, Da,' said John Henry equably. 'You'll like her.' It was a good time to speak to his father without immediately walking into a thunderstorm. Douglas would have had his first drink of the day, enough to calm his nerves, but wouldn't yet be far enough gone to be angry.

'Oh? Well, better be on your way yourself, boy, like Wee Dougie. Ye don't want the sack, do ye, for being late?'

The younger Douglas, although a tall, strong young man at least as big as his father, was known, in the habit of the country, as 'Wee Dougie.'

John Henry went.

As he bicycled along the narrow country road towards the linen factory, in the bright June sunshine, he wondered if he was doing the right thing in introducing Rose to his family. Suppose she found herself in the middle of an outburst of bigotry from his father? Was it fair to her, to expose her to that possibility? But they had to meet her sometime, and if they liked her – and John Henry couldn't imagine anyone not liking his Rosie – then they might accept her religion better, when eventually they had to be told about it. Better not mention it just yet, though.

But John Henry was reckoning without Rose.

Chapter Four

Sunday came. John Henry picked Rose up just down the lane a bit from her house, waiting five minutes or more for her to arrive. He walked impatiently to and fro, picking at the honeysuckle on the hedge beside him, holding one blossom after another to his nose to smell the sweetness, and then sucking the end of each flower to taste the delicious nectar. He hoped his father wouldn't have drunk too much yet.

Rose finally appeared, looking even prettier than usual with a new blue ribbon tying up her light brown hair and an apprehensive sparkle in her blue-grey eyes. The blue of the ribbon made her eyes more blue than grey.

'All right, Johnny?'

'Aye. You're looking grand, Rosie.' And he put his arm round her as they walked along, and leaned over to kiss her.

'You're looking very smart yourself, Johnny,' Rose said mischievously. 'You've put something on your hair, haven't you?'

'Aye. Well. I have to live up to you, Rosie, don't I?'

Peggy was in the garden when they arrived, picking flowers to put in a vase in the dining room. She darted over to John Henry and Rose as they opened the gate and came through.

'Hullo! You must be Rose! I'm so pleased to meet you!'

They followed her into the house, and after initial greetings they sat round the dining table, eating a carefully laid out meal of salad with tinned salmon and bread and butter. Martha brought in the teapot and poured tea in everyone's cup, then went out to fill up the pot again from the huge kettle kept on the boil on the kitchen stove.

Rose, although feeling better because of the welcome John Henry's family was giving her, was a bit overawed. This was a much larger and more impressive house than the cottage where she had been brought up. Although she could see that it hadn't been kept in proper repair, she still realised that John Henry's family must be better off than her own.

'So, Rose,' Big Douglas began when they had all had tea poured for them and the bread and butter had been handed round, 'I hope you can eat salmon?'

'It's a real treat, Mr McClintock,' Rose assured him. 'It's something my family only have on special occasions.'

She could see that John Henry's father was pleased, although all he said was, 'Humph.'

'So you come from Dromore, Rose, Johnny was telling me?'

'Well, not exactly,' Rose said innocently. 'I was born down in County Monaghan, but we moved up here about ten years ago, when my father was looking for work. He got a good job in the end working as a caretaker at the church.'

'Ah, well, work's hard for all of us to find, these days.'

'Then my mother died, two years ago, and my father went just a wee while ago.'

'So, are you on your own, girl?'

'No, Mr McClintock, I live with my two big brothers and my wee sister. And I have a good job myself working for the Reillys at their farm, mostly in the kitchen.'

'I'm glad to hear that, Rose. It's a good thing for the childer to bring in some contribution to the family's support, as I've told Johnny here many a time.'

'Have some more bread, Rose?' Martha intervened, offering the plate. She didn't want her father to get started again on John Henry and his desire to stay on at school. She'd heard quite enough of that. It was three years ago now, after all.

Peggy offered more tea, and took her turn in going out to fill up the teapot. Wee Dougie, always a bit shy, said nothing. Douglas McClintock took up the conversation again.

'So, which church was this that your da worked in, Rose?'

John Henry started. He hadn't expected the conversation to focus on this sort of thing straight away today. He should have known his father would try to inquire into Rosie's background, he reflected. He tried desperately to think of something to change the subject, but he was too late. Just as he was opening his mouth to ask his father if he'd been out for a walk earlier, Rose was answering the question in all innocence.

'It was St Martin's, Mr McClintock. They're very kind people there. It was Father Donnelly who got me my job with the Reillys, two years ago when my da was still alive. They go to St Martin's, so Father Donnelly knew they were looking for some help in the farm kitchen.'

John Henry watched as his father's face grew gradually redder and redder. The broken veins began to throb in his cheeks. His thick eyebrows came further down over his glaring eyes in a hard and terrifying frown. For a moment he said nothing. Then he spoke quietly. 'Are you telling me you're a Papish?'

Rose stared back at him.

'I'm a Roman Catholic, Mr. McClintock. I'm not ashamed of it.'

Douglas McClintock sprang up from the table pushing his chair backwards with so much force that it fell with a deafening crash to the floor.

'A Papish in my house, eating my food at my table!' he roared. 'John Henry McClintock, what do you mean by bringing a Papish into my house?'

John Henry in turn sprang up. 'Don't speak to Rose like that, Da!'

'I'll speak whatever way I like in my own house, ye wee skitter!' roared McClintock. 'Get that wee heathen out of here before I do something I'll be sorry for!'

'You've done that already, Da,' said John Henry. He turned to Rose, who was sitting frozen in her place, a slice of bread and butter in one hand halted halfway to her mouth.

'Come on, Rosie,' he said gently. He gave her a quick, apologetic smile. 'I should never have exposed you to this. I'll take you home.'

'If you go out of this house with that wee Papish you'll not come back!' thundered McClintock, his fist raised as if to strike.

'I wouldn't want to come back, not after the way you're behaving.' John Henry turned away from his father, took Rose's hand and raised her to her feet. His brother and sisters sat in stunned silence.

Rose set down her bread and butter, pushed back her chair and got to her feet.

'I wouldn't want to come between you and your da, Johnny,' she began, but John Henry interrupted her.

'If you have, it's by his choice, Rosie,' he said firmly. He led Rose to the door. Turning round to face his father, he said, 'I'll not be back, then, Da. So goodbye.'

Douglas McClintock stared at his son for a long moment. Then his fist dropped. The anger faded from his face, and he collapsed back into his chair.

'Johnny, Johnny, don't go! I didn't mean it!'

Tears began to stream down his face and he fumbled clumsily in one pocket for a handkerchief.

'Don't go, Johnny! Don't go! I couldn't bear it!' He sat shaking and trembling, all his anger turned to grief, the scowl on his face transformed into a crumpled childlike fear.

John Henry gave Rose's hand a pat and let go of it. Then he went over to his father and knelt beside him, putting both arms round Douglas and holding him tightly.

'I don't want to go, Daddy. But you mustn't talk to Rose like that.'

'I'm sorry, Johnny, I'm sorry!'

John Henry found his father's handkerchief and began to wipe his eyes.

'Daddy, Daddy, why must you make a fool of yourself like this with the drinking? You were never like this years ago when Mammy was alive.'

'I know, Johnny, I know. I can't help it, Johnny.'

'Well, never mind. I think I'll just take Rosie home now, anyway, But I'll be back, don't worry.'

Douglas McClintock put out a trembling hand and seized his son's. 'Don't ever leave me, Johnny. I couldn't bear it.'

'It's all right, Da. I'll be back. So why don't the rest of you finish up your tea? You don't want to let the salmon spoil, do you?'

Peggy laughed shakily. 'We'll keep you your share, Johnny.'

John Henry, his arm round Rose, walked away.

Chapter Five

Rose, as John Henry found out within a few minutes, wasn't nearly as upset as he was himself.

'It's all right, Johnny,' she told him as they walked arm in arm along the country lanes which ran through long miles of fresh green fields and hedges to her home. 'If it had been you meeting my brother, it would have been just as bad, boy. And you know what, I stirred it up myself by talking about the church my da worked at. Mr McClintock was bound to ask more about it after me saying what I did.'

'But he didn't have to get so angry, Rosie.'

'No, he didn't. But I knew he might. I thought it was better to have everything out in the open right at the start, Johnny. I'm sorry that I've caused you grief.'

'Ach, no, Rosie, don't be saying that! The thing is, Rosie – I should have made it clearer to you before, but I don't like to talk about it – my da's a heavy drinker. A real souse. When he's sober he's a good man. He's been good to me. But since my ma died he's drunk more and more. All the money goes there. That's why the house is in the state it is – you can't have helped noticing. And when he gets to a certain level of drunkenness, he gets angry at the least wee thing. And then a minute later he's in tears and saying how sorry he is. I wish he wasn't like that, but it's the truth, and no use saying otherwise.'

'You love him, no matter, don't you, Johnny?'

'Aye, Rosie, I do. He's an awful old git, but he's the same man used to sing me to sleep when I was a wean, and give me rides on his back round the garden, and take me and Dougie for walks down to the river to catch spricks in jamjars. He's changed, aye, but he's still my da.'

'Oh, Johnny, I'd glad you do love him! It makes me love you all the more!'

John Henry stood still. He looked Rose in the face, saying nothing, and watched as her cheeks gradually grew pinker and pinker.

'Did you mean that, Rosie?'

'And why should I have to tell you if I did or not when you haven't said anything yourself?' retorted Rose spiritedly.

'Well, then, I'll say it too. I love you, Rosie Flanagan.'

And he bent his head down and kissed her, there in the middle of the lane with the smell of honeysuckle and wild roses floating out from the hedges – and the manure the farmers had been laying down on the fields to add to the good country mixture.

And Rose kissed him back with all her might, and knew that she had been given her heart's desire.

'I'd like to meet your own family, Rosie,' said John Henry when he could breath again.

'Well, I'd better warn you here and now, Johnny, that my big brother Hughie won't like it any better that your da did,' Rose said. 'But I'm having no pretence about it. I'm telling him before you arrive there that you're a Protestant, and warning him to behave himself. He knows, for I told him, about me going forward at the tent mission, and I mean to explain to him that you and me believes the same things, and that it's none of his business anyway.'

'You've a brave girl, Rosie,' was all John Henry said. 'Come on, give us another kiss!'

Chapter Six

When Rose went home that night, her brothers Hughie and Sammy were still out with their mates, but she knew they would be turning up before long looking for their tea.

Rose had no problem with Hughie or Sammy. By and large, they were decent enough brothers, she thought. They expected her, as the woman of the house, to do the cooking and housework, even though she, like both of them, was out working for most of the day. But so did every other Irish man Rose knew, so there was nothing unusual about that. At least they carried in the daily buckets of water from the pump and the coal and wood for the fire.

Emily, their younger sister, was still at school, and although she did her share of the housework, Rose tried to give her as much time as possible to do her schoolwork. Emily was a bright girl, a 'good scholar,' and Rose had hopes that she might go further than the Reillys' kitchen when she looked for a job. Hughie and Sammy worked as farm labourers, hard work and not well paid, but all there was available for them.

Rose wrapped an apron round her good dress, and began at once to peel the potatoes and put them on to boil. There was some cold bacon, and she cut a few slices from the side and threw it into the frying pan, accompanied, a few minutes later, with some cabbage she'd chopped rapidly. Hughie loved bacon and cabbage fried together.

Above the sizzling from the frying pan she heard the clump of heavy boots outside, and a moment later the door was pushed open and Hughie came into the kitchen, followed a minute later by Sammy.

'Ah! That smells good, Rose,' Hughie exclaimed, putting an arm round her waist and giving her a brotherly hug. 'Is it nearly ready?'

'It'll be ready as soon as the two of you've taken off your mucky boots and washed your hands, Hughie boy,' said his loving sister, twisting round to give him a peck on the check. 'See if Emily's finished her homework, will you?'

It wasn't long before they were seated comfortably round the kitchen table. Rose, who had eaten quite at lot at John Henry's house, didn't really want anything more, but for the sake of family unity she gave herself a small helping and worked her way through it, knowing neither her brothers nor Emily would notice how much or how little she ate.

'I was round at John Henry McClintock's house earlier on, Hughie,' she said when she felt he had eaten a reasonable amount and would probably be feeling fairly satisfied. 'You remember I told you I'd been walking out with him for the last two months?'

'Aye.' Hughie shovelled up a forkful of potatoes, cabbage and bacon into his mouth.

'Well, I'm going to ask him round next week – next Sunday – to have tea with us. You'd need to be here, all of you, and cleaned up and ready to eat, when he gets here.'

'What's he like, Rose?' Emily asked, her mouth full of potato.

'Well. I think he's nice looking. I wouldn't be walking out with him if I didn't, would I? He has dark hair and his eyes are the same colour as mine, I suppose, sort of blue grey. He's tall. I don't know what else I can tell you.'

'He sounds nice,' breathed Emily. 'And are you going to marry him?'

Sammy laughed. 'Hey, hey, wee Emily, let Rose have time to make up her mind about that.'

'It's all right, Emily,' Rose said. 'As it happens, I think I probably am going to marry him. But you should all know, I met him at that tent mission I told you about, and although we both believe the same things, he wasn't brought up Catholic like us. He was brought up Protestant.'

Three pairs of eyes gaped at her. Three mouths fell open.

Hughie was the first to speak.

'Dear save us, Rose, you're not going to marry a Black Prod?'

'And if I am, whose business is it except mine and his?' retorted Rose.

Hughie, soft as butter for all his great size, quailed under the spark in Rose's eye.

'Oh, aye, oh aye, it's your own business, all right. But what will the neighbours say? And the Reillys you work for, and Father Donnelly?'

'Nothing bad, I hope,' Rose said soberly. 'But if they do, Hughie, it just can't be helped, because it won't make any difference to either of us, see?'

'Ach, Rose, it's just like Romeo and Juliet!' breathed Emily happily. 'We're doing it at school this year. Our teacher says it's the best love story ever written.'

'Maybe.' Rose spoke drily. 'The best if you're outside looking on, Emily pet. Maybe not the best if you're on the inside.'

Emily's face fell. 'I s'pose.'

Rose smiled at her young sister. 'It's all right, Emily. Nothing for you to worry about. Me and Johnny'll work it out okay.' She glanced over at Hughie, sitting dumbfounded, but not so shocked that he was forgetting to go on shovelling potatoes, cabbage and bacon into his mouth, and at Sammy, his eating suspended as he took in the news. 'And listen to me, Hughie, and you too, Sammy, I want to know right now, before I bring Johnny here, that you're going to treat him right.'

'Ach, well, Rose ...'

'Because if you're not, you needn't turn up for your tea next Sunday when he's coming. You can get something to eat somewhere else – from one of the neighbours you're so worried about, or from the Reillys, or Father Donnelly.'

'Rose, Rose!' Hughie spluttered through a mouthful of potatoes, 'I didn't mean I wouldn't treat him okay. If you choose to bring him here, I'll behave like I would to any guest of yours, girl.'

'Like, sit there feeding your face and not bothering to speak?' Rose laughed. 'It's all right, Hughie, I'm only joking. But just see you remember what you've said. And what about you, Sammy?'

'Oh, aye, oh aye, it's your own business, all right, Rose,' said Sammy, deliberately mimicking Hughie's earlier reply in a put on voice. 'I'm like Hughie, I'll be as nice as pie to your boy, see? Just as long as you go on making my tea for me.' Sammy gave her a grin, and Rose smiled back at him. She'd known, anyway, that easygoing Sammy, who liked a laugh and a joke more than anything else, would cause no trouble.

John Henry was apprehensive enough about the projected meal with Rose's brothers and sister, but he put on a brave face and turned up in his best clothes at five o'clock on the following Sunday as he'd agreed to do. Rose opened the door to him and greeted him with a smile.

'Come on in, Johnny, it's good to see you.'

Twelve year old Emily was hovering in the background, also smiling. This didn't look too bad so far, John Henry thought.

'Come and meet Johnny, Emily,' Rose invited her, and Emily came forward with a rush. Her eyes were big with excitement, and as she spoke she stuttered slightly from nervousness. 'H-h-hello, Johnny.'

'Hello, Emily. Pleased to meet you,' John Henry said gravely. 'See, I'm not a strange monster, am I?' A smile suddenly lit up his face, and Emily, seeing it, relaxed.

'Ach, I never thought you were, Johnny!' she protested, blushing.

'No, she thinks you're Romeo – and I'm Juliet,' Rose contributed.

'Rose! Why'd you tell him that?' Emily blushed scarlet.

'Well, let's hope we don't both end up dead, then,' John Henry said. Then, seeing Emily's reaction, he saw he'd put his foot in it. 'You haven't got to the end yet? Sorry I've spoiled it for you, Emily. But it's a beautiful ending anyway. Nothing to be sad about, really.'

Emily looked doubtful, but had no time to ask more, as Rose swept them both into the kitchen where Hughie, knife in one hand and fork in the other, was sitting at the table sniffing at the tasty aroma of boiled beef and carrots coming from the huge pot on the stove.

'This is my brother Hughie, Johnny. Stand up and say hello, Hughie, will you!'

Hughie stumbled to his feet. 'Hello,' he muttered, eyes downcast.

'Hello, Hughie.'

'And this wee skitter is Sammy.'

Sammy grinned. 'See what's she's like, Johnny? No respect for her betters.'

'Betters, indeed – I don't see any here, except maybe Johnny!' retorted Rose, waving a dishcloth at Sammy in pretended threat.

'Maybe?' murmured John Henry, and everyone laughed. It was a good start to the meeting.

'Now,' said Rose briskly, 'sit down everybody, and I'll get the food out.'

'So, Johnny, you're walking out with my wee sister?' Hughie said. It was hard to know if he was trying to be pleasant or the opposite, and John Henry decided to take it well for as long as possible.

'That's a fact, Hughie. For a wee while now. We met at the tent mission. Rosie's told you that, she says.'

'Aye. Well, you'll be quare and glad to get your feet under the table at last.'

'Yes, I've been wanting to meet Rosie's family. She came round and met mine last Sunday.'

'So she said. And what did your da think of all this?'

'My family all think Rosie's a great wee girl,' John Henry said firmly, ignoring the initial reaction. It was true by now.

'Oh.'

Hughie turned his attention to Rose. 'So we're having beef today, Rose. Well, I'm not complaining. It's a rare good treat. But have ye fell into a fortune?'

Rose flushed angrily. The truth was that she'd cut down on the house-keeping money for the last week and for several weeks to come, to give John Henry a better than usual meal today.

'We can manage it okay, Hughie.'

John Henry hastily changed the subject.

'Do you follow the hurling, Hughie? Or are you a Gaelic football man?'

Hughie was eager enough to talk about his favourite sports. John Henry, who mainly enjoyed cricket, but if the truth were told wasn't greatly interested in sport at all, listened patiently, occasionally putting in a word to show he followed what Hughie was saying.

When the meal was over, John Henry rose to go.

'Good to meet you, Hughie. And Sammy and Emily. Rosie, walk a bit of the way with me, will you?'

Rose came with him willingly.

'They like you, Johnny,' she told him when they were well out of hearing from the cottage.

'I think Emily does – though I did spoil Romeo and Juliet for her. And maybe Sammy,' John Henry grinned. 'But I'm not so sure about your older brother. I think he was just putting it on, so's not to make a row in the house.'

'Ach, maybe. But he'll accept it – he'll have to.'

And sure enough, when she got back to the house, where Emily had cleared the table but the dishes were piled up waiting for Rose at the sink, the first thing Hughie said was, 'Smarmy git. Asking me about the Gaelic, as if he'd ever watched a match.'

'He was trying to be friendly, Hughie.'

'Aye. Well, I was friendly too, Rose, wasn't I? But don't bring him here too often, because you'll end up trying me too far if you do!'

'Did you get me the water to wash these dishes, Hughie?' was all Rose said. 'And make sure there's enough for breakfast tomorrow, see?'

And Hughie grabbed the big tin bucket and slammed out of the house to the nearby pump.

Chapter Seven

John Henry had developed a habit of seeing Rose every Sunday after she'd been to church. He would wait for her afterwards, and they would walk together through the country lanes, like other young courting couples.

On their first walk John Henry had picked the spring flowers, especially the early wild roses, 'Your flower, Rosie,' and the bluebells whose scent filled the air for such a distance around their full bursting beds. He gave them to Rose, who pressed a single wild rose in her Bible when she returned home that night and kept the withered petals safely there, between the leaves, for many years.

Both their families now seemed happy enough with the understanding that had come about between Rose and John Henry. There was no immediate prospect of marriage for them. They had no money and nowhere to live. But they had begun to save up, hoping to get enough over a few years to manage. It was the advent of the First World War which changed things.

Suddenly there were posters all over the place. 'The lamps are going out all over Europe, we shall not see them lit again in our life-time,' said Sir Edward Grey, and it became a familiar saying very quickly.

On August 4th 1914, Great Britain declared war on Germany. Britain, led by Prime Minister Herbert Asquith, had given Germany an ultimatum to get out of Belgium by midnight August 3rd. Belgium's neutrality had been guaranteed by Great Britain as far back as 1839. Asquith had a very simple decision to make – but one that would have a cataclysmic impact on Britain. He could either turn a blind eye to a war in mainland Europe that might have little impact on Britain if she stood as a neutral. Or the British public could see Asquith as the man who stood up to the bullying of Germany and who stood for righteousness and decency. A future Prime Minister, Winston Churchill, described the scene in London in the hours that led to the declaration of war:

'It was eleven o'clock at night – twelve by German time – when the ultimatum expired. The windows of the Admiralty were thrown wide open in the warm night air. Under the roof from which Nelson had received his orders were gathered a small group of admirals and captains and a cluster of clerks, pencils in hand, waiting. Along the Mall from the direction of the Palace the sound of an immense concourse singing

'God save the King' floated in. On this deep wave there broke the chimes of Big Ben; and, as the first stroke of the hour boomed out, a rustle of movement swept across the room ... I walked across the Horse Guards Parade to the Cabinet room and reported to the Prime Minister and the ministers who were assembled there that the deed was done.'

But the Kaiser said, 'With heavy heart I have been compelled to mobilise my army against a neighbour at whose side it has fought on many a battlefield. With genuine sorrow do I witness the end of a friendship, which Germany loyally cherished. We draw the sword with a clean conscience and clean hands.'

The newspapers had large black headlines. The Daily Mirror said,

Great Britain Declares War on Germany

Declaration last night after 'unsatisfactory reply' to British ultimatum that Belgium must be kept neutral. Great Britain declared war against Germany at 7pm.

War was Germany's reply to our request that she should respect the neutrality of Belgium, whose territories we were bound in honour and by treaty obligations to maintain inviolate. Speaking in a crowded and hushed House yesterday afternoon the Prime Minister made the following state-ment, 'We have requested to the German Government for a satisfactory assurance as to Belgian neutrality before midnight tonight. The German reply to our request, officially stated last night, was unsatisfactory. Great Britain is in a state of war with Germany.

It was John Henry's own idea to join up to fight in the war. No one wanted him to go. His father was heartbroken at the idea.

'Da, I'd have thought a man like you, always talking about being a loyalist, would have wanted me to fight for my country,' John Henry said, when, to his dismay, Douglas had received the announcement of his intention with cries of protest.

'It's not that I don't think people should join up,' Douglas McClintock said mournfully. 'But not you, Johnny, not you! What'll I do without you? And by the time you come home, if you ever do,' – tears filled his eyes at the thought – 'I may not be here any more.'

'Why, are you thinking of moving, Da?' John Henry asked, trying to joke his father out of this melancholy mood.

'Ach, Johnny, you know rightly what I mean. I'm getting on – and my health isn't the greatest. I may be dead, is what I mean, if you want it in plain words.'

'Not you, Da! You're as tough as an old boot – you'll outlive us all.' John Henry bent over the old man and hugged him.

'And what about Rose?' his father asked him. 'She'll not be wanting you to go away and fight, will she? She's got more sense than you, Johnny, not that that's saying much. Johnny, if you go I may never see you again, one way or the other.'

'I'll look after myself, Da, don't you worry. And as for your own health, if you'd just cut down on the drinking you'd live twice as long, wouldn't you?'

'Well, now, Johnny, I did cut down on it that time you told me off, the first day you brought Rose here. You know I did.'

'Well. You cut down, yes. But you could do with cutting down a lot more, Da, to tell you the truth. Ach, Da, I don't like talking to you this way, but you brought up the subject of your health, didn't you?'

Douglas was silent.

'Sorry, Da. I didn't mean to upset you. And I'm sorry you don't want me to go and fight, but my mind's made up. You're right, Rosie doesn't want me to go, either. But it's a decision I have to take by myself.' His face was firm.

Douglas McClintock could see that John Henry wasn't going to change his mind. There was nothing to do but accept it. His son was going away to fight, and the chances were that he wouldn't come back. But there was nothing Douglas could do about it. He said nothing more.

Chapter Eight

Rose was, indeed very much opposed to John Henry's decision. She could see no reason for John Henry to go, and indeed held a strong conviction that all war was wrong.

But John Henry held to his equally strong belief that it was his duty to go and fight. And although Rose was no moral weakling, and was not to be persuaded out of her conviction, John Henry, a man of great strength of purpose, remained firm in his own belief.

'You, of all men, Johnny,' Rose said to him, when the subject first came up, one warm September evening as they walked arm in arm through the woods near Rose's home, stepping on the first of the fallen leaves, and hearing them crackle underfoot. 'You who's such a firm Christian! Why should you want to fight? What about turning the other cheek, and loving your enemies?'

'Ach, Rosie, you're getting it all mixed up,' John Henry said. He spoke the more vehemently because he wasn't completely convinced that Rose was wrong, for her words had touched something in him. As he walked, he reached up above their heads, and pulled down a thin branch, whose slight attachment to the mother tree made it dangerously easy to snap off. John Henry broke it quickly, and held it in his left hand, while his right arm still encircled Rose. He began to swish with it angrily at the trees and bushes they were passing, knocking the leaves from bramble and whin alike.

'Turning the other cheek, that's about private fights, quarrels with people who do you down some way. It's nothing to do with a whole country going to war. If we didn't fight, we'd have Kaiser Bill over here, forcing us to do things his way, before you could turn round. Is that what you want for your country? If the Irish don't fight for the country's freedom, can you tell me who will? We're the bould fighters, and proud of it, Rosie!'

'Some of us think we should be fighting for Ireland, not for England, Johnny,' Rose retorted, but he would have none of it.

'That's a different matter, Rosie,' he said firmly. 'I don't deny there are problems enough at home, now they've passed the Home Rule Act, and are promising that it'll be carried out as soon as the war's over. But we all need to pull together here, girl! This war is against the Kaiser, and we need to put our private differences aside, and stand shoulder to shoulder, or we'll have no country left, either England or Ireland!'

'I still think fighting's wrong, Johnny,' she said, not trying for a new argument, but simply sticking with what she was sure of, for all his efforts to change her.

But there was something fighting against her, which she wasn't even aware of, and that was John Henry's ardent desire to get out of his dead-end job, to go somewhere, to do something, to make a success of his life. He told himself that the desire sprang from a need to do his duty, as a Christian and an Irishman. But if he had looked a little deeper, he would have had to recognise the burning need to get away from the daily round that was trivialising his life. And which, day by day, he hated more. Joining up, if he did it, would create an opportunity for him to escape.

So all at once he was angry at his failure to bring Rose round to his point of view, and near to throwing up the whole understanding.

It was the sight of the tears beginning in Rose's eyes, as she murmured, 'Oh, Johnny, I don't want you to go away to war! Suppose – suppose –'

She couldn't bring herself to put into words what she feared, but John Henry understood what she was thinking without the need for words.

Rose feared, and with good reason, that if John Henry set off to go to war, she would be left, like the heroines of so many sad Irish songs, with only his memory, and the announcement, some day, that he had died 'gloriously, for his country.' And what use would that be to anyone?

It was the first real disagreement Rose had had with him, and although it was made up before he sailed, it left a sour taste in her mouth.

The following day, John Henry enlisted. For Rose, it was the beginning of five long years of waiting for him to come back. For John Henry, it was the start of a new life. But not necessarily a better one.

Chapter Nine

John Henry was a volunteer; for Irishmen in those days were not conscripted. He went up to Belfast to sign up, and found himself surrounded by eager crowds of boys of his own age, mostly not old enough yet to be called young men. John Henry was just turned eighteen, but he recognised some faces in the milling crowd of boys whom he knew were younger than him. Artie Baird, one of the friends who had gone with him to the tent mission, was there, hovering anxiously from foot to foot as he waited for his turn. When he saw John Henry he rushed over full of excitement.

'Are you joining up, too, Johnny? It's going to be great, isn't it?'

John Henry frowned. 'Artie, you know rightly you're just turned seventeen. What are you up to, trying to enlist?'

'Ach, Johnny, don't be telling them that, now! Sure, I want to go and fight for my country, just like yourself.'

'So, I suppose Tommy Maguire and Willie Morgan are about here somewhere, too?'

Artie turned red with embarrassment. He hung his head. 'Well, no, Johnny. Tommy and Willie didn't see it the same way as me.'

John Henry asked no more. He could see that Artie was disappointed in his idol Tommy.

Presently as the queue moved forward it came to his turn to sign up. There was a medical, and John Henry was pleased to come out of the embarrassing experience (he had never stripped in front of anyone before) with a grade of A2. 'Why two?' he asked, and was told that his eyesight wasn't quite perfect – but it would do.

Coming away he ran into a disconsolate Artie Baird. The youngster had been turned down.

'They said I wasn't strong enough, Johnny. Well, I know the doctor's been saying I've a weak heart for years now, but I didn't think they'd be able to tell.'

'Never worry, Artie. Maybe you're well out of it. It won't be a game, you know.'

But Artie refused to be comforted.

There would be twelve weeks' training before anyone could be sent to France. The two Northern regiments, the sixteenth and the thirty-sixth, would be sent to Aldershot. To John Henry, who had never been across the water, it was an exciting prospect. The first, he thought, of many new experiences. He was a bit nervous, too, but by now he had put Rose's views behind him, and was sure he was doing the right thing.

He was kitted out with a new uniform, given a rucksack to carry his belongings, and told that he would sleep overnight in Victoria Barracks. He would sail, with the rest of the new recruits, on the following day.

Early next evening they left. It wasn't many minutes out from Belfast, in fact they were still sailing down the Lough, when a dreadful, demoralising sea sickness made him question his sense in letting himself in for this.

'I'm dying, Paddy!' he gasped, to a boy standing beside him, who had shown himself friendly. 'What'll I do?'

'Hang over the side,' Paddy advised, 'and bring up everything you can. You won't feel just as bad then.'

Paddy O'Connor, who had worked with his father on the family fishing boat at Ardglass, was used to the sea and although well past sickness himself, he had seen enough of it to be reasonably sympathetic to others.

John Henry took his advice, but it didn't help much. For what seemed like hours he hung over the side of the ship, retching continually long after there was nothing left to bring up. At some unidentified time, he staggered away from the rails to the corner of the deck where he had piled his kit, wrapped his greatcoat round him, and managed a few hours of disturbed sleep.

Liverpool looked grey and gloomy, teeming with rain, when the ship drew in to harbour next morning. John Henry, however, had no sooner stepped onto firm ground again than his spirits began to rise. Presently, when the sun came out, watery at first but soon growing in strength, lighting up the strange docks, with their piles of boxes and coils of rope spread everywhere, he even found himself whistling.

'Rock of Ages, cleft for me!' whistled John Henry.

Paddy, struggling over the roughly concreted dock at his side, weighed down by rucksack and greatcoat, looked at him. 'Religious, are you?'

'Aye,' said John Henry, always a man of few words, and they left it there.

The next stage of the journey was by train. John Henry was surprised to see the platform filled with cheering crowds, most of them women, many from Liverpool's large Irish population.

'There's the brave lads!' called one woman. 'Shoot lots of Germans for me, ye boys, ye!' She was red-faced, dressed in too-bright colours, and swaying dangerously from side to side. If they had been at home, John Henry would have known what to make of her, but being in a strange place, he gave her the benefit of the doubt. Maybe respectable women dressed like that over here. He'd been told that you could believe anything of people who lived in England.

However, one thing he was in no doubt of at all, and that was that she was drunk. He thought it was sad, so early in the day, too.

Inside the train, it was the lucky first-comers who got seats, crammed tightly into the carriages, while the rest sat on rucksacks in the corridors. John Henry had hung back to help Paddy, who was struggling more than ever with his load, and now he found himself condemned to the corridor. He didn't really mind. At least like this he could stretch out his long legs; unlike the soldiers in the carriages, who could hardly move, packed as they were like sardines in a tin, but without the lubricating oil.

As soon as the train had started, someone who had a mouth-organ started to play, *'Pack Up Your Troubles In Your Old Kit Bag'*, and all around, people joined in enthusiastically (in so far as they knew the words, and even a bit further.) After that came, *'It's A Long Way To Tipperary,'* and then, *'The Mountains Of Mourne.'*

A boy sitting in the corridor not far from John Henry joined in, softly at first, then with growing confidence. He had a sweet Irish tenor voice, high and piercing. Like John McCormack, whom John Henry had once heard sing at a concert in Belfast. As his voice soared up into the words of the last verse John Henry listened and felt as if his heart was being squeezed. *'So I'll wait for my wild rose, who's waiting for me ...'*

The words brought him a painful vision of his own Rose. Only a day gone, and he was missing her already. Maybe he would never see her again. Then he gathered up his courage. Never mind, he thought. We'll certainly be home by Christmas, if not before. The recruiting officer had told him so and, anyway, everyone was saying the same. I'll see her then, John Henry thought.

Chapter Ten

The twelve weeks of training dragged.

John Henry, used to an indoors job in a factory, found himself pushed to the utmost to carry out each day's programme of long marches, drill, practice with gun and bayonet, early rising, confinement to the training camp except for a few hours on a Saturday evening. And above all, the constant sharing of a limited space with nine other people, the other members of the ten-man unit to which he had been allocated.

He was used to some degree of privacy, if not during the working day then at least after it. At home, he had spent quite a lot of his free time wandering around the countryside, through the woods and fields, often with Rose, but more often still on his own. The removal of this freedom was the thing he found hardest to come to terms with.

As a substitute for his freedom, he learnt to enjoy the sense of comradeship that grew steadily among the boys in his hut. As he grew stronger physically, and found he could manage the increasingly strenuous daily training programme without falling into bed exhausted at the end of each day, so John Henry found himself with time available to take part in the chat and banter of his companions, and to join in games of football and other sports with a pleasure he had not experienced until now.

He even found time for a few walks in the open air, discovering more beauty in the English countryside than his insular Irishness had led him to expect. Autumn was fully present by now, but the multi-coloured leaves, with their melancholy voices sighing of death, had their own beauty for John Henry. As he walked through them at his ease, he thought about life and death, and the war he was about to experience, where inevitably he would find himself killing people, and he wondered if he could do it.

There was more blasphemy from his companions than he was used to, although his time in the linen factory had to some extent inured him to that. Whether because it came naturally to them, or because they thought this was how real soldiers should talk, his companions used more foul language, too, than John Henry found comfortable.

However, after the first few weeks, he noticed a considerable dropping off in this. He suspected that the reduction was only in his presence, that when he was not there, they spoke as crudely as ever. But he was happy to escape the worst of it.

One man in particular, a thin, red haired soldier in his early twenties, was especially foul-mouthed. John Henry tried not to let this prejudice him against the man, known as Foxy, but he realised early on that Foxy seemed to have taken a dislike to him. John Henry wasn't aware of anything he had done to cause this, and gradually decided that it made Foxy feel guilty to be around someone who didn't swear and who was considered 'good living' by the other men.

He was struggling with his heavy equipment on one of the first days of training – awkward rifle, heavy greatcoat, and rucksack packed full – when Foxy bumped into him, making him drop the rifle on his own foot just as he was getting sorted out.

'Sorry, mate,' Foxy said. He didn't sound sorry. There was an unpleasant sneer on his face.

'That's all right, boyo,' John Henry said easily. Then, a moment later, Foxy bumped into him again, and managed to trip him up. John Henry sprawled painfully on the muddy ground, rifle, rucksack and cap flying in all directions.

John Henry stood up and carefully brushed himself down. He walked over to where Foxy stood sniggering a few feet away. John Henry loomed over him. He said nothing for a moment. Foxy, looking up at him from lowered eyes, grew noticeably paler.

'Foxy, I hope you won't do that again,' was all John Henry said. His tone was quite mild. But Foxy backed hastily away, and in his turn tripped over the end of his rifle. There was a roar of laughter from the watching crowd.

John Henry was careful not to join in the laughter although he was hard put to it to prevent a grin creeping over his face. He turned away, leaving Foxy to get up in his own good time. He realised that he had made an enemy. There was no point in making things worse by laughing.

His friendship with Paddy O'Connor grew. The fair haired young fisherman from Ardglass was generally to be found in the middle of any practical joke, but he spent some quiet time with John Henry too, questioning him about his beliefs and listening avidly to the answers. John Henry usually found it hard to talk about such personal things, often struggling to put his meaning into words, but he did his best, because, like most people, he couldn't help liking Paddy.

'So, what do you think about this story that the troops saw angels at Mons, before the battle?' asked Paddy.

'I don't see why not,' John Henry answered slowly. There were some things he still had to work out for himself. He was never ready with quick, glib answers. But that did him no harm in Paddy's eyes.

Then one evening Paddy asked, 'What do you think of this?' Each of them was stretched out on his own bed, speaking in low voices just before lights out. Paddy produced a string of rosary beads from beneath his pillow, and held it out for John Henry to see, keeping it scrunched in his own hand, so that it stayed out of sight of people passing. 'My ma gave me it just before I left to sign up,' Paddy said. 'I suppose, you not being a Catholic, you would think little of it.'

John Henry took a few minutes to decide. 'If it helps you to pray, Paddy, and to concentrate on what you're praying, I don't see how it can be anything but good,' he said at last.

Paddy laughed. 'Well, I don't know about that,' he said. 'I suppose I think it's a kind of good-luck charm. I mean, my ma wouldn't think like that, but me, I'm different from her, see?'

'I suppose you are,' John Henry agreed.

'Yer man Ian Stewart saw me with it the other night and he told me it was superstitious nonsense. He's good living, like you, Johnny.'

Ian Stewart was a tall, thin, Belfast man who for some reason John Henry found it hard to like, in spite of their common faith.

'Well, I suppose he has a right to his own opinion, Paddy.'

John Henry didn't say that maybe Ian should be a bit slower about forcing his opinion on a young man who was looking for comfort and who had serious things to face soon, like them all.

Paddy looked at him anxiously, wanting more. 'But when I have it in my hand just before going to sleep, it gives me a good feeling, that's all.'

'Well, we could all do with something like that, these days, Paddy,' John Henry said. 'Here comes Corp. It's lights out.'

There was another plus, during this time of training, which made up to John Henry for all rest. As part of the training, they were each given the opportunity to follow courses, to learn things which would better fit them for their return to civilian life after the war, and John Henry eagerly chose to extend his curtailed schooling. He quickly gained certificates proclaiming his successful qualification in Mathematics and English, and went on to add French and German to the list. It meant working for most of the few hours that would otherwise have been leisure time, but John Henry rejoiced in the opportunity to make use of his talents at last.

Markie Stevens, the young man whose Irish tenor voice had moved John Henry so much on the train journey as he sang *'The Mountains Of Mourne'*, was another soldier who was eager to do well in the courses. He and John Henry often helped each other, speaking to each other in French and hearing each other's vocabulary lists.

Markie was a small, bright-eyed boy, about John Henry's own age, with fair hair which the army had cropped short but which tended to grow fast and to flop over his forehead, until the Sergeant Major would bark at him on parade, 'Stevens! Haircut, before you come on parade again!'

Like Paddy, Markie came from a Catholic background, but unlike Paddy he was established and confident in his faith, and John Henry found him comforting to talk to.

Chapter Eleven

During this time, and especially over the first weeks, when the physical work and the mental strain of never being alone were at their height, John Henry lived mainly through the letters Rose sent him regularly.

Rose was missing him desperately. Without the full programme that filled John Henry's days, she had too much time to brood, to wonder if he would come safely back, if he would stay faithful. She worried less about this last than about his survival. She knew he was a man of his word. He would not easily break the promises he had made to her.

But as she stood by the farmhouse sink, with her arms plunged into the greasy water as she scoured the pots and pans, or as she peeled endless potatoes for the farm workers' meals or kneaded the dough for another batch of soda bread, she found herself continuously wondering how soon it would be before Johnny was under fire, and how soon the war would be over, and if he would then come safely back to her.

She prayed for him every night; it was all she could do for him. She wrote him long letters daily, and in them she enclosed a wild flower, an autumn crocus or a Michaelmas daisy, and, as winter drew on, a holly berry or the leaf of an ash tree which she found one day still hanging from its branch. She discovered long afterwards that the official censorship authority removed these tokens before they got to John Henry.

At last the training was over.

One evening a few days before the end of the final week John Henry was surprised to be called to the hut of the camp commander, Major Fitzpatrick.

The major was a tallish man. Although born in Ireland, he had gone to a school in England and there had acquired an accent that to the troops under his command sounded English, although his English friends would have said he had a definite brogue. He had a fair bushy moustache, slicked back, light-coloured hair, which was mostly hidden under his uniform cap, and the beginnings of a pouch above his Sam Brown belt (which he hoped would diminish once he was out in the field again away from the fleshpots of the training depot, and the officers' mess there).

In so far as he had seen anything of the man at first hand, John Henry quite liked him.

Formalities over, the major said, looking at a paper on the desk before him, 'I understand, McClintock, that you've done well in all your subjects. English, Mathematics, French and German. Your sergeant instructor recommends that you be promoted and begin to teach some of these subjects from now on. You'll be a corporal at first, and if all goes well, you'll be promoted to sergeant instructor yourself, before too long. Are you willing to take this on?'

For a moment John Henry could say nothing. His delight was too great. Here was the recognition, the opportunity, he had been longing for.

The major, seeing he was dumbstruck, kindly filled the gap for him. 'You realise, of course, that that means remaining here at the home base, instead of going to the front.'

John Henry stared at him. No, he hadn't realised that. His pipe dream burst in his face like a wet, soapy bubble, stinging his eyes. 'I'm sorry, sir,' he said, 'but if I have the choice, I'd rather do what I signed up for. I'm here to fight the Germans, sir.'

Major Fitzpatrick frowned. 'Are you sure, man? It's not everybody who's offered an opportunity like this. Don't decide in a hurry.'

But John Henry had already decided.

A few days later, he sailed for France with his small unit and the rest of his battalion.

They landed in Calais, and started marching.

Chapter Twelve

John Henry's later memories of those first weeks in France were confused. They marched by day, camped overnight, marched the next day. They covered an unbelievable amount of ground. He was glad, now, that the twelve weeks' training had toughened him up or he would surely have collapsed by the second day.

Then came a stage when they were transported by train, packed even more tightly than they had been on the journey from Liverpool. The soldier with the mouth-organ still played to them as they travelled, but the tunes were stale now to most of the men.

The final stage, bringing them up to the line, was by cattle wagon.

Almost before he could register that they had reached the place where they would fight, he and the others were set to digging trenches. He worked alongside Geoffrey Poots, a slightly older man from Coleraine, and Liam Kilpatrick from Tyrone. Liam worked hard, but was so clumsy that his spade regularly threw mud over John Henry's uniform, whereupon Liam would apologise fervently and attempt to brush it off, actually making the stains worse.

Poots, although he always gave the impression of working hard when the corporal drew near, tended to lean on his spade and sigh a lot at other times. John Henry quite liked them both. Poots, he learned in conversation, wasn't quite sure why he'd signed up and was already regretting it.

'I wanted to do the right thing, Johnny,' he said earnestly, leaning on his spade again. He seemed unable to work and chat at the same time. 'My Da brought me up to do the right thing. He died last year, but I thought he'd have expected me to sign up and fight for my country. If I'd been able to ask him, I think he'd have said that. But now I don't know if it was the right thing or not. I wish I was home again, Johnny, to tell you the truth.'

'You did what you thought was right at the time, Pootsy,' John Henry said, digging away. 'You can't go back and change it now, but if it was wrong, the Lord won't hold it against you. It's better to try to do the right thing and get it wrong, than never to even try.'

And Geoffrey Poots looked happier.

They were in Belgium now, not France, he found when he asked the corporal in charge of his unit. Their job was to defend the line near a town that the corporal, Jimmy Colman, called Wipers. There had already been heavy fighting there in October, while John Henry's unit was still in training. The troops were billeted in one of the nearby villages during their off duty spells. On their arrival, the Sergeant Major gave them a short talk, aimed at helping them to settle in.

'Don't rob the locals. You get paid enough to buy cigarettes, beer and even some extra food in the village shops and pub. Don't rape the local girls – we want these people on our side. We're here to help them, not set them against us. There's a 'Red Lamp,' as we call it – a brothel, for you ignoramuses – just down the road. Don't go to the 'Blue Lamp,' that's for the officers. Be sure to keep back enough money from your pay for a regular visit.'

John Henry was horrified. Not so much by the Sergeant Major's assumption that the men would automatically be looking for sex. He'd learnt enough from his time in the linen factory back home to realise that this was to be expected. But from the way it was made almost official, acceptable, by the Sergeant Major's attitude. He had expected that authority, while aware that it happened, would have frowned on such activities. It would have been different at home, he was sure.

But perhaps the main difference was that these men were at war, and the Sergeant Major knew that.

So regularly every week after pay day whenever his unit was off-duty John Henry watched his companions in the battalion, even young Paddy O'Connor, heading off to the Red Lamp, and rolling back slightly drunk just in time before lock up. He said nothing. What was there to say?

All the same, he found himself talking to Paddy about it, one night.

'I'm surprised that you, who pray and have your rosary beads, should go along to this brothel, with the other boys, Paddy.'

Paddy was silent with embarrassment for a few minutes.

'Well, Johnny,' he said eventually, 'I have to go. I'm only human, you know.'

'So am I, Paddy. But I don't go.'

'Oh, you're a saint, Johnny!'

It was John Henry's turn to be embarrassed. 'I'm no saint, Paddy,' he said at last. 'But I know it's wrong. And I think of my Rosie, and how hurt she'd be if she ever knew I'd done that, and that makes it easier not to go.'

'Well, there it is, Johnny. You have your Rosie. I don't have anyone at home.'

'But you will have one day, when you get back there, Paddy. When the war's over.'

'If it ever is.' Paddy suddenly sounded cynical. 'But suppose I don't ever make it home, Johnny? There's lots of good fellows gone west already. I could be one of them next time we're in the trenches. I don't want to miss out on the things in life that other people are enjoying.'

John Henry found himself with nothing more to say.

It was lonely sitting in the billet on his own when all the other lads had gone out, most of them to the Red Lamp. John Henry got into the habit of walking round the village, enjoying the fresh air, chatting in his reasonably adequate French to the locals he met and improving his vocabulary and accent.

It was as he was strolling around the outskirts of the village one dark evening that he heard strange sounds in the distance. Someone was sobbing, but he could make out a few French words.

'Maman! Oh Maman!'

It was the voice of a girl, quite a young girl, John Henry thought. He quickened his steps and hurried in the direction of the sounds.

Chapter Thirteen

The sounds were coming from a dark alleyway which ran between some warehouses, deserted at this time of night.

As he drew nearer he could hear the girl's voice sounding desperate, and muttered growls from a man. British, from the words John Henry caught.

'Shut up, ye trollop or I'll shut you up!'

John Henry began to run. Bursting into the alleyway, he saw dimly through the darkness that two figures were struggling at the farther end of the place. The smaller of the two was being forced back against the alley wall in spite of her struggles. A stray moonbeam lit up the girl's face, white and terror stricken. John Henry could just see in the frail light that the man attacking her was ripping at her blouse and had tugged the thin material down nearly to her waist. Her small hands clawed feebly at his huge ones, trying in vain to prevent his savage assault. The big male hands ignored her weak efforts, and John Henry could see that her attacker was thrusting his powerful body against hers.

'Stop that, you!' John Henry leapt for the man, who instantly, hearing his voice and his approach, let go of the girl, swung round without a second's pause and hit out. John Henry took the blow on his raised forearm and seized his assailant by the throat. His training came into use without conscious thought and he struck out, punching the man directly on his Adam's apple. The man gave a faint sizzling sigh and sank to the ground. John Henry bent over him, assured himself quickly that he was still alive, and then turned to the girl. She was cowering against the alley wall, her hands over her eyes.

No sooner had he taken his eyes off him than the man leapt to his feet and ran, his feet pounding down the alley back to the main street at what seemed the speed of light. John Henry took one step to pursue him, then realised it was more important to reassure the girl.

'It's all right! You're safe now!'

But did she understand English?

'C'est bien – vous etes bien!' His French, so painstakingly learnt, deserted him in the moment of crisis.

'Merci – thank you!' The words came as a faint moan. The girl raised panic-stricken eyes to his. She was wondering, he realised in horror, if he was going to carry on where the first soldier had left off. As he watched she tried awkwardly to pull her ripped blouse back up over her exposed breasts, and John Henry hastily looked away until he felt that she must have sorted out her clothing. When he looked back the tears were streaming from her eyes, down over her colourless cheeks, drained into pallor by the moonlight.

The necessity of comforting her took over. John Henry found his French again.

'It's all right. I'll take you home. Where do you live?' he asked her in her own language.

She pointed along the alley, out of the town, towards the countryside.

'I'll take you home. Don't worry, you're safe now. Lean on me.'

She rested on his arm and stumbled along with awkward steps as he led her slowly through the darkness in the direction she indicated. The moon ducked out from behind a cloud occasionally to point out the pathway, then grinned mockingly and hid its light so that they tripped and almost fell on the rough country lane. Now that he had both time and occasional moonlight to look at her, John Henry saw that she was a very pretty girl, with curly dark hair and bright eyes which were shining at him in admiration. She was of medium height, a little taller than Rose.

Presently a small building could be seen looming up not too far away, against the momentarily lightened sky. John Henry thought it was a farmhouse, or maybe just a farm labourer's cottage.

'Do you want to tell your parents what happened?' he asked her. 'Or would you rather try to keep it to yourself?'

She stopped her stumbling progress and looked up at him fully for the first time. 'Why –? How could I do that?'

'Well – I don't know – perhaps you might just say you slipped and hurt yourself, and ripped your blouse, and I found you and helped you home?'

John Henry knew that in his own country – and from what he'd heard, in this country too – a girl might be very ashamed of being assaulted and would even be considered the guilty party, someone who had 'asked for it,' although the man concerned wouldn't be blamed, even when he'd been guilty of rape. One law for the men, another for the women, thought John Henry drily. It made him angry to think of it. It was completely against his Christian principles.

'I don't want to lie to my parents,' the Belgium girl said firmly. 'They trust me. They will believe me when I tell them what happened.'

'So, why were you out on your own in that dark alley?' John Henry couldn't help feeling curious.

'I was visiting my granny. She's old and not very well, and it cheers her up to see me. I baked some bread for her and took it round. I should have left hours ago, but she was so pleased that I'd come, and she needed help to get to bed, so I stayed much longer than I meant to. She kept saying, "Please don't go yet, Marie Louise, please stay a while." I didn't notice how dark it was getting.'

'But still, it was madness to go down that alley alone – is it a short cut or something?'

'I didn't – I kept to the main road! That soldier jumped out at me as I was passing the mouth of the alley. There just happened to be no one around at the time. It was getting late, people had gone to bed. He put his hand over my mouth to silence my screams, and dragged me up the alley. If you hadn't heard me, and come running, I don't know what he'd have done.'

I do, thought John Henry grimly. 'Do you know who it was, Marie Louise? Did you recognise him?' he asked.

'No. He had a rag tied over his face, I don't know who he was.'

John Henry hadn't seen his face either, but there had been something familiar about the attacker, all the same. He was sure it had been someone he knew. Someone who was too broke to go to the brothel, clearly. He'd look into it as soon as he got back.

They were nearly at Marie Louise's home, a small neat farmhouse set amid tidy fields obviously well tended. The door of the house opened as they approached – Marie Louise's parents, growing anxious as the time went by, had been on the lookout for her. Inside, the house matched its external appearance. The room into which John Henry was ushered was lit by an oil lamp on a well scrubbed kitchen table. A warm fire burnt cheerfully in the chimney place and the floor was of rough granite tiles in various colours. A rocking chair covered in a patchwork blanket still swayed gently from the force with which Marie Louise's mother had sprung up from it.

Marie Louise's parents were at first overcome with relief to see her arrive home safely, then very angry when she told them what had happened. They couldn't say enough in praise of John Henry and in thanks. Marie Louise's father, Jean Claude Desjardins, was a small, sturdy man in his early forties with a normally placid face, currently streaked with worry, and his wife Berthe was a round, merry looking woman with dark curly hair like Marie Louise's, already beginning to go grey.

'Any time you would like some extra food, come to us!' Jean Claude insisted. 'We will be so happy to feed you, it's the least we can do.'

And Marie Louise's mother Berthe, hardly able to speak for tears both of horror and of thankfulness, told him, 'Every day I will pray for you, my dear son. You are an angel sent from on high to rescue my baby!'

Embarrassed and tongue tied, John Henry didn't know what to say. 'It was nothing,' he mumbled. 'Anyone would have done the same. I must get back – I'll be in trouble if I'm late for duty.'

And he escaped, but not without promising to come for dinner on his next free evening.

Chapter Fourteen

Back in the hut, John Henry, still very angry at what had happened, began at once to do his best to investigate the attempted rape and to try to find out who had been responsible for it. He hadn't quite recognised the man. His face, as Marie Louise had pointed out and as John Henry now realised, had been partly covered with some sort of cloth. But for all that, there had been something very familiar about him.

John Henry was pretty well convinced that the rapist had come from his own hut, his own unit, not just from the battalion. He was one of these men whom John Henry knew fairly well. A bad thought. He hated to believe it of any of them, although some of them were friends and others were just people he knew.

'I suppose everybody in the battalion but me went to this brothel, did they, Paddy?' he asked his friend casually, as they lay on their neighbouring bunks later on that same night. 'Am I the only one who thinks it's wrong?'

'Ach, no, Johnny. There's a few others who'd agree with you – Ian Stewart, and Geoffrey Poots and Markie Stevens for a start. And then there were quite a number who'd spent their money on booze and cigarettes during the week and had nothing left – Mustard, for one. And Foxy and Liam, and Matt. I've maybe forgotten some of them, but I don't think so. I think that was the lot. But, no, you weren't the only one, for goodness sake!'

'Ach, well, glad to hear it,' John Henry said, and moved off to stretch out on his bunk.

The names ran through his head. The three who'd refused to go, like himself, for moral reasons, could probably be ruled out, he reasoned. But the other four? It had to be one of the seven people Paddy had named – everybody else had an alibi, such as it was. And wouldn't have needed another woman on the same night, surely, in any case. But Paddy had said he might have forgotten one or two. John Henry sighed. It wouldn't be easy to identify Marie Louise's assailant.

Mustard, the corporal, so called because he was tough and ready for anything, as hot as mustard – and also because his name was Colman, now John Henry came to think of it – was a small wiry man. Not him, then. The rapist had been tall, wide shouldered, much bigger than Mustard in every way.

Foxy was the red haired man who'd caused trouble for John Henry when they were first learning to use their gear and going for practice marches, tripping him up and bumping into him so that he dropped everything. Could it be him? But, no, like Mustard he was too small to be the figure John Henry had seen dimly in the alleyway. Two ruled out.

Liam and Matt. John Henry tried hard to remember, to visualise their build. Neither of them fitted into the mental picture he retained of Marie Louise's attacker. Matt, like Foxy and Mustard, was too short, too thin. And as for Liam Kilpatrick, he was far too tall and much too clumsy. He hadn't enough control over his body. It certainly hadn't been big Liam who'd swung round on John Henry so deftly. No, neither of them.

Was it someone whose name Paddy had forgotten? Would he have to question some of the other boys who'd been to the brothel that night? John Henry sighed, and wondered whom he could ask. It needed to be someone he could trust to tell him the truth and someone who wouldn't be too suspicious of his questioning. He didn't want to shame Marie Louise by spreading abroad the fact of her assault. Marty, that was the man. Marty was friendly and truthful, but he wasn't too bright. He wouldn't pause to wonder why John Henry was asking.

He rolled out of his bunk and wondered along the hut until he reached Marty's bunk.

'Sleeping, Marty?' he asked casually.

A moan came from the bunk, and Marty reared himself up, leaning on one elbow.

'Well, I was until some bugger woke me up! Oh, it's you, Johnny – sorry about the language.'

'I've heard worse, Marty. Not that it's a good thing,' he added hastily. 'So, you've exhausted yourself tonight?'

'I should think so! If you'd come along, you'd be sleeping, your-self, now, not wandering around waking up your friends, Johnny!'

'I still don't understand how a good Derry boy, brought up like you, could go there, Marty. I suppose everyone else was there except me?'

'Well, most of us, Johnny.' Marty ignored John Henry's first remarks. 'Except a few good livin' boys like yourself, and the ones who were broke.'

'Oh?'

'Yes.' Marty reeled off the same names as Paddy. There didn't seem to be any others without an alibi.

'Listen, I want to get back to sleep,' he mumbled. 'It's not like you to come preaching at a man in the middle of the night like this, Johnny. Go away!'

'Sorry, Marty. I wasn't meaning to preach. You have to make your own choices – and live with them. Go back to sleep.'

'Sorry, Johnny – didn't mean it. Night night.' Marty rolled over in his bunk and was snoring again in a few moments.

But John Henry was perplexed. Paddy had thought there might have been some other absentees, but Marty had been certain that there had been none. And John Henry had already ruled out all of them.

Except the three men who, like himself, had refrained from visiting the brothel on moral grounds.

Surely it wasn't one of them?

John Henry knew that temptation could overcome anyone. Had one of these three, after refusing the easy sex on offer, seen Marie Louise walking along the empty main street of the village, and been overcome with lust? Had he found it too hard to resist such an attractive girl apparently available to a man much stronger than her?

But if so, which of them?

John Henry, lying on his bunk again, thought back to the events of the night, picturing exactly what had happened, what he had seen.

And suddenly he had a clear vision of Marie Louise's attacker. And shuddered with horror as he recognised the figure beyond all shadow of doubt.

Chapter Fifteen

The next day he was kept too busy to do anything except carry out his various duties. It wasn't until evening, free from the routine jobs and for a few days free also from duty in the trenches, that John Henry knew he had to speak to the man he had recognised.

He was glad it wasn't either Markie or Pootsie. He liked them both. Ian Stewart was a different matter. He'd always found it hard to like the big Belfast man. But was he letting his feelings prejudice him? Did he think it was Ian he had seen just because he didn't like him? Couldn't it have been someone from another unit, a semi-stranger?

But, no. He was convinced that he had recognised the man. Not his face, certainly. The rag tied round it had concealed him well enough to make that impossible. But his build, his movements – they identified Marie Louise's assailant as Ian Stewart, now that John Henry had thought of him, beyond further doubt.

Ian was lying on his bunk reading when John Henry approached him.

'I'd like a word, Ian.'

The tall, thin man sat up and laid aside his book. John Henry saw, with some unhappiness, that he'd been reading the Bible. Was he a plain and simple hypocrite, or what?

'Now? Won't it wait?' Ian Stewart asked.

'No.'

Stewart swung his legs over the edge of the bunk and slithered down to stand on his feet beside John Henry. Like Marie Louise's attacker, he was much the same height. John Henry looked into his face for a moment, then turned and led the way out of the hut.

When they were some distance away and at no risk of being heard, Ian Stewart halted and said impatiently, 'Well? Are you going to tell me why you've dragged me out here?'

'Let's keep on walking,' John Henry suggested. 'What I want to say will come easier that way.'

'Right.'

They walked towards the nearby wood.

'I see you've got a bad bruise on your throat, Ian,' John Henry said presently.

Stewart said nothing.

'And I've got a sore place, a bit rubbed and raw, on the knuckles of my left hand.'

'Have you?' Stewart's voice sounded dull.

'It would be a strange thing, now, if there was no connection between those two things, wouldn't it?'

No response. But Stewart drew his breath in sharply as he waited for the inevitable.

'We both know it was you in that alley last night, Ian. You who attacked that poor wee Belgian girl.'

'You've got no proof!' Ian Stewart burst out savagely.

'I don't need proof.'

They walked on in silence for a few minutes.

'What are you planning to do?' Stewart asked at last in a low, shaken voice.

'Nothing.'

'But – ' Stewart stood still and swung round to look John Henry in the eye for the first time.

'I thought you might like to talk about it. About why you, who read your Bible and claim to be a Christian, should have done such a thing.'

They were well into the wood by now, walking along a rough, winding path which was just beginning to widen out into a small grassy clearing. John Henry sat down casually on a fallen tree trunk and motioned Stewart to sit beside him.

'I understand the force of temptation, Ian,' he said. 'None of us can throw the first stone. But talking to a friend can help.'

Stewart's head fell forward unto his hands, and John Henry could hear him groan. There were tears trickling down his face.

'Oh, Johnny, Johnny, I never meant to do it! I swear it was the first time! And if you won't tell on me I promise I'll never do such a thing again!'

Chapter 15

John Henry smiled. 'Amn't I telling you I've no intention of saying anything about it? What good would that do? But I'd like to help you, if you're willing.'

'How?' Stewart raised his head and looked at John Henry in bewilderment.

'I thought we might spend more time together and encourage each other – especially when most of the rest of the lads head off to this brothel, boy!'

'Why would you want to spend time with me?'

'Sure, aren't we brothers, Ian?' He smiled at the bewildered face next to him. 'There's many a time I could do with a bit of encouragement myself, when some of the lads try to be annoying to me because of my beliefs, like yer man Foxy bumping into me and tripping me up on purpose back when we were in training, for instance.'

'We could read the Bible together!' suggested Stewart eagerly.

'Aye, we could do that. Or just talk and share how things are going, maybe?'

'I'd like that, Johnny,' Ian Stewart said humbly. And from then on, John Henry sacrificed some of his free time, and the two men walked and talked together. They never became close friends, or not to John Henry's mind. But they came to understand and support each other in a way which both found helpful.

Chapter Sixteen

On his next free night John Henry took up Marie Louise's parents on their offer of a meal. It was an experience which turned out to be a great pleasure, in fact, since Berthe, like so many French or Belgian women, was an expert cook, with many recipes at her fingertips.

John Henry sat at the big kitchen table in the warm room with its appetising smells and its atmosphere of love and friendship, its feeling of safety and peace, with Marie Louise sitting shyly at one side, Jean Claude sitting opposite him, and Berthe taking the seat on his other side when she had finished serving; and he relished the cassoulet, the Coq au vin, the Sole Bonne Femme, the Crepes Suzette, and the other marvellous French or Belgian dishes, on many nights after that.

After the meal, Berthe and Jean Claude developed a habit of disappearing and leaving him alone with Marie Louise, who more often than not would suggest that they should go for a stroll round the farmhouse outside. At first John Henry in his innocence agreed to this quite happily, but it was not long before he realised his mistake. It happened on his second visit, when he and Marie Louise were walking past the stable where Jean Claude kept two worn out horses, well past their prime but still essential to the work of the farm. Jean Claude had told John Henry that he would love to replace them, but it was too difficult. Money had been far too scarce for quite some time now.

'Let's go in and make sure the poor horses have enough water for the night, Johnny,' suggested Marie Louise in a soft voice. Slipping her hand into John Henry's arm she led him inside the shadowy building.

'I was supposed to check on this much earlier,' Marie Louise whispered, 'but I forgot all about it this evening because I was so excited that you were coming to dinner, Johnny.'

She leaned over the trough where the water was kept. 'Oh, dear, it's not very full! Will you help me to get a bucketful from the well, Johnny?'

John Henry was quite happy to be of help, and with his country background he was familiar enough with wells to be able to carry out the job speedily enough. Emptying the bucket into the trough, he handed it back to Marie Louise. She placed it by the door, then came over to him where he stood by the trough, drying his hands on the seat of his regulation trousers.

Suddenly she tripped on something John Henry couldn't see, and next moment she had fallen helplessly against him, forcing him to catch hold of her. He wondered afterwards just what it was she had tripped on, but although he looked for it carefully later on, meaning to put it out of harm's way, it turned out that he could find nothing which could have pitched Marie Louise headlong into his arms like that. A funny thing, John Henry thought in his innocence.

'Oh! Johnny! Thank you for catching me!' Marie Louise breathed into his ear. John Henry was hastening to set her back on her feet and disentangle himself when he found that Marie Louise was pushing very close to him in the darkness of the stable and that she had twined her arms around his neck. She stretched up towards his face, and whispered gently, 'Johnny, you are such a lovely person.' Then she turned her face up towards him and a moment later John Henry found that he was kissing her. And such a kiss, long, passionate, and with something in it which made it almost impossible for him to stop.

It was Marie Louise, in fact, who finally pulled back.

'Oh, Johnny. You are wonderful!' she sighed in her own language. 'This is such a beautiful night. Can you smell the last of the roses in the tubs outside?'

What John Henry could mainly smell was the straw and the horses, but he didn't say so. The mention of the roses had pulled him sharply back to reality. Roses. These were cultivated roses, not wild roses. The season for wild roses was long over. *'So I'll wait for my wild rose, who's waiting for me.'* His Rosie. How could he be doing this to her?

He disentangled himself gently from Marie Louise's arms.

'I'm so sorry, Marie Louise,' he said as kindly as he could. 'I should never have kissed you. The truth is, I have a girl back home. I love her very much, Marie Louise. I like you, I can't say I don't, but it's different. You'll find someone of your own soon, my dear. But it won't be me. I'm already taken.'

It occurred to him, seeing her stricken face in a streak of moonlight, that maybe he was being too blunt. 'I'm so sorry, pet,' he added to soften it. 'Rosie and me plan to marry as soon as this lousy war is over, do you see? I can't let her down.'

Marie Louise looked up at him, her eyes full of tears. 'I understand, Johnny,' she said. 'I like you – a lot. But maybe just because you rescued me that time, and because you're so nice. I don't want to come between you and your girl. Rosie, is it? I hope you and Rosie will be very happy. And please don't let this stop you coming round here for meals. My parents would be so disappointed if you stopped coming. I'd like us all still to be friends.'

'We will be, Marie Louise,' John Henry promised. 'Like I said, I like you and your parents a lot. But I don't want you to get the wrong idea. I have to treat Rosie right – see?'

'Yes, Johnny. I see. And Johnny – I'm glad you think like that. I just hope my own man will think like that too.'

'If you pick the right one, he will, Marie Louise,' promised John Henry. 'With a lovely girl like you, he's bound to.'

But he made a mental note to avoid any further walks with Marie Louise in the moonlight. A meal inside, in the company of her parents, was one thing, but emotional or, worse still, sexual involvement with Marie Louise was quite another.

In spite of all this, his friendship with the family continued to blossom, and it added a very pleasant note to John Henry's time in that part of Belgium. It certainly beat digging trenches.

Chapter Seventeen

In the end, the trenches were ready. Then came weeks of cold. Of sleeping on muddy ground, when it was his unit's turn to supply the guard. Of rising in the middle of the night to take his turn on duty. Of near misses from bullets, and often hits. One evening a bullet that just missed John Henry killed his fellow sentry, tearing through the boy's brain.

Time moved on, so full of work that he hadn't taken in its swift progress, till one evening John Henry realised, with dismay, that tomorrow would be Christmas, and the fighting, far from being over by then, for him at least had hardly even started.

He strolled out for a walk late on Christmas Eve. The sky was clear and cold, full of bright, white stars. The stars, he remembered vaguely from a line of Shakespeare, were said to sing to the angels – *'Still quiring to the young-eyed cherubim.'*

As the line ran through his head, he heard them singing. No, it wasn't the stars, he realised after a moment. It was an earthly voice, although it sounded angelic. It reminded him of Markie, singing on the train. But it came from the direction of the German lines, and the words were German:

> *Stille Nacht, heilige Nacht,*
> *Alles schläft; einsam wacht ...*

But John Henry knew the tune. It was the carol known to him as, *'Silent night, holy night.'* As he listened, more voices joined in, the first voice soaring above them. John Henry couldn't remember when he'd heard anything so beautiful.

Tears came to his eyes, and he wondered why he and his companions should be fighting these men who had so much in common with them.

As the singing drew to a close, he heard a voice calling across No Man's Land. 'Hey, Tommy!' The words were English, but the accent was German.

John Henry hesitated, but someone else was calling back, 'Hi, Fritz.'

'Merry Christmas!'

'And Merry Christmas to you, too!' called the voice from the British lines. And suddenly voices on both sides were chiming in.

'Merry Christmas!'

'Ein gesegnetes Weihnachtsfest!'

John Henry recognised the German version, and attempted it himself.

For the rest of that night, there was no firing from either side.

Next morning, there was still no firing. Just after breakfast John Henry, who happened to be looking in that direction, saw four hands raised in apparent surrender above the German trenches. Then two men scrambled out, one of them carrying a board with 'Merry Christmas' printed neatly on it. They stood waiting for a response. John Henry and Paddy were among the first to raise hands above the trench in return.

Pootsy hurriedly scribbled, 'Merry Christmas,' on a piece of board and handed it to them. John Henry and Paddy climbed out holding the board high in the air in front of them, and the two parties advanced cautiously towards each other. Moments later, as they met in the middle of no man's land and shook hands, the rest of the battalions on both sides scrambled out of the trenches behind them and surged forward. Men were laughing, slapping each other on the back, shaking hands.

John Henry found himself greeting a young soldier, probably, like John Henry himself, still in his late teens. He was typically German in looks, with blond hair, blue eyes, and a fresh complexion, and his English was about on a par with John Henry's German.

'My name is Johan,' the German soldier said after the initial greetings.

'Isn't that funny? My name is Johnny!'

They laughed and slapped each other's back again. 'We're twins, see?' John Henry joked.

The commanders on both sides, who at first had tried to prevent the men from fraternizing, gave up and approached each other.

'Why not have Christmas dinner together?' suggested Major Fitzpatrick. 'We can pool our food, mainly corned beef, I'm afraid, on our part.'

'And we can contribute some barrels of French beer,' the German commander offered. 'It's terrible beer – very weak. No one will get drunk on it, I'm afraid, but maybe that's a good thing!'

The food was produced, the barrels of beer rolled out, and the British and German soldiers sat companionably in No Man's Land, chatting and smoking together and celebrating the peace of Christmas Day.

John Henry found a place beside Johan, and they chatted in a strange mixture of English and German. Presently he found himself telling Johan about Rosie, and how she hadn't wanted him to go to fight. Johan sympathized, and shyly produced a snapshot from his breast pocket of a pretty, dark-haired girl. 'This is my Heidi,' he said. 'When the war is over we will marry. She, too, begged me not to fight. I think now perhaps she was right.'

After the meal, someone suggested a football match. John Henry was picked for the team, as was Johan for his own side, and they spent a happy, relaxed afternoon battling against each other, but without injury or bloodshed. The Germans won, to John Henry's surprise. He hadn't thought they would be good at any sport. He realized how little he really knew about ordinary German people. His knowledge was only of Kaiser Bill and his desire to dominate the world. But wasn't his own country's desire very similar, he wondered suddenly? Was there so much difference between them?

The troops retreated to their own lines as dusk fell. But although both sides waited all night for the first sound of gunfire across the lines, there was none. Neither side was willing to fire on the men they had got to know, the men they had spent a happy day with. The night passed, the morning came, and not one bullet had been fired.

Chapter Eighteen

On the following morning, word came that the troops on the line who had been fraternizing with the Germans over Christmas were to be moved back and replaced with fresh companies who had no reason to be reluctant to fire. John Henry didn't know whether to be glad or sorry.

He and his unit were put to work away from No Man's Land, being trained in the use of some new weapons which had just arrived. But it was only a temporary measure. When the commanders felt that the men had had time to recover their fighting spirit, they were moved back to the trenches.

John Henry lay awake at nights, in the huts where off-duty units were allowed some shelter, unable to sleep for the pain of his blistered hands (still raw from the recent digging) and tried to read the end of Matthew's gospel by the light of a candle stump, seeking a little peace. When at last he fell asleep, his dreams were troubled by pictures of the young German, Johan, whom he'd met on Christmas Day.

One particularly bad dream came repeatedly. They were in the middle of a battle. John Henry was charging over the top of the trench, his bayonet at the ready, following his commander. Out of the blue Johan appeared, leaping towards him, bayonet equally ready to thrust out. In his dream, John Henry was horrified, but in spite of his horror before he knew it he had thrust forward and his weapon had pierced Johan's heart. Blood spurted everywhere, and the young German lay dead at his feet. At that point John Henry woke, his tears flowing freely enough to soak the edge of his blanket. And then he would lie awake, unwilling to sleep again and dream the same desolation over and over.

There had been no attack, no 'over the top' charge, as yet, for John Henry and his battalion. But each of them knew as they waited that it must come soon. There was a mixture of dread and excitement building up as each day brought the moment closer when they would be given their battle orders and told to that this was it. Then at last there came the day of the first attack.

Just as in his dream, John Henry found himself charging over the top, cutting the barbed wire and sliding under it, then charging on, bayonet at the ready. His companions of so many weeks, the men – or boys – in his own unit were by his side. The heavy guns thundered and it was hard to see anything ahead. John Henry found himself blundering against someone who was thrusting at him with a matching bayonet and he felt the sudden gash in his left arm followed by a spurt of blood. He thrust back in his turn and found before he had time to realise it his enemy was lying dead at his feet. John Henry gave a sob and charged on.

His ears were bursting with the noise of the cannons and his eyes stung with the gun smoke. He had lost sight of the men around him. Only the groans and shouts told him that his comrades were still there. Or some of them were.

Out of the smoke he saw the tip of a bayonet thrusting towards him. It was too late to avoid it. His own bayonet was ready to thrust back, but he knew without thinking about it that he would be too late. Then suddenly another bayonet, thrusting from the direction of the enemy in front of him, struck the first bayonet and pushed it aside. John Henry looked in disbelief. A German soldier had saved his life. But why?

Dashing the sweat and smoke out of his eyes, he saw, in a moment, the face that had haunted his dreams. Johan.

'Okay, Johnny?' came the familiar voice with its German accent. He understood. Johan had recognised him. He had been unable to allow his fellow soldier to kill the man he had met on Christmas Day, the man who had become a friend.

'Thanks, Johan!' he gasped out. For a second the two men stood still and smiled at each other as the war went on all around them.

Then John Henry heard the sound of feet charging up behind him, and as he turned to see who it was, Ian Stewart's face loomed up by his left shoulder and Ian's voice was shouting, 'It's okay, Johnny boy! I've got him!'

Then John Henry saw with unbelieving eyes the flash of Stewart's bayonet across his vision, and heard the shriek as the sharp blade pierced Johan, the young German, straight to his heart. For a moment Johan hung, transfixed, on the bayonet, then he tumbled in a heap at John Henry's feet. John Henry stumbled down after him, feeling for a pulse, but the blood was spurting out in a fountain and by the time John Henry could feel his neck the pulse was gone. Johan lay there dead.

Ian Stewart pulled out his bayonet and leapt on into the heart of the battle. And a minute later, John Henry followed him.

It was much later that night, when the few survivors were resting uneasily back in the huts, that John Henry had time to think about what had happened. He knew he couldn't blame Ian Stewart. Really, he knew he should be grateful to Stewart. Stewart had thought he was saving John Henry's life. But in spite of his rationalising thoughts, John Henry felt a black surge of hatred mounting up within him. He had always found Ian Stewart a difficult person to like, with his black and white judgements and his hypocrisy in action.

Recently John Henry had been managing to overcome this. He and Ian had spent some time together and John Henry had come to understand a little of the dark urges which sometimes took control of Stewart, and of his difficulty in trying to overcome them. He had, he hoped, been of some help to Stewart. Maybe not. He'd tried, certainly. Tried to be understanding, not to judge, to listen rather than give advice. He had learnt some time ago that no one wanted to hear advice. Mostly advice would be ignored. But a listening ear, while someone thrashed things out for themselves and thought about what they needed to do, was another matter. That sometimes helped.

But now, with the vision of Johan's dead face springing up in his eyes again, of the moment when such surprise had shown on the young German's face, before Stewart's bayonet drove into his heart, John Henry felt bitterness overwhelm him. Why couldn't Stewart have waited to see what was happening?

He knew that was stupid. In battle, waiting was the last thing anyone should do. If John Henry had really been in danger, waiting would have meant that he was dead.

He refocused his anger. It wasn't Ian Stewart who'd been to blame. It wasn't himself, either. But couldn't God have stopped this from happening, arranged things differently? He didn't know.

Presently he found the release of tears. But it was almost morning before he managed a few unhappy hours of sleep, haunted by dreams and constantly disturbed by terrifying nightmares which jerked him abruptly awake. Then he would turn over and try again to sleep. Without much success.

Chapter Nineteen

It was getting colder all the time. John Henry, when he was given the chance to sleep, took to piling his army greatcoat and any spare clothes on top of him and rolling into a bundle. He was so tired most nights that he fell asleep very easily, cold or not.

It was on a particularly cold night that he was wakened by a voice whispering softly in his ear, 'McClintock! McClintock! Wake up!'

John Henry started up with a gasp, and felt a strong hand cover his mouth. 'Shut up, you fool! We don't want to wake the others.'

He rolled round sufficiently to see who was speaking and found that it was his Commanding Officer, Major Fitzpatrick.

John Henry knew that his eyes were starting out of his head.

'Get dressed and come outside,' said Major Fitzpatrick in the quietest whisper. 'I want your help.'

John Henry obediently rolled off his bunk and threw his top layer of clothes on quickly. He had no idea what Major Fitzpatrick could want with him in the middle of the night, but it didn't do to argue with a senior officer.

He stumbled out of the hut and found the Major waiting for him impatiently.

'Ah, McClintock. Come away a bit. We don't want any of the fellows to hear what I have to say.'

The two men moved well out of hearing distance of the sound sleepers inside.

'I've had instructions from the Brigadier,' Major Fitzpatrick said softly. 'He asked me to pick one man to assist me, and I immediately thought of you. You have all the qualities necessary. Courage, intelligence, loyalty. I was very impressed when you turned down promotion because you wanted to actually fight the Germans, rather than have a safe post at home. Also, of course, you know and can speak some German, which might be important.'

'Thank you, sir,' John Henry mumbled. He wondered what was coming.

71

'I've been asked to carry out a reconnaissance at night as soon as possible, to see if I can pick up some idea of the opposing forces and their artillery, and so on. Since it needs to be done quickly, I would like to do it tonight. I know I'm springing it on you, but I think that may be the best way. Prevent you thinking too much about it in advance and building up the nerves. Are you happy to come with me?'

John Henry replied without hesitation. 'Yes, sir!'

'You understand that anything we learn tonight will be confidential, McClintock? I'll report it to Brigadier General Montrose but no one else is to be told anything either about our expedition or about what we learn. Do you understand that?'

'Yes, sir.'

'And do you swear to keep it all secret?'

'Yes, sir. I swear.'

John Henry fully understood the need for secrecy. Rumours spreading round the camp, whether true or false, were the worst possible thing for morale. He made the promise to keep everything secret without a second thought.

He could see in the faint moonlight the white gleam of Major Fitzpatrick's teeth as he smiled.

'Good man, McClintock. I knew you'd be for it.'

John Henry stood ready, waiting for the Major to give him his instructions.

'Have you got your pistol? And your knife?'

'No sir, but I can easily slip in quietly and get them. Will I be needing my rifle?'

'No, your rifle would be too clumsy. It would just get in your way. We'll be mostly crawling, man. But bring your greatcoat and your gloves. It'll be cold.'

John Henry slipped back into the dark hut, as quietly as possible. Someone groaned, and turned over in his bunk. John Henry stood stock still.

Marty was mumbling in his sleep. 'Aw, Mary Ann, I'll be back soon, don't be going with that eedjit Murphy, sure, I love you, darlin', I need you to keep lovin' me ...'

John Henry felt that he shouldn't be hearing this. He edged quietly away, his legs shaking. Moving as silently as possible, and trying to shut his ears to Marty's dreaming voice, he pulled out his knapsack from beneath the bed and felt in it until he could identify the knife and the pistol which he kept there for regular use. Slipping them out as quietly as he could he pushed the gun down into the holster attached to his belt, and slipped the knife into his pocket.

Time to go. Moving as softly as his heavy boots would let him, he picked up his greatcoat and slung it round his shoulders. Reaching the hut door he twisted the doorknob silently, his breath held as he listened for the possible squeak. Then he pulled the door gently open and slipped through the small gap.

It was important, he realised, to be just as careful in closing the door again as he had been in opening it. He held onto the handle as he drew the door carefully shut behind him. Then he very cautiously reversed his actions and allowed the doorknob to turn slowly round into the closed position. When he was satisfied that the action was complete, he released his grip on the handle and stepped silently away from the door.

He looked around him, and found that he could see a vague figure looming up against the faint moonlight not too far away. Major Fitzpatrick.

John Henry made his way slowly and carefully across the distance between them.

'Got what you need?' the Major whispered.

'Yes, sir.'

'All right. Follow me.'

They moved quietly out across the rough ground beyond the trenches until they reached the barbed wire which signalled the start of No Man's Land. The Major stopped, signalling a halt to John Henry with a downward gesture of one hand. John Henry stopped obediently and watched as the Major took an implement from the small bag attached to his waist and began to work on the wire. It was, John Henry soon realised, one of the regulation wire cutters, which would make it possible to get into the wide space between the lines.

A small click, followed by a satisfied grunt from Major Fitzpatrick, told John Henry that the first strand had been successfully broken. But it seemed quite a while later, minutes during which John Henry felt his heart constantly jumping into his mouth, before the last of the wires was broken and the major turned to him and whispered, 'All done.'

The relief which surged through John Henry was so strong that it took him a while to recognise that the broken wires were not the end of the journey. On the contrary, they were the beginning. The beginning of something dangerous and frightening.

'Now,' said Major Fitzpatrick, 'time to get down, McClintock. As flat as you can. And let's start crawling. Watch what I'm doing, and follow me. Keep your head down as much as possible. It's the eyes shining in the dark, when they turn the lights on you, that tell the Germans just where you are. That's why so many poor wee animals get shot. Foxes and weasels and the like, aye and a wheen of rats of course, that get their eyes lit up in the cross lights. So don't be caught like them, boy. Right, we'll go for it. And no talking from now on, unless it's something serious.'

John Henry obediently dropped to his knees and lay face down across the mud of No Man's Land. He kept his eyes turned down, crawling after Major Fitzpatrick across the difficult ground, his nose distressed by the harsh muddy smell, using his hands and his knees to propel himself on, aware continually of the dirt clogging his clothes, particularly the knees of his trousers which seemed to be several inches higher than the rest of his body as the mud fastened on to them and built itself up in thick layers.

The chill of the mud crept over him. He hadn't expected it to be so cold. His fingers, even inside the thick Army Issue gauntlets, were beginning to freeze, to feel like frozen sticks of wood. The crawling continued for what seemed like an eternity.

It was so dark that it was hard to see anything. John Henry fastened his gaze on the soles of Major Fitzpatrick's boots, moving before him like some weird creatures from *The War Of The Worlds* or some other Science Fiction story. Abruptly John Henry froze. What was he crawling over?

'Major!'

The boots stopped. A face appeared as Major Fitzpatrick twisted his head round over his shoulder.

'What?'

'We're crawling over something – something strange.'

John Henry's voice sank to a whisper.

'Well?' The Major's voice came in a hard bark, made more frightening by the attempt to keep it at a low level.

'It's – I think it's a body.'

'Well? What do you expect? This is No Man's Land. It's chock full of bodies, man!'

'Oh. Yes.'

'I told you not to speak unless it was something important!'

The major's face twisted round again out of sight and his boots continued their forward progress.

John Henry followed on. A man's body wasn't important, it seemed. Silly of him to think it was.

He crawled on.

Something ran across his eye line, a few inches in front of his face. A huge, brown rat, fat and sleek from the bodies it had fed on. John Henry groaned with disgust. He hoped Major Fitzpatrick didn't hear him.

He wondered how far they had come. The cold continued to sink into his bones. He was bitterly aware of it with one part of his brain, but with another he had almost blocked it out. His body was cold. All right. Forget about it, and keep moving, said this other part of his brain, and John Henry obeyed it. He wondered if they were anywhere near the enemy lines as yet. The whole idea was to get across them, wasn't it, and try to eavesdrop on conversations which might tell them something, or alternatively to view the various artillery in the enemy's possession?

'Stop.' John Henry just about heard the sound, whistled through the Major's teeth. But he saw that the Major's boots had stopped.

Raising his head cautiously he peered around him in the semi darkness. Faint moonlight allowed him to identify something ahead of them as a fence made of strands of more barbed wire. German barbed wire, this time. John Henry wondered if it was any different from their own sort. Probably not. And that was strange, in itself. Like the German soldiers on Christmas day, so like his own comrades. He wondered again why two sets of people with so much in common needed to sort out their differences by killing each other.

The Major was extracting something from the bag attached to his belt. The wire-cutters again, John Henry knew.

He could hear small noises, hard to pick up even for him, so near to their source, as Major Fitzpatrick worked as silently as possible at strand after strand of wire. Every so often there was a rather louder sound, a crack, as a strand sprang apart.

After a long quiet time, Major Fitzpatrick turned his head enough to whisper, 'Go.'

John Henry crawled forward. The Major was holding back the strands of wire to allow them to slide, one after the other, through the gap he'd created in the fence. John Henry went first. Then he held back the wire to allow the major to follow him and to take up his position as leader again.

John Henry felt a shudder run through his body, partly fear and partly excitement. They were behind the German lines.

Chapter Twenty

Not far off they could catch glimpses of campfires, and see shadowy figures moving about. Sentries, John Henry thought. Armed and on the lookout for just this sort of thing. He wondered how many times while on duty he himself had missed the enemy presence as two or less German soldiers wriggled through cut wire to explore their own set up. Never, he hoped. But he couldn't be sure. He realised that while on sentry duty he had been more concerned with snipers than with spies.

Spies. That was what he and the Major were right now. John Henry hadn't put this name to their activities before. They were spying. Something he had always despised. But he could see for the first time that it might be necessary in times of war, even essential. And that it would be the action of brave men.

Meanwhile, once more, nose to the ground and eyes lowered, he was following Major Fitzpatrick's boots.

Instead of proceeding straight forward, he noticed, they were moving along the wire fence. He supposed this made sense. They needed to give the sentries a wide berth, to skirt around the edge of the encampment rather than plunge straight in. But at some point, surely, they would need to move in closer.

Yes, sure enough, the boots were turning in a direction diagonal to the fence, and heading towards what should be the outskirts of the trenches and huts. John Henry hoped that the Major and his boots had judged the distance right. It would be too bad if they found themselves crawling into the middle of the soldiers, sleeping or not.

He knew from the rising heat that they must be nearing the campfires. For the first time in ages he became aware again of the bitter cold permeating his body. The sensation of heat coming from somewhere to his right reinforced his awareness once again of the chill that penetrated right to his bones.

As his forehead bumped against something he noticed that the major's boots had halted once again. He heard the soft hiss. 'Stop. To the right.'

The right. That was where the heat was coming from. And also, he saw now, where a light was twinkling against a block of darkness. He thought it out. The men would be asleep, except for those on duty. The only people likely to be awake, with a light shining, would be the commanders. Possibly discussing strategy. And that was what he and the Major had come there to hear, if possible.

Sure enough, Major Fitzpatrick's boots swung to the right and slowly, laboriously, John Henry followed them. The twinkling light drew nearer. He could see now, while still doing his best not to raise his eyes too much, that the light came from one of the huts. The end hut – that also suggested that it might be the hut belonging to the camp commander. He would want to be in a position to oversee everything that was going on.

Major Fitzpatrick was now crawling around the side of the hut which had the light. John Henry followed. They were, he was pretty sure, safe from being observed by any of the sentries. There was a window at the side as well as the front of the hut. Major Fitzpatrick stopped beside it, sat up, and waited for John Henry to draw up beside him.

The window was slightly open. That was good. Otherwise they would have been wasting their time. John Henry strained to hear what he could of the muffled conversation inside the hut. It was clear enough soon that the speakers were the senior officers of the German brigade.

With a mental struggle, John Henry managed to adapt his mind to the German language and to follow what they were saying. It was doubly hard because only a few words could be heard clearly.

'... next time ... it will make all the difference ...'

'... it seems so wrong ...'

'... our fatherland deserves the best ...'

'... but is this the best?.. ...'

'... not for us to decide ...'

'... the Kaiser ...'

'... we need a weapon which will work ...'

'... gas ...'

'... it has to be done We need to use it ...'

John Henry, gasping in horror, missed the next few sentences. Were the Germans seriously deciding to use gas?

It seemed that the decision wasn't being left to these men on the spot. If he'd understood the conversation correctly, the decision had come from the very top. So nothing was going to stop it.

Major Fitzgerald tapped John Henry on the arm.

Chapter 20

'Time to move, McClintock.'

John Henry obediently shuffled back down to crawling position, and the two of them began to make their way silently back at an oblique angle across the camp.

'I want to check out their artillery,' the Major said very quietly. 'Over in that direction, I think.' He indicated the large looming blackness etched against the faint light of the sky and at once, head down, began again to move in towards whatever it was. John Henry, from the brief glimpse he'd had, was reasonably confident, also, that this must be the big guns. He wondered if there might be a soldier on guard there, then shrugged off the idea. If there was, there was. Nothing to be done about it except be even more careful.

The decisions were not up to him, as he was very well aware, but he thought if he'd been Major Fitzpatrick he'd have wanted to get straight back with the information they'd already picked up. Surely it was more important to get that warning back to the commanders rather than risk being caught for the sake of some unnecessary details about the types of gun in use? They already knew the enemy had a lot of artillery and would certainly use it. They had fully experienced its strength and fire-power. But so far, no gas had been used. If that was about to change, and the words they had overheard made that only too clear, then it was important that the essential preparations for such an attack should be made.

They had nearly reached the artillery. John Henry, taking a quick glance, thought he saw something moving beside the nearest gun. A sentry?

He just caught Major Fitzpatrick's whispered command, lower than ever. 'Stay there.'

John Henry obeyed. Major Fitzpatrick moved forward. If he hadn't known he was there, John Henry didn't think he would have heard or seen him.

There was a pause of several minutes duration, which seemed even longer to the waiting soldier. Then he heard a very faint sound, half a groan, half a cry, and knew instinctively that Major Fitzpatrick had dealt in his own way with the patrolling sentry. It was no worse than killing the enemy in battle, John Henry supposed. It only seemed so much worse.

A moment later, the major crawled back. He held something in his right hand which gleamed in the starlight. As John Henry watched he wiped the knife on a rag taken from his pocket and sheathed it again in the attachment on his belt. 'All clear.'

The Major turned away and crawled back towards the big guns, with John Henry following close behind. John Henry wasn't sure what Major Fitzpatrick expected to learn, but he was willing to find out.

Each individual gun seemed huge. Major Fitzpatrick reached the nearest and stood up slowly. In spite of the moonlight which occasionally crept out from behind the clouds his shadow was completely hidden by the huge shadow of the gun. 'Stay down, McClintock. And memorise the details I give you.'

John Henry did his best.

This first gun was an sFH 13. It weighed 93 pounds. No wonder, John Henry thought, it seemed so colossal. The Major relayed to him rapidly, apparently from previous knowledge, that this gun fired High Explosive rounds which caused maximum shock. It could fire three rounds per minute and had a range of 9,400 yards. It was the gun which the Germans had mostly been using against them.

Major Fitzpatrick dropped to the ground again and crawled on to the next piece of artillery. This one loomed up even higher against the sky from John Henry's lowly perspective. A monster, he thought. Again, the Major detailed the information to John Henry, as if to a copy typist who would keep a safe record of everything said. This one was a Schalnke Emma – 'Skinny Emma.' It weighed eight hundred and forty-eight pounds, and used nickel steel projectiles, three hundred and five mm shells. It could fire a round every three and a half minutes. A far more terrifying and devastating enemy than the sFH 13. They proceeded along the line. The Major identified three more guns, one of them a Skinny Emma and the other two the lighter sFH 13s.

He turned at last to John Henry with relief, and forgot himself so far as to whisper the good, but non essential right then, news. 'No sign of a Big Bertha, thank goodness.'

Even John Henry, not over familiar with the German weapons, had heard of Big Bertha, named after Bertha Krupp, the heiress and sole proprietor of the Krupp industrial empire since the death of her father. It was said that her husband actually ran the company in her name, but Bertha Krupp was still a force to be reckoned with. The Big Bertha gun had been around for years, and had become well known after the siege of Port Author during the Russian Japanese war, when the Japs had used it to enormous effect, to sink the Russian navy from land.

The Germans, not unnaturally, had produced some Big Bertha's for their own use, and at the start of the war, John Henry had heard, they had used it at Liege to lay waste the Belgian defenses in four days. If the artillery he and Major Fitzpatrick had just been examining was big and heavy, Big Bertha cast them into the shade, weighing in at forty-three tons and able to propel shells of eighteen hundred pounds nearly eight miles. It took a crew of dozens six hours to assemble Bertha, and ten railway transport cars were necessary to bring her up to the line, to carry her dismantled parts.

It had never been all that likely, John Henry thought from his scanty knowledge, that the German commanders would have bought up one of their few Big Berthas to this part of the line. But he supposed that it was possible. He was glad to learn that it hadn't happened.

Meanwhile, time was going on. It occurred to John Henry, as it must have done to Major Fitzpatrick, that the sentry he had killed would be replaced at some point when his spell of duty reached its end. Not quite yet, possibly. But when the time came, the new sentry was going to discover his comrade's body, and give the alarm that the enemy was here. It would be good to get safely away before that happened.

It still seemed to John Henry that the information they had overheard about poison gas was of far more importance than the strength and power of the guns lined up against them. The soldiers needed to be prepared with gas masks for the assault. They already knew that there would be big guns firing against them. He was relieved when the Major, dropping down from the final gun, whispered, 'Back now, McClintock.'

They resumed their painful, freezing progress across enemy territory until they reached the edge of the camp and then turned down again towards the fence. Crawling carefully along, at last they reached the place where Major Fitzpatrick had cut the wire. So far nothing had gone wrong. It mustn't go wrong now. They needed to take this information safely back.

Suddenly a shrill warning blast of whistle and bell pierced their ears. The relief sentry had arrived.

Chapter Twenty-one

For a moment both men froze. Then Major Fitzpatrick tugged John Henry's arm gently and indicated without words that he wanted them to move on. It was pointless to stay behind the German lines where sooner or later they would be discovered and either killed or taken prisoner. Moving as quickly as possible, the Major crawled forward and pulled back the cut wires to enable John Henry to get past. Then John Henry, in turn, held back the wires for his commanding officer, until both men were safely through. The worst was over. But there was still a long way to go.

Once again John Henry found himself crawling across No Man's Land. They had slipped through the wire fence which marked the start of the German lines, passed through the open cut without triggering off any alarms, and now began the last long, freezing journey. John Henry tried not to think about some of the objects which he was crawling over. He must simply keep going.

And yet before they were more than halfway across he suddenly stopped. What was that he had heard?

Over to his left there was a faint moaning. John Henry listened. Presently he could make out some words.

'God, oh God. Help me, someone. Will no one ever come?'

This time he was sure the situation was serious.

'Major.' A whisper, but with enough force in it to reach Major Fitzpatrick's ears, he hoped. Yes. The Major twisted his head round. John Henry could see his face just showing in what moonlight there was.

He said nothing, which was almost worse than if he had shouted angrily.

'Major, can you hear? Someone asking for help, just over there.'

Major Fitzpatrick took the time to listen. 'You're right, McClintock. Well, I suppose we must have a look. But I warn you, man, it may be someone in extremis, and in that case the best thing we can do for him is to dispatch him quickly.'

Everything in John Henry rebelled at the idea. He offered up a quick prayer. 'Don't let it be like that, Lord.'

Major Fitzpatrick, followed closely by John Henry, made off in the direction of the sounds. As they neared the injured man, both of them could hear his words and groans more clearly. John Henry caught his breath.

'Sir. I think it's –'

'I think so too, McClintock.'

The man was lying on one side, his right leg stretched out, but his left bent away from his body at an awkward angle. They could see his face as they came closer.

'Markie.'

'Corporal Stevens.'

It was the boy with the beautiful tenor voice which John Henry had first heard on the train from Liverpool. He had been promoted to Corporal a short time ago when Mustard, Corporal Colman, had been shot, but hadn't lasted long in that position. He had been missing for two days, since the last engagement. The mystery was how he had managed to survive for so long.

Major Fitzpatrick spoke briskly. 'All right, McClintock. Keep a look out while I check how badly he's injured.'

John Henry did as he was told. And as he looked carefully round, he continued to pray silently, all the more now that he knew who the injured soldier was.

'It's his left leg. And a few cracked ribs. That's it.'

John Henry breathed a sigh of relief. 'Not too serious, then.'

'Serious enough,' snapped Major Fitzpatrick. He sounded all the harsher because of necessity he was keeping his voice as low as possible. 'Now we need to work out some way of getting him back without making things worse.'

There was silence for a moment, spent by John Henry in giving thanks.

'Get your greatcoat off, McClintock.'

John Henry hastened to remove his coat, realising that Major Fitzpatrick had already removed his own.

'We should be able to make a type of stretcher from these. Done it before.' The Major worked busily, fashioning a makeshift carrier from the two coats, fastening them together by their buttons.

'Belt, McClintock.'

John Henry removed his belt and passed it over.

'Now, help me slide him onto the coats. We'll use it like a sleigh, just pull it along the ground between us, understand? And we'll use our belts to fasten him securely onto it.'

Markie had passed out during Major Fitzpatrick's examination of him. It was just as well, John Henry realised. Working quickly and carefully, the two men slid the injured soldier onto the coats, strapped the belts across his waist and legs, and then, one on each side and still crawling, they began to drag Markie Stevens across the remaining part of No Man's Land.

If it had been cold before, when he was muffled in his thick warm Army greatcoat, John Henry knew that it was more bitter than ever now. But somehow he didn't mind. He was so glad to be involved in the rescue of the young soldier and so thankful that they had come along in time before Markie died of his wounds and of thirst and starvation and cold.

Unlike the outward trip, the return journey to their own lines went quickly, in spite of the continual exertion involved in tugging Markie along. John Henry felt the flames of extreme effort flashing through his arm and leg muscles, and the cold which cramped his fingers and numbed his legs, but then he could see the faint outline of the wire fence which marked their own lines and knew that they were within a stone's throw of safety.

'McClintock.' It was the Major's voice, so soft he could just about hear it.

'Yes, sir.'

'This is where we need to be especially careful. Remember that the enemy snipers are on the lookout for any movement around this fence. Don't do anything sudden. Certainly don't begin to stand up until we're well clear. I'll need to cut a few more strands of wire if we're to get this boy through them without hurting him any more than we can help.'

John Henry said nothing. No point in replying and making more noise by doing so.

Major Fitzpatrick crawled forward alone and John Henry knew that he was engaged in cutting more strands of wire to widen the opening. It seemed a long time before he returned.

'Now. Let's get him moving.'

The took up their familiar positions, one on each side of Markie, and half dragged, half pushed the injured boy up to and then, very carefully, through the fence. It needed the joint strength of both of them to manoeuvre him forward, and there was no one to hold back the wire this time. But the Major had done a good job with his cutting, and they took him through without damage. Then Major Fitzpatrick hurried off to get help, while John Henry stayed with Markie. Soon he would be warm and well looked after, with a doctor treating him who knew what he was doing.

John Henry thought this must surely be a 'blighty one,' an injury serious enough to ensure that the victim would be sent home to hospital to recover. He would miss Markie. But he'd have missed him even more, he thought philosophically, if he had died of his injuries out there on the battlefield.

Presently he heard the sound of men approaching. First came two soldiers led by Major Fitzpatrick. They were carrying a light stretcher, a real one this time rather than the two coats fastened together which Major Fitzpatrick had manufactured in No Man's Land, and they set it down beside Markie before lifting him carefully into it. John Henry took the opportunity to seize his greatcoat and belt and put them back on. By the time he had done this the doctor had arrived. After a cursory examination the doctor pronounced, 'This man will have to be taken to the field hospital. Get moving, you fellows.'

'Will Stevens be all right, sir?' John Henry ventured.

'Stevens? That's this soldier's name? No reason why he shouldn't be,' the MO replied shortly. 'I'll do what I can for him in the field hospital, and then see about getting him shipped back home for further treatment.' He turned on his heel and walked away.

'Now, McClintock, you and I need to agree on what we found, collate it and report it. Come along to my hut and we'll compare notes.'

Major Fitzpatrick also turned and marched briskly away. Markie was forgotten. And that was the way it had to be, John Henry reflected as he hurried after his Commanding Officer. Markie was one man, and the army was doing its best for him. But the information he and the Major had collected that night might mean the difference between victory and defeat, and the lives of thousands.

Chapter Twenty-Two

John Henry knew that the Commanding Officer of the Brigade had a hut to himself at the far end of the camp, but he had never been inside it. Major Fitzpatrick was leading him towards it now.

Just before they reached it, the Major stopped. 'Let's just make sure we're in agreement about our information, McClintock, before we go in to report,' he said. He ran quickly over the list of heavy artillery he and John Henry had noted. 'Have I left anything out?'

'No, sir, that's all correct. And then, there's the conversation we heard about the gas, of course.'

'Gas?' Major Fitzpatrick looked blank.

'When we were listening outside the hut, before we went to look at the big guns,' John Henry prompted him. 'The officers were talking in German. It's a really important bit of information.'

'Ah. The conversation in German.' The Major coughed in embarrassment. 'Your German is a lot better than mine, McClintock. Well, that was one of the main reasons why I brought you, as I said. Er – what exactly did you hear?'

John Henry stared at him in amazement. Had Major Fitzpatrick really missed the gist of that conversation?

'I didn't hear it all, sir. But from what I did hear, orders have come down from higher up – from the Kaiser himself, as far as I could be sure – to use gas in the next push.'

'My God!'

'It seemed to me very important to warn the CO, sir, so we can all be prepared. Gas masks, and stuff, I mean.'

'Well, this certainly justifies me in picking you to come with me, McClintock! Your German language skills, I mean. But I never dreamt –'

He thrust out his lower lip, clasped his hands together low down his back, and began to stride around in circles.

'You're absolutely positive this was what you heard, McClintock?'

'Yes, sir,' said John Henry without hesitation. He hadn't realised that Major Fitzpatrick hadn't understood the conversation. That would be why he hadn't hurried straight back to report, but had taken time to inspect the artillery. John Henry had been surprised by this delay at the time. Now he understood it.

'All right.' Major Fitzpatrick stopped walking round in circles and came to a halt at the door of the C.O.'s hut. 'I'll report on the guns, but you'll have to tell your story about the gas yourself. He'll probably want to ask you questions about what exactly was said.'

'Yes, sir.'

Major Fitzpatrick knocked briskly on the door of the hut. A voice inside barked, 'Come!' The Major opened the door and went in with John Henry at his heels.

Three men were seated round a glowing stove, managing to look official in spite of the way they were huddling round it for warmth. John Henry recognised them. Brigadier General Montrose, whose voice had ordered them to come in. He was a large, almost fat man with a red face, and a thick white moustache bristling over his mouth. Colonel Johnston-Smythe, the next in command, a much thinner, more distinguished looking man, whose uniform always looked as if he'd put it on straight from his tailor that morning. And Colonel Watterson, a pleasant man with a kind face who often smiled.

Of the three, John Henry instinctively liked Watterson the best, although he'd had no personal dealings with him. But others who had had such dealings reported him as ready to listen and understand, not the sort to jump down your throat and assume that you'd been in the wrong in whatever situation it might be. These men were Major Fitzpatrick's direct superiors. And John Henry's own superiors, of course, at a much further distance.

'Come to report, sir,' said Major Fitzpatrick, saluting smartly and addressing himself to Brigadier General Montrose. 'Private McClintock and I carried out a reconnaissance behind enemy lines in accordance with your instructions.'

'Ah ha. Good man, Fitzpatrick. Just back?'

'Yes sir. I thought it best to come straight here to report, sir. As you instructed, sir.'

'Yes. So, give me your report, Fitzpatrick. Word of mouth will do for now. You can write it up later.'

'We examined the field artillery, sir, and made a list. You'll be glad to know, sir, that there was definitely no Big Bertha. The guns we saw were sFH13s and Skinny Emmas.' Major Fitzpatrick rolled off the list of guns and the number of each, and then said, 'Private McClintock will confirm that this is an accurate list.'

John Henry drew himself up smartly, saluted in turn and snapped out, 'Yes sir!' in true military style.

'Hmm,' said Brigadier General Montrose when they had finished. 'Valuable information, Fitzpatrick. Now go away and put it into writing while the Colonels and I consider what we've learnt.'

'Yes, sir.' For a moment John Henry thought Major Fitzpatrick was about to turn on his heel and march out, but instead he said hesitantly, 'There was just one other thing, sir. I think it may be important.'

'Yes?' The Brigadier raised his thick, bushy white eyebrows and glared under them at both men.

'We listened outside the hut where the senior officers were, sir, before looking for the guns. As you are aware, sir, my German is not of the best. That was one reason why I chose Private McClintock to accompany me, sir, because his German is said to be first class. We overheard a conversation, but since it was in German I picked up very little of it. My main concern was to assure myself that the officers were in their hut and not out prowling around near the artillery, sir. However, Private McClintock understood the conversation, and with your permission I suggest that he should report what he heard to you directly.'

'Very well,' barked Brigadier General Montrose, his eyebrows now lowered over sharp eyes. 'Go ahead, private! What did you hear which Major Fitzpatrick considers so important?'

'Sir, to be brief, I heard the German officers discussing whether or not to use gas during their next attack, and deciding that they would do so.'

The thick white eyebrows shot upwards again.

'Are you serious, boy? It's not very likely, is it? An evil weapon. So far no one civilised has used it.'

'The French used tear gas against the Germans in August last year,' observed Colonel Johnston-Smythe in a drawling voice. His thin, distinguished figure which had been crouched over the stove was suddenly drawn upright.

'I said no one civilised, Colonel,' snapped the Brigadier. 'That hardly includes the French.'

Colonel Johnston-Smythe smiled reluctantly.

'Moreover, when the Hague Convention of 1907 expressly forbade the use of poison gas and said it would be considered a war crime,' Brigadier General Montrose continued, 'tear gas was not included in the category of 'poison gases.' Which may to some extent excuse the French use of it. I find it impossible to believe that the Germans, who are, after all, men much like ourselves, could stoop so low as to use actual poison gases such as Chlorine or Mustard.'

'Perhaps it would help if Private McClintock would give us some more detail of the conversation he overheard, if he can remember it,' suggested Colonel Watterson, smiling at John Henry.

'Very well. You heard the Colonel, McClintock. What exactly did you hear?'

John Henry attempted to repeat the snatches he had overheard as accurately as he could.

'I heard bits and pieces, sir – not always whole sentences. It was hard to pick up everything through the walls, even though one window was slightly open. I'll give you the things I definitely heard clearly. Someone said, "... next time ... It will make a difference ..." and then another officer said, "... it seems so wrong ..." Then either the first one, or it may have been another, said, "Our fatherland deserves the best ..." and the second man said, "But is this the best?" And others joined in, saying things like, "... It's not for us to decide ...". One of them mentioned, "... the Kaiser ..." and talked about, "... a weapon which will work ..." Then I definitely heard the German word for gas, and the first man said, speaking in a tone of great authority, "... It has to be done. We need to use it ..." I didn't hear any more, sir, but I thought –'

'I don't need to hear what you thought, private. Only the words which you overheard. That's all.'

John Henry nodded, and then hurriedly corrected himself and said, 'Yes, sir.

'Well, gentlemen? What do we think?'

'It sounds serious,' Colonel Watterson said, and for once he was not smiling.

'The boy certainly heard a discussion about the use of gas,' contributed Colonel Johnston-Smythe. 'And apparently he also heard these men deciding to use it "next time."'

'But,' said Brigadier General Montrose, leaning forward impressively towards his subordinates, 'while that seems clear enough, I still question whether they meant to use anything we could classify as poison gas. I suspect they were simply considering copying the French and using tear gas.'

Chapter 22

'I suppose that's possible,' said Colonel Johnston-Smythe slowly.

'It's not only possible, it's almost certainly true,' the Brigadier said energetically. 'Do we really believe these men, enemies at present or not, would dream of using such a weapon any more than we would ourselves? Why, before the war I've met on social terms with any number of German officers, and a nicer, more gentlemanly bunch of fellows you couldn't find anywhere. They haven't changed into criminals overnight!'

'I'll grant you that, sir,' Colonel Watterson agreed. 'I myself have visited in country houses before the war where there were some very pleasant German officers as fellow guests, and I remember that I liked them enormously. Nevertheless – Private McClintock has brought us what is potentially very valuable information, and I don't think we should reject it in a hurry.'

'I'm still convinced nothing worse than tear gas was discussed. And I'm not convinced that even that was actually going to be used. Who knows what the final decision was? Not to use anything of that sort either, if I'm any judge of my fellow man. You say you heard the German word for gas, Private,' he said, suddenly swinging round towards John Henry again, and glaring up at him from his seat by the stove. 'Are you sure it was a word which meant poison gas, or did it only mean tear gas, eh?'

'It w- was g- giftgas, sir – poison gas,' stammered John Henry, taken by surprise. 'Not Trynengas, I'm quite sure.'

'And you expect me to turn the whole brigade upside-down, making preparations for an attack by poison gas, simply on the word of one young private?' the Brigadier said contemptuously. 'I'm not ready to waste time on such a huge exercise because one private thinks he understands German well enough to be sure about such a matter. I don't claim to speak German expertly myself, but I would expect that either word might be used for the harmless substance.'

'As a matter of fact, sir, McClintock has the meanings correctly,' drawled Colonel Johnston-Smythe reluctantly.

'And who's to say he's remembered which one was used at the time? No, I'm not prepared to put much weight on what Private McClintock thought he heard, and that's final. It would be another matter if Fitzpatrick had also understood what these officers said. A great pity he doesn't claim to speak German well – like myself, ha ha, Major? Nothing wrong with that! Still, it leaves us without the corroboration of an officer as to what was heard.

'The lower ranks aren't running this war quite yet, gentlemen, in spite of the growing revolutionary tendencies worldwide. We're living in dangerous times, gentlemen, when a labourer can take upon himself the right to question his superiors. I've seen too much of it on my own estate before this war started. Well, at least we can keep it out of the army. Major Fitzpatrick, I don't doubt you thought you were doing right in letting me hear what this private had to say, but I've now made my decision. There will be no scaremongering, no suggestion to the men of a threat of gas. You and the private may go now.'

Major Fitzpatrick made haste to leave. So, of course, did John Henry.

When they were safely outside with the door tightly shut behind them, John Henry could contain himself no longer. 'Are they really going to make no preparations in case the Germans use poison gas in the next attack, Major?' he blurted out. 'I can't believe it! Isn't there anything we can do?'

'No, McClintock, there isn't. Decisions like these are up to our commanders. Our job is to obey and not to spread dissension in the ranks. I hope I can trust you not to repeat any of this, McClintock. You understood at the start that everything we learnt would be confidential, didn't you?'

'Yes, sir,' John Henry said miserably. He knew well that he had been sworn to secrecy before they set out, and he supposed that it would be wrong not to keep his word.

Chapter Twenty-Three

When he went to bed shortly afterwards, John Henry spent the worst night he had ever had in his life, tossing and turning and wondering if there was anything he could do about this dreadful situation. Would there be any point in breaking his word and warning his fellow soldiers? If he thought it would make any difference, save any lives, he knew he would do it without a moment's hesitation. But gas masks would only be issued on the command of the Brigadier General. And that command was not going to be given. What would be the sense in worrying the men by telling them what to expect, when there would be no protection available?

And yet John Henry felt guilt weighing him down. Could he have said more, convinced the senior officers to believe him? Colonel Watterson had been prepared to accept his version of what he had heard. Even Colonel Johnston-Smythe might have gone along with it. But they had been out talked and trounced by Brigadier General Montrose, with his view of the German officers as friends and gentlemen.

John Henry prayed for guidance. Was there anything he could still do? But the answer seemed to be that there was nothing. Instead, he felt that he was being told to be at peace, to relinquish the guilt which he was holding on to, to realise that he had done everything required of him. He had tried hard to persuade Brigadier General Montrose of the accuracy of his report. The Brigadier has refused to listen. In the end, John Henry surrendered himself to the sense of peace which he felt flooding over him, and fell asleep, believing that he had done what he could.

The next day was quiet. A few random shells, some injuries, some deaths. It was on the following day that the Germans launched their next attack.

Led by Major Fitzpatrick, John Henry and his comrades leapt over the trench tops, reached the barbed wire and cut their way underneath it, and advanced across No Man's Land into battle against the German forces. It was April 1915, the second Battle of Ypres. For the first time in the war, the German forces used gas. The gas they used was chlorine. Nothing like as deadly as Mustard gas, but nevertheless it could kill and damage.

The first thing the soldiers noticed was a yellow-green cloud moving towards them – gas delivered from pressurized cylinders dug into the

German front line between Steenstraat and Langemarck. They and their officers thought that it was a smokescreen to disguise the movement forwards of German troops.

All troops in the area were therefore ordered to the firing line of their trench – right in the path of the chlorine. Its impact was immediate and devastating. The gas chocked their lungs and terrified them, so that they fled back to what they thought was safety in the trenches.

Their understandable reaction created an opportunity for the Germans to advance unhindered into the strategically important Ypres salient.

Although Major Fitzpatrick rallied his forces bravely, and led them over the edge of the trenches again in response to the initial German offensive, it soon proved impossible to force their way on into the gas which polluted the air all around them.

John Henry at first found himself charging after Major Fitzpatrick across no man's land, for some reason wasting his breath by shouting. Bullets and shells flew on all sides of him. To his right, a shell exploded, killing what must have been at least a dozen men. He saw torn pieces of a human body jump through the air, and found more underfoot as he continued to run forward after the major. Some pieces, with sick horror, he thought he recognised as belonging to friends.

Then it was retreat. They were back at the trenches. But there was no safety there, for the air of the trenches was also permeated with the poison gas.

So they were still running; and still running.

Chapter Twenty-Four

The Allied line was chased back so many miles that day that a new battle line had to be drawn up, beyond the place where John Henry had completed his journey by train.

'Could have saved theirselves the fare,' observed Paddy, the only other member of John Henry's unit, as far as he knew, who had survived.

'I don't think they paid ...' John Henry realised it was a joke.

How could Paddy still joke after what they had seen that day?

The new line was drawn up, the new trenches dug. John Henry and Paddy were allocated to a new unit, created from the remnants of several others. It was a strange feeling. Most of the men who had become his comrades were gone, either dead or so badly injured that they were in process of being sent home. Pootsy, who had written 'Merry Christmas' on the board they had carried with them to greet the German soldiers on Christmas day, was dead, blown to smithereens by those same German soldiers. Ian Stewart, the rapist who had become, in some sort, a companion to John Henry, was likewise destroyed. Time to make some new friends. But was there any point? How long would those new friendships last before these men too were dead and gone?

To John Henry, one of the worst things about the trenches where he spent so much of his time for the next year was the absence of all the beauty of nature which meant so much to him. Mud, mud, mud stretched on all sides. Puddles of dirty water, rats constantly overrunning the area, men groaning as they suffered the horrors of trench foot, caused by prolonged exposure of the feet to damp, unsanitary, and cold conditions. The affected feet became numb, turned red or blue, and smelt of decay. It was essential to treat the condition before gangrene set in.

The drainage pipes had been damaged and broken by the shelling and could no longer do their proper job. Instead, they allowed the water to flood out over the battle field, so that the trenches were constantly swamped in spite of all attempts to bail the water out. Keeping the trenches operational was a constant struggle. Bailing, digging, working, this was John Henry's life. And short gaps when he slept, or when from time to time his unit was off duty. There seemed at times to be little else. Where, John Henry sometimes asked himself, was God to be found in all this?

He was no longer within reach of his Belgian friends the Desjardins, Jean Claude and Berthe and their daughter, Marie Louise, the friends whom he had made in the small local village now many miles away, and he badly missed not only Berthe's appetising meals, but the solid company of ordinary people who were not directly involved in fighting and killing their fellow man.

He was glad to realise that what he missed most was not Marie Louise – indeed he was quite relieved to be away from her – but instead the quiet sensible conversation of Jean Claude, and the Belgian man's objective approach to the war and the ongoing battles which made up so much of John Henry's life. He would have enjoyed a chat with Jean Claude some evening, and he was sad that this wasn't something which could happen any more.

He read, in an English newspaper passed to him by Major Fitzpatrick, who knew that McClintock loved to read, an article written by a Sergeant Munro. The major told him Munro was in the Royal Fusiliers, but wrote under the name 'Saki'. The article was called 'Birds on the Western Front'. Munro, apparently, on throwing himself to the ground to escape enemy fire on one occasion, had found his face pressed into a nest of baby larks. Some were injured, but the rest seemed to be thriving in the middle of the battlefield. John Henry wished he could have a similar experience.

And yet, as he began to look around him more carefully, he saw some signs of the nature he loved. Trees, smashed by shellfire, but still standing up as stumps with some ragged leaves. And new shoots growing recklessly, ignoring the repeated lessons that should have taught them how foolish it was to try to survive. And one day, a lark sang high above the trenches, soaring into the heights of the sky, lifting John Henry's heart in the old way.

There must have been a nest somewhere nearby, but though he looked for it, he never found it. The song was enough.

One night when he was on sentry duty he was kicked awake by Paddy, who had completed the shift before him. 'Get up, you lazy blurt!' Paddy said, with a grin to take away the sting. 'Get out there so's I can get to my pit!'

John Henry scrambled guiltily to his feet. He tried, normally, to wake in good time, and to be dressed and ready to take his stint, so as not to keep the man who was coming off his shift waiting. For he knew, none better, how ready a guard was to collapse straight into bed the minute his hours of duty were over. 'Sorry, boyo!' he said. He dressed hurriedly, and took up his rifle.

Chapter 24

'I'll just lie down here, mate,' Paddy said. 'I don't have the energy to crawl away over to my own place, when you'll have been keeping this one nice and warm for me. You can have my bed when you finish your duty. Don't be coming back here and waking me up, now!'

'Fine with me.'

John Henry went out to walk up and down beside the trenches, watching for enemy activity. He ducked occasionally as a bullet headed in his direction. No need to report that: it would make itself known without his help. He was there to give advance warning of troop movement, of an attack across the lines. But for most of his shift, with nothing happening but the occasional shell falling well short, or a bullet easily dodged, John Henry felt secure enough.

It was one of those lovely, quiet nights that he had always enjoyed. The stars shone in a clear navy blue sky. The night air felt warm against his cheeks, a reminder that summer was approaching again. John Henry looked up at the sky, and for almost the first time since he had arrived at the battle lines he felt a presence there, someone watching him, loving him.

The shift came to an end. John Henry prepared to go and wake the next man on duty.

Suddenly he heard another German shell soaring through the air towards him. He threw himself down instinctively, and waited.

The shell landed, a direct hit, in the trench just behind him. He heard noises, groans, exclamations. Clambering down into the trench, he looked around. People on all sides were crying out with the agony of injuries caused by shell splinters.

John Henry looked at the spot he had claimed for his own bed, where Paddy should have been sleeping peacefully. Instead he saw blood. Torn, reeking remnants of flesh. The remains of the exploded shell. The unrecognisable remains of a body.

Nothing, no one, alive.

The Germans had scored a direct hit on Paddy O'Connor.

Chapter Twenty-Five

It was Willie Woodbine who helped John Henry through his grief. And through the guilt, however senseless, that he couldn't help feeling at Paddy's death.

Willie Woodbine was a Church of England vicar who had picked up his nick-name because he made a habit of offering cigarettes as well as comfort to the soldiers he met. When he offered one to John Henry, he met with a firm refusal. John Henry, very much a man of his time and country, considered that a Christian should neither smoke nor drink. All the same, Willie Woodbine was one of the few men John Henry had met since he joined up who seemed to share his own beliefs. Of the others, Markie had gone home to hospital, and Ian Stewart had been blown to pieces in the last offensive. But now here was Willie Woodbine. Talking to him helped.

He soon found that the vicar's own experiences on the battlefield were rapidly turning him into a pacifist. And since the things John Henry had seen were producing in him a bitter hatred of war and fighting, he was glad to meet him.

Since coming to France, he had seen every last one of the unit he had trained with killed. Day after day, there had been senseless death after senseless death. He no longer knew where to find God in the horror and muddle of the fighting. Sometimes he would remember how he had looked up at the sky, and knew that he had felt God there, just before Paddy's death. There was an irony in that which he couldn't cope with.

He shared his sense of guilt with Willie Woodbine. 'It should have been me, see? In that bed. It was my bed. Paddy was only there by accident.'

'That's one way of looking at it,' the older man said slowly. 'There are others. You were where you were supposed to be, out on sentry duty, when the shell exploded. You might like to think you were being looked after but if that only makes you feel worse, think of it from Rose's point of view.' (For John Henry had spoken to his new friend of Rose and of the far-off days when they had walked the country lanes in peace. And of Rose's belief that war was wrong, which he himself was fast coming to share.) 'How would Rose have felt if you had been in that bed at that moment? Be grateful for her sake, if not for your own.'

Gradually, John Henry began to come to terms with what had happened.

It was only by looking at the date on one of Rose's letters that John Henry noticed that he had been on the battle line for nearly two years. Although it was summer, the Flanders plain was turning into a swamp under increasingly heavy downpours, now that the natural drainage had long since been destroyed by the bombardments of shell and gunfire. The rain had nowhere to go. John Henry and his comrades spent long, repetitive, boring hours bailing out the water that filled every shell hole and crept higher and higher up the trench walls. Much of the time they spent up to their knees in muddy rain water.

Rumour had it that very shortly they would be going over the top again in an attempt to drive the Germans back and retake the ground they had held at the beginning of the fighting.

John Henry, like most of his comrades, looked forward to the day when the advance would begin. The endless monotony of living in the ever-lasting mud, in company with scavenging rats swollen from feasting on scattered human remains, was something he wondered if he could bear for much longer. And yet what alternative was there? Only the advance, when it came.

One day they were lined up in front of the huts, most of them so inundated with rain water that their clothes hung heavily on them and it was an effort even to shoulder their guns. The battalion commander addressed them: 'This is what you've been waiting for, boys!' he said. 'This is where you show your courage, what you're made of! This is your opportunity to join your names with those of the men who have defended our country all down the centuries! With Marlborough! With Clive! With Wolfe! With Wellington! This is your hour, the battle you joined up to fight!'

The men, dizzy with fatigue, tormented with lice, found themselves cheering, excited and exhilarated.

They were to go over the top the next day.

Chapter Twenty-Six

So, for John Henry, began the long-drawn-out horror of the third battle of Ypres, a battle that was to last, with repeated advances, until, in November, it ended with the capture of the place that afterwards gave its name to the series: Passchendaele.

Next morning, as often before, a mist hung over the Flanders plain, and the summer rain continued to sheet down.

John Henry, woken by the reveille, prepared with his unit for the attack. The moments while he waited for the signal to advance seemed longer than the years he had been away from home.

Then, suddenly, they were charging over the top of the trench, himself and the men, or boys, he had lived with for the past months. Beside him was Charlie, a farm labourer from up near Derry, who last week had shared a bar of chocolate, sent from home, with John Henry and a few chosen friends. On the other side was Geordie, an illiterate Belfast boy, whose letters home John Henry had helped to write.

John Henry followed Major Fitzpatrick's broad, uniformed back as if in a dream. This had happened before. And, as before, John Henry was uttering strange war cries he hadn't thought he knew, charging at top speed across no man's land towards the German trenches.

He had no time to look around, but he knew that on all sides the line of British troops spread for what must have been miles. Not simply his own battalion, but all the others who had been holding this part of the line were being thrown against the Germans in an all-out attempt to drive them back and retake the ground lost more than a year ago.

He could see only vaguely through the enveloping mist and the clouds of gunsmoke like a blanket pulled over his eyes. Over to his left, he was dimly aware that something had exploded – a mine, he thought. He heard men scream, and when he glanced sideways, Geordie was no longer running beside him.

Still he charged on, grimly now, the first exhilaration fading to something like despair. Now he could no longer see Major Fitzpatrick's back in front of him. What was going on?

He continued to move forward. His foot caught against something, and then he was down on his knees, his left hand flung wide to support himself. It came down on something that felt like cloth.

Major Fitzpatrick was sprawled before him. He leant forward. 'Sir! Major ...' It was too late. The major's eyes were wide open, staring.

His commanding officer certainly did not rank as a friend, but John Henry had nothing against him. He had shared some important experiences with him, and had often found him kind and helpful.

He looked more closely. Major Fitzpatrick's head was more than half destroyed by the exit wound of the bullet that had killed him. Brains oozed out. Flesh had disintegrated. The blood was already beginning to congeal. John Henry's sadness turned to horror, to disgust.

He stumbled to his feet again.

During the minutes he had knelt by his dead commanding officer, he had been left behind. He looked around, but could see no one.

Aiming towards the sound of the screams and gunfire, he began to run again, in what he thought must be the right direction. He continued for several minutes, but the noises grew fainter, and there was still no sign of his comrades or even of the enemy.

Stopping in his tracks, he tried to orientate himself.

He thought he could identify the direction of the sounds of battle. He began to move again, not so rapidly this time. The moment for speeding up would come when he was sure he wasn't moving further away with each step.

If only the mist would lift. And the gunsmoke made it yet more difficult to see, even though the guns seemed now to be further away. Presently he found himself tripping over roots, held back by thick undergrowth. He must have stumbled by mistake into a wood. Clearly, his first move must be to get back out.

He turned to retrace his steps. After what seemed a long time, but was probably only five minutes, he found the trees getting thicker about him. He must be going further into the wood.

Ahead of him, an owl, one of the many that frequented the battlefield, screeched, and flew up at an angle away from him.

John Henry felt like giving up, and would have done if giving up had been in his nature. He ploughed on, taking first one direction, then another. After a while, it occurred to him that at the very least he could prevent himself taking the same wrong turning if he marked one of the trees as he passed it with a strip of cloth. He ripped a small piece from his shirt tail and tied it round a branch.

Sure enough, eventually, although he could have sworn he was following a straight line, he came to the tree marked with a piece of his shirt. So, he should try to go back from here.

But when he came to the same piece of shirt for the third time, and then a fourth, even John Henry could not force himself onward.

He sank down beneath the accursed tree, rested his head on his arms, and wept a little. Was he to die here in this wood, not even in the heat of battle, but from exhaustion, hunger and thirst?

Chapter Twenty-Seven

He had been sitting there for some time when he noticed that the top of his head, still bent over his arms, was surprisingly hot. He reached up a hand and felt it cautiously.

John Henry raised his head. Through a gap in the trees, the sun was shining down on him with an unexpected power. He stood up.

The mist had lifted, and the sun was lighting the ground in all directions. John Henry realised that if he went about it carefully, he should be able to see enough to find his way back out of the wood.

Still stumbling from time to time over tree roots, he tracked his previous route by broken branches and occasional footprints where the ground was wet. In a surprisingly short time, he found himself back at the place where he had unwittingly entered the wood. It was really not much more than a clump of trees and bushes, he now saw. He was appalled that he had been so completely lost in it. Like someone drowning in a few inches of water, he thought.

He was out on the wide Flanders plain again, and once more his first duty was to find his way back to the battle and contribute whatever he could to his side.

He made his way across the broad space, squelching across the acres of mud, needing all his remaining strength to lift one foot after the other. His ears remained alert for any sound of voices or gunfire.

As he grew accustomed to his surroundings he saw with growing revulsion that what he had at first taken for bumps and uneven places in the ground were people – dead or dying soldiers, sunk into the mud and partly covered, their clothes so caked and filthy with it that many blended into the landscape unobtrusively as human wreckage.

John Henry looked more closely as he plodded on his way. Expecting, yet dreading, every moment to see a familiar face. Before long he had seen more than one, and he wondered if anyone at all had survived the battle except himself. Then he heard a feeble voice crying out to him from a short distance. He made his way across the sea of mud and recognised a boy he had rather disliked.

'Micky,' he said, going down on one knee beside him. 'What can I do for you?'

Micky groaned. He was a farmer's boy from County Antrim, who had made a point of teasing John Henry about his beliefs, and had, John Henry was reasonably sure, been responsible for the disappearance of his Bible some weeks ago before its equally mysterious return. But all that was in the past.

John Henry remembered that he still had some water in his flask. Unscrewing the top, he held it to Micky's lips, and the boy drank gratefully.

'Where are you hurt, mate?' he asked.

'I dunno. I don't seem to be able to move. But I don't feel any pain, 'cept for my left arm. I reckon it's broke. But my legs and all, they don't feel nothin'.'

John Henry, who remembered enough from his basic first-aid training to have a fair idea of what was wrong, tried to keep his voice cheerful. 'Well, Micky, that doesn't sound too bad. Sure, there'll be people along soon with stretchers for the wounded, don't you think? We'll not try to move you until then, see?'

'Don't leave me, Johnny.' The boy's face was white and frightened. 'I'm sorry I hid your Bible, Johnny. Don't leave me.'

'I'll not leave you, Micky. Don't worry about the Bible – sure, it was only a joke.'

He knew that Micky's back was broken. It was likely he hadn't long to live. He took the boy's hand in his, and sat down beside him.

'What happens when you die, Johnny?' Micky managed to say. 'Johnny, say a prayer for me, will you?'

So John Henry, still holding the boy's hand, tried to bring him what comfort he could, until, long after, Micky's voice sank below a whisper, his eyes closed for the last time, and, like a flickering candle, his life went out.

John Henry was filled with anger. What was this war they were all fighting, which did such things to men not much more than children?

He wanted someone to blame.

He stood up. 'This shouldn't have happened to you, Micky,' he said loudly.

In the middle of the mud and misery of no man's land, he began to stamp up and down. His feet struck hard against the soggy earth, producing a squelchy, sucking noise. He wanted to hurt, to punish. He waved his fists wildly, and shouted. Someone was responsible. Someone had brought about this vileness.

He went on shouting and stamping for some time.

At last he stopped. He was shaking, hardly able to keep to his feet. He felt as if, after a long drinking bout (something he remembered from his early teens), he was sober again but hollow and sick.

It came to him, standing beside poor dead Micky, remembering Major Fitzpatrick, remembering Paddy, remembering the other boys in his training unit, all gone, that there was no one he could hold to blame but himself.

'Rose told me this wasn't what You wanted,' he said, shouting once more. But now he was no longer speaking to dead Micky. 'You said, *"He who lives by the sword shall die by the sword."* By the guns and the shellfire, too, then. You didn't want any of this. I'm here, taking part in this damned bloody war, by my own choice, just like all the rest of the poor fools. But it wasn't by Your choice.'

He shook his head and knelt down, took Micky's hand in his again, and began to weep quietly.

At last, he began to speak again, quite softly now. 'You've kept me safe, so far,' John Henry said. 'If you'll bring me home safely to Rosie, I'll tell her how wrong I was, and I'll never go to war again.'

He went on holding Micky's hand for some time, but eventually, stiff and sore, he released it, and stood up.

There was nothing else for it.

Staggering slightly, he continued to make his way across the plain of Flanders. Until at last he heard, in the distance, the continuing sound of battle.

Chapter Twenty-Eight

Rose continued to struggle through the years of John Henry's absence. She drove herself hard at work, with the result that she finished for the day, and was ready to go home, all the sooner.

She spent the extra time trying to help her younger sister Emily with her school work, with some difficulty, for Rose was not much of a scholar herself. Emily was a clever girl, and with Rose's help she was learning to concentrate and work hard. She was at the top of her class now, and had passed the school leaving age, but Rose had insisted to her brother Hughie that Emily must stay on and get good qualifications, and he had muttered and grumbled and finally agreed. So Rose felt she wasn't wasting her time.

One night, when John Henry had been away for more than two years, her older brother Hughie brought a friend home with him after work, expecting Rose to make dinner for them both.

Rose didn't mind. She worked at least as hard during the day as any of her family, but when she was at home she was quite well aware that the other three believed it was her job to cook whatever meals might be required.

It was later than usual for Hughie to come home, and the meal Rose had made for herself and her younger brother Sammy and sister Emily was long since over and cleared away. However, she set to readily enough, and began to peel more potatoes and put them on to boil at the side of the fire, swinging the hob out over the heat; then added a saucepan of cabbage. When everything was ready, she mashed the potatoes with buttermilk and a little salt, and put plates from the dresser on the table.

The two men, Hughie and his friend Bernie O'Hagan, sat down to eat, and Bernie at once remarked, smiling at Rose, 'Aren't you the lucky man, now, Hughie Flanagan, with a wee sister that's a good cook like Rose, here? Many a man would be happy to take her off you, so you'd better be watching out.'

Rose expected Hughie to make some response, but his mouth was full, and he did no more than grunt, so Rose took it on herself to answer. 'My man went to the war, Bernie, but I've been promised to him for nearly three years now, and when he's safely back we'll be getting wed.'

Bernie's face fell. Rose recognised, with some surprise, that his words, although delivered in a joking manner, had been meant seriously. She felt sorry for him, and would have been even sorrier if she had thought him anything but a great lazy lump of a boy, only too like her brother Hughie with whom she had never got on well.

When she leant over the table to gather up the dishes and take them into the scullery to be washed, she was annoyed to find Bernie picking up some of the dishes and at the same time trying to put his arm round her waist. Rose wriggled free, and gave him a look that she hoped made her feelings quite plain.

But when she carried the dishes out into the scullery, to her annoyance Bernie followed her, took the plates gallantly from her hands, and set them down for her beside the washing-up bowl. 'Now, Rose, see what a good man you'd have, to give you a bit of a hand in the house, if you took me!' he said, giving her what she supposed he thought was a winning smile.

'I've already told you, Bernie O'Hagan, that I've a man of my own already, who's away at the war!' she snapped.

'Ah, but Rose!' insisted Bernie, coming a step nearer. Rose stood with her arms akimbo and her eyes flashing. Beside her stood the bucket of water that her younger brother Sammy had brought home from the pump to supply all that day's needs. Rose was unwilling to turn her back on Bernie, and scoop up water from the bucket to wash the dishes. She had an instinct that, if she turned her back on him, Bernie would grab at her again. 'Rose, for all you know the man may be well dead by now. Who's to say he'll ever come home again?'

'I hear from him every week, Bernie O'Hagan,' Rose told him, 'so I know fine he wasn't dead when he wrote me his last letter, not so long ago. I'll believe he's not coming home when I get the telegram, and not before. And I'll tell you straight, you're doing yourself no good by making suggestions like that.'

'Well, and I'd no intention of upsetting you, Rose, but I'm just being realistic, see? And I'll tell you what, Rose, you should remember that for all you know he'll have been going with any number of other girls all these long years when he's been away from you. What soldier wouldn't? And so why should you stick by him if you can't be sure he's been sticking by you?'

Rose picked up the saucepan that had held the potatoes, and brandished it at him. 'Don't judge everybody by yourself, Bernie O'Hagan!' she shouted, waving the pan in his face. 'And get on out of here before I give you a clout! Johnny wouldn't break his word to me, I know that fine!'

Chapter 28

Bernie ducked away from her, laughing. 'My, my!' he said admiringly. 'You're just like my old ma when you shout like that, Rose. You needn't think you're putting me off, at all, girl!'

But at least he went out of the kitchen.

But from then on, he was back in the house regularly, annoying Rose, already tired at the end of her long working day. And, moreover, raising doubts and worries in her mind about Johnny. Not about his faithfulness, but about whether he would ever return to her.

Things came to a climax one summer evening when Rose's brothers had gone into the village to an entertainment in the church hall, and Emily had gone early to bed. Rose, too exhausted by a particularly strenuous day, and not especially drawn to the entertainment offered (coloured slides of the Jesuit Fathers' work in Africa – no doubt a good thing, but not of riveting interest to Rose just at this minute), had opted to have a quiet night at home.

She had just made up the fire, and settled down beside it to mend some of the shirts and socks that had begun to pile up in her work basket, when she heard someone knocking vigorously at the door.

Who on earth ...? she thought. Then it occurred to her that it was probably a neighbour, short of bread or some other necessity, coming in the hope of borrowing enough to get them through tomorrow's breakfast.

With a sigh, she stuck her darning needle into the top shirt, set it to one side, and went over to open the door.

On the threshold, swaying slightly, stood Bernie O'Hagan.

Chapter Twenty-Nine

Rose stared at him.

'Is Hughie there?' he mumbled.

Taken a jar, was all Rose thought at first. 'No, he's not, Bernie, so you may go away on home,' she said.

But Bernie moved forward, over the threshold.

'And so I may, indeed, when I've got my breath back,' he said, sounding quite reasonable. 'You won't turn me away from your door without so much as a mouthful of cold water, will you, Rose?'

'Well, come in a minute and I'll get you a glass,' Rose said, stepping back and opening the door wider. 'But when you've had it, you'd better be going. You can sit down over there while I fetch it.'

'You're a great girl, Rosie.' Rose was annoyed to hear him call her by the name no one but John Henry had ever used. She turned away in irritation, and went to dip him a glass of water from the tub in the scullery.

When she came back with it, she found that, far from sitting down to rest, he was standing, straddling the gap between the table and the fireside chair, which would be the easiest approach to the doorway. 'Come here to me, Rosie,' he said coaxingly.

Then, seeing anger in her face, he went on, 'There's no one here but me and you, Rosie, excepting the wee girl asleep upstairs, so you can't say no to me this time can you?'

Rose backed away.

'Indeed I can, you great lump!' she said. 'I can say, "No!" and I can say, "Clear off!" and I can say, "Have a titter of wit, ye eedjit ye!"' She was still more angry than scared.

Bernie laughed. 'My, my, Rosie, you're a great girl,' he said admiringly. 'Just the girl for me, darlin'!'

Moving forward, he grabbed Rose round the waist and tried to kiss her. Rose was still holding the glass of water in her right hand. Twisting in an attempt to struggle free, she raised her arm and emptied it over Bernie's head.

His face took on an ugly expression. Spluttering and gagging he seized Rose even more roughly.

'That's enough of that!' he said. His furious tone made Rose aware of the danger she was in. Bernie's brutal strength shocked her. Through her head, thoughts ran haphazard. What did he intend? How far did he mean to go?

She struggled and kicked, wishing she still had her heavy working shoes on instead of the soft, flimsy slippers she always changed into when she was at home in the evening. Bernie's red, scowling face, meaty, fleshy, ugly, was very near to her own, and she could feel his hot breath sour on her cheek, smelly with the onions from his last meal, reeking even more with the smell of the whiskey he had been drinking. He was pushing her backwards, dragging her down to the floor, while with one hand he attempted to tear at the buttons on the front of her dress.

Rose saw that she would be lost if she let him throw her to the floor, where the weight of his body would pin her and allow him both hands for the purpose of stripping off her clothes.

'Help me!' she found herself praying, as she tripped on the edge of the hearthrug and felt herself borne downwards.

A thought slid into her mind and she acted on it without hesitation.

In her right hand she still held the empty glass. In one instant, she had smashed it against the hearthstone just beside her. Now she was holding a jagged piece of glass in her hand. With an upward thrust of her arm she slashed the sharp edge along Bernie O'Hagan's cheek.

Bernie cried out in pain.

Rose, hardly aware of what was happening, felt blood dripping over her. And noticed, still numb, that her own wrist had suffered in the blow.

Bernie rolled away from her, swearing and crying. His left cheek was ripped from just beneath the eye to the jaw.

You'll need stitches in that, Rose thought automatically.

Then the horror of what she had done came home to her. She had only just missed Bernie's eye. And she thought, 'So much for my lectures to Johnny!' The words she had quoted came to her lips and she spoke them aloud: 'Turn the other cheek.'

'No!' With a howl of terror, Bernie, believing Rose was about to cut his other cheek now, sprang to his feet and bounded towards the door.

'Get out of here, Bernie O'Hagan!' she said softly. She still held the jagged glass in her hand. 'And don't ever come back, unless you want me to tell my big brother Hughie on you. And then see what he'd do! It'd be a lot more than me!'

Bernie found the door handle and blundered out, still sobbing.

If Rose had not been shuddering in every bone, she knew she might have laughed.

Foremost among her emotions was shame. Why, she didn't know. What was there for her to be ashamed of? But she knew she didn't want anyone ever to hear about this. Least of all John Henry.

She was confident that Bernie would say nothing. He would make up some story for the doctor who stitched his cheek, and for his mates; probably about an accident while drunk. The story of his failed attack on Rose wouldn't redound to his credit.

Rose shivered at her narrow escape. She knew well that if Bernie had succeeded in his assault on her, her brother Hughie would have heard about it straight away from him, and Hughie would have tried to force her to marry Bernie, brute though he was.

But she was safe enough now.

No one would ever know.

She needed to sit down and recover. But Hughie and Sammy would be home soon, and she needed to clear up the mess – broken glass, blood, disorder of rug and chair – that Bernie had left in his wake.

Buttoning her dress, thanking heaven it wasn't ripped, she went to wash the scrape on her wrist in the scullery, then wrap some clean cotton round it, pulling her sleeve well down to conceal the signs. Then she fetched a dustpan and brush, and began to tidy the room.

She wished with all her heart that the war was over, John Henry safely home, and they wed.

Chapter Thirty

For John Henry, the war dragged on. Most of his time was spent in the trenches, but every so often there would be another push, leaping over the top, cutting through the barbed wire, and charging with fixed bayonet against the German soldiers.

And this was a problem now. John Henry had sworn to his God that if he came safely home he would never again try to solve his problems by fighting. He would no longer 'live by the sword.' But equally, he had signed up to fight for the duration of the war, and that meant continuing to fight and to kill German soldiers when called upon to do so.

He thought about what would happen if he went to his new commanding officer and told him that he had decided that fighting was against his principles, and asked to be released and sent home. The idea made him laugh. If it had still been Major Fitzpatrick, he might at least have had a fair hearing. But Major Fitzpatrick was dead, killed in action, and John Henry's new Commanding Officer, Major Warren, was a very different man, hard and very far from being interested in his men or their problems.

And in his heart of hearts, John Henry knew quite well that even though Major Fitzpatrick would have listened with sympathy, the outcome would have been the same. No one was allowed to change his mind about this war. Each soldier had signed up, and that was all there was to it. To try to stop fighting would be considered the act of a traitor.

So John Henry made up his mind that there was nothing to be done about it. He'd put himself in this position and he would have to carry on until the time, whenever that might be, that peace was declared.

Others were not so philosophical. John Henry, constantly losing his friends to death or serious injury, and constantly making new friends, had become particularly close to a young man from Kilkeel in South Down, near Newcastle. Newcastle, where the mountains of Mourne sweep down to the sea, held a special place in John Henry's heart since he had heard Markie Stevens singing the song in his sweet tenor voice on their first train journey to the front. It had reminded him then, and continued to remind him whenever he heard it, of Rose, his 'wild rose,' waiting for him at home.

Maybe that was why he'd taken an immediate liking to young Kevin Donavan. Or maybe it was because Kevin, with his fair hair and bright, happy face, reminded him, painfully at times, of his first friend in the early stages of the war, Paddy, the young fisherman from Ardglass. Kilkeel and Ardglass weren't too far apart, and sometimes Kevin's accent was upsettingly similar to Paddy's, bringing back memories to John Henry which he would have been glad to do without.

John Henry and Kevin were sitting in the trench one evening, supposed to be resting before their respective turns on duty, but neither of them feeling ready for sleep, when Kevin said, 'Do y'know something, Johnny, I don't think I can stand this much longer.'

'Stand what exactly, Kevin?' John Henry was half asleep and not sure he was understanding what Kevin meant.

'This lousy war!' Kevin broke out violently. 'I hate it, everything about it! The trenches, the bullets and shells, the bloody officers!'

'Keep your voice down, Kevin, you don't know who may be listening – an officer patrolling nearby, even.'

'Not them.' There was a sneer in the young soldier's voice. 'Tucked up in their billets nice and warm, as far away from us poor rank and file as they can get.'

John Henry said nothing. He knew there was a lot of truth in what Kevin said.

'Johnny, I've heard that some of the men in other units have shot their officers in the back as they went over the top – they hated the officer more than any German.'

'I've heard that, too, Kevin,' said John Henry cautiously. 'You can see why, but shooting someone in the back's a terrible thing.'

'Maybe. And maybe forcing us to fight on and treating us like scum is even worse, Johnny.'

'I'll not argue about which is worse. But, Kevin, you wouldn't be thinking of doing such a thing?'

'I don't know, Johnny, to tell you the truth. We go out with orders from these people to shoot German soldiers who are men like ourselves – so why not kill a few officers instead, and maybe bring an end to the war all the sooner? I tell you, Johnny, I hate that Major Warren more than any German!'

John Henry found this conversation worrying. He did his best to joke Kevin out of his opinions, but knew he was getting nowhere.

It was a few days later that Kevin turned up on parade with his uniform jacket buttoned up wrongly.

'Donavan!' barked Major Warren. 'Step forward!'

Kevin, sill exhausted after a night on duty and only a few snatched hours of sleep, stumbled forward.

'Stand up straight, man! You come on parade improperly dressed and then you can't even stand to attention correctly! Sergeant, put this man on fatigues for twenty-four hours, and see that he doesn't appear before me again dressed like that.'

'Yessir!' roared the sergeant smartly, and poor Kevin was led away to scrub the latrines with a bucket of icy water and a hard scrubbing brush until his hands were blue with cold, and then made to stand correctly at attention for hours before going back to his scrubbing.

There were angry murmurs among his comrades, but there was nothing anyone could do. John Henry went to Major Warren's office and attempted to speak to him about it, but the only result was that he himself was put on fatigues for two hours with the threat of longer if he complained about his Commanding Officer's decisions again.

A week later there was another push. John Henry, going over the top beside Kevin, remembered the times when he had followed Major Fitzpatrick instead of Major Warren. Those hadn't exactly been good days. The constant deaths and injuries of his fellow soldiers made it impossible to describe them like that. But they had been better in so many ways than the current times, with the bad atmosphere which had grown up between the men and their leaders.

There was never time to think much in the middle of an attack. John Henry was charging on when he heard the sound of a hand gun firing just beside him. He looked sideways as he continued to run, and saw Kevin with something which looked like a gun in his hand. Then he twisted his head forward again. Just ahead of him was Major Warren, a dark stain beginning to spread across his back. Then, so slowly that John Henry almost bumped into him, the Major began to crumple. He stopped moving forward. Then he collapsed in a neat heap almost at John Henry's feet. When, seconds later, John Henry bent over him to feel his pulse, there was nothing there. Major Warren was dead.

John Henry swung round and stared at Kevin, who was in the act of replacing his gun in its holster. As John Henry stood there Kevin moved his bayonet back into his right hand and took it in the correct two handed grip.

'One problem solved, Johnny,' he said.

'And if I charge on, will I be the next, Kevin?'

'Ach, Johnny, don't be daft, why would I want to hurt you?'

John Henry could say nothing. Turning on his heel, he began to charge onwards towards the enemy, leaving Kevin staring at his back.

It wasn't wise to stop to think in the middle of battle. John Henry automatically continued to run as he had been trained.

But Kevin, standing for too long watching his friend, was an easy target for an enemy sniper. Major Warren didn't lie alone for long. John Henry didn't know it until afterwards, but that night he heard that Kevin Donavan had been found lying across the body of his commanding officer, shot through the head.

Chapter Thirty-One

Then there was Brian Murphy, a man some years older than John Henry, but an enlisted private like himself. Brian was an intelligent man, a reader like John Henry, a man who had joined up in the first fervour of enthusiasm but had lived to regret it bitterly. He and John Henry went for walks together in their off duty time, lent each other the few books they had acquired, and talked about literature, Ireland and its problems, and life.

John Henry enjoyed these times. The war had been dragging on for nearly four years now, and John Henry had been promoted to corporal, but he and Brian had found that they could still be friends. Talking to Brian helped John Henry to remember that there was another life out there. He liked to watch Brian's thin face crinkle up with interest as they shared their views, and he liked Brian's dry, quirky sense of humour.

But as time went on, and the war showed no sign of ending, Brian's humorous remarks became fewer and fewer, he became quieter, and his face grew more and more unhappy. John Henry knew something was wrong, and at last, one evening as they walked in the woods well behind the front line, he ventured to ask what it was.

'If you don't want to tell me, that's all right, Brian,' he added hastily. 'I'm not meaning to pry into your business. I just thought maybe I could help, if I knew what was wrong, see?'

'Let's sit down,' Brian said abruptly. There was a large hummock beside the path which they had been wandering along. Brian collapsed unto the hummock. John Henry lowered himself unto the grass nearby, drew up his knees, clasped his hands round them, and prepared to listen.

'I just don't think I can go on,' Brian said at last. 'I don't think I can stand this war any more.'

To John Henry's ears the words came as a disastrous echo of Kevin's words months ago. He went on listening, half afraid that he was about to hear some story of how other men had shot their officers as they went over the top, and what a good thing that was, and wondering what he could say this time round which might do more good than the things he had said to Kevin. He hoped seriously that he could be more effective than he had managed to be the last time. But Brian Murphy's approach was not the same as Kevin Donavan's had been.

'I have to get away from here, Johnny,' he said. 'I'm going off my head. Day after day, in the mud and water of the trenches, or going into action and seeing my friends killed all round me, and knowing I'm killing other men who aren't any different or any worse. And the noise of the guns is driving me out of my mind. I tell you, Johnny, I can't stand any more of it. I need to escape!'

'But, Brian, where could you go?' asked John Henry gently. 'If you tried to run away, you'd be caught and brought back before you'd gone more than a few miles.'

'Oh, I know. And then I'd be court-martialled and shot, like that poor fellow last month. No, Johnny, I'm not fool enough to risk that.'

John Henry sighed with relief. But Brian was going on.

'No, I've got a better idea than that. You remember Davie O'Henry? Oh, well, maybe you never met him. He was in the same unit as me months ago, before we all got shot to pieces in one of the pushes and the remains of our unit were sent to make up the numbers in other units. That's when I was sent here.' He paused for a moment, remembering his dead comrades. 'No, you wouldn't know Davie. He wasn't here for as long as the rest of us. He was like me, couldn't bear the thought of any more fighting, hated the whole thing. He was determined to get away and be free of it all.

'He told me beforehand what he was planning to do, so I wasn't surprised when the next time he was on sentry duty, he shot himself in the foot, and pretended it was a bullet from an enemy sniper that did it. He was sent home. He told me it was well worth the pain to know he was getting away from all this.'

'But, Brian, that must have been in the early years,' John Henry protested. 'Sure, I've heard stories like that, but the officers caught on to that stuff long ago. They wouldn't be so easy to fool these days.'

'Maybe not. But for the past week, I've been making up my mind whether or not to risk it,' said Brian grimly. 'And I've just about decided that it would be worth the risk as well as the pain.'

'The risk of being court-martialled and shot?'

'Just that, Johnny. Aren't we all risking being shot every moment we're on duty, anyway?'

'Don't do it, Brian.' John Henry spoke quietly. 'The war can't last much longer.'

Chapter 31

'Oh, yes, it'll all be over by Christmas!' Brian stood up in a sudden access of anger. 'That's what they told us when we joined up. But there've been four Christmases since then, Johnny, haven't there? I'm not waiting for another one.'

John Henry was horrified. He knew, as had been the case with Kevin, that his words had fallen on deaf ears.

Brian must have needed more time to work himself up to the shooting. At any rate, nothing happened on his next bout of sentry duty, or on several further occasions. Then one night Brian went off drinking in his free time, and when he came back to the hut started talking wildly in the same vein about getting out somehow. He even mentioned shooting himself in the foot if necessary. John Henry did his best to shut him up, and the other men mostly laughed and ignored him. But time passed, and John Henry had almost decided with relief that Brian would never carry out his threat.

Then, out of the blue, one stormy night when Brian was on outside duty and John Henry was resting in the trench ready to relieve him, he heard a shot, and a voice screaming in pain. Brian's voice.

Chapter Thirty-Two

John Henry sprang to his feet, his heart racing. What had happened? Had Brian done it? Or was it a genuine shot from an enemy sniper?

He raised his head to look out, and saw Brian writhing on the ground in agony, his rifle lying beside him. John Henry got out of the trench and made his way cautiously over.

'What happened, Brian? You've been shot?'

He realised as he spoke how unnecessary his question was, and knelt down to see where his friend was wounded. Blood was pouring from low down on Brian's left leg, but as John Henry examined it he saw that the wound was probably not serious. It needed immediate treatment to prevent infection, and it needed a tourniquet to stop the flow of blood. John Henry was beginning to apply his basic first aid skills when he felt rather than saw a shadow looming over him. Turning his head, he saw Sergeant Campbell. John Henry's experience of sergeants had never been good, but he thought Campbell was the one he had found it hardest to get on with. It was immediately clear that Sergeant Campbell was not offering sympathy.

'I've been expecting something like this, Murphy!' he snapped out. Brian could not answer. By this time he had passed out from loss of blood. He lay on the ground, with the cloth John Henry had used to try to stop the worst of the blood loss bound round his leg, and heard nothing.

'Well, it's to be expected that someone on sentry duty will be shot sooner or later,' John Henry offered. 'So far, both Murphy and I have escaped it. It couldn't last for ever.'

'That's not what I meant, Corporal McClintock, and you know it right well! I've had my eye on this man for some time. I've heard some of his mutterings, discouraging his fellow soldiers, talking about getting home by whatever means he can.'

'He never discouraged anyone!'

'That's not what Private O'Halloran says. A couple of weeks ago he came to me, and told me Murphy had been talking wildly one night in the hut about how he couldn't stand this war any more, and that he'd do anything to get home. He said that next time he was on sentry duty, he'd fake an enemy wound by shooting himself in the leg. O'Halloran said he'd been drinking or he might not have spoken so freely. O'Halloran also said that he felt it was his duty to tell me this, because he could see it was upsetting and discouraging the other men, and even he himself didn't like hearing it.'

Sneaky O'Halloran – surely no one would believe him? He was a man most of the soldiers despised. John Henry realised that he must have been going behind all their backs, reporting to the sergeant what people had been saying in the privacy of their own hut. He knew, also, that there had been suspicions of Sneaky. No one much liked him. His nickname spoke for itself. John Henry found it hard to believe he would have sunk so low. Still, the sergeant wouldn't be lying about it. And it was clear that the sergeant had learned what Brian had said, by some means or other. He must have heard it, as he himself said, through Sneaky.

'But, sergeant, that doesn't mean that Murphy wasn't actually hit by an enemy sniper!' John Henry protested.

'Oh, yes, it does, McClintock! I told you I had my eye on him. I was watching him tonight when he positioned his rifle to fire at his left leg. I know what he did, I saw it clearly, and I know why. Go and fetch the MO, Corporal McClintock. We'll get this wound patched up – and then we'll see.'

John Henry was thunderstruck. Sergeant Campbell had actually seen Brian shoot his own leg. There could be no hope for him now.

Brian Murphy was carried off on a field stretcher to the nearest field hospital. Once there, he was treated by the MO and as soon as he had recovered consciousness he was put under arrest. John Henry was forbidden to visit him. None of his friends were allowed to see him.

It was some weeks before Brian Murphy was considered well enough to be put on trial. John Henry asked to speak at the Court Martial. He was prepared to say anything he could in defence of Brian, to emphasise Brian's long service and his courage in action, to talk about the dark stormy night when the shooting had occurred and how unlikely it was that Sergeant Campbell could have seen anything clearly enough to swear to.

If necessary, he had told himself, he would lie if asked if Murphy had ever spoken to him about shooting himself to get home. The lie would be justified, he believed, in order to save Brian's life. The Lord would understand. But he was told firmly that he would not be required as a witness. Instead, Sergeant Campbell and Private O'Halloran would be the only witnesses required.

Sneaky O'Halloran – he was going to stand up and report the things Brian had said. What chance did that give Brian?

Chapter 32

The Court Martial was held in private shortly afterwards, at the start of October 1918. Brian Murphy was found guilty of being a traitor and duly sentenced. On the following morning he was taken out, placed before a firing squad, and shot.

John Henry found it hard to believe. He was racked with guilt, wondering if he could have done anything more. He found relief in prayer, and at last found peace again. But what sort of war was this that they were fighting, where men – Major Warren, Private Brian Murphy – could be shot by the people who were supposed to be on their side?

On 11 November 1918, just a month after Brian's death, the Armistice was signed. The War in Europe was over. But the war in Ireland was just beginning.

Chapter Thirty-Three

It was to be more than a year and a half before John Henry was demobilised and could return to Rose.

Before that, matters in Ireland had been steadily reaching a climax. Two years before the Armistice was signed the Easter Rising, an armed insurrection which took place in Dublin during Easter Week 1916, was mounted by Irish republicans, with the intention of ending British rule in Ireland and establishing an independent Irish Republic.

The Rising was organised by seven members of the Military Council of the Irish Republican Brotherhood. It began on Easter Monday, 24 April 1916, and lasted for six days. Members of the *Irish Volunteers*, led by Patrick Pearse, and the smaller *Irish Citizen Army* led by James Connolly, along with 200 members of *Cumann na mBan*, seized key locations in Dublin, including the General Post Office in O'Connell Street, and proclaimed the Irish Republic independent of the United Kingdom.

But the British had immensely superior numbers and artillery. They were quickly able to suppress the Rising, and Pearse agreed to an unconditional surrender on Saturday 29 April. Most of the leaders were executed following court martial, but that was far from being the end. The executions horrified many people who had not been in support of the Republican movement before that. Feelings among those who wanted a free Ireland rose even higher.

In the December 1918 election in Dublin the Irish republican party Sinn Féin won a landslide victory in Ireland. On 21 January 1919 they formed a breakaway government (*Dáil Éireann*) and declared independence from Great Britain. That same day, two members of the armed police force, the Royal Irish Constabulary, were shot dead in County Tipperary. This was seen as the beginning of the Irish War of Independence.

At first the Irish Republican Army concentrated on capturing weapons and freeing republican prisoners, but in September that year the British Government outlawed the *Dáil* and *Sinn Féin*, and the conflict grew worse. The IRA began ambushing RIC and British Army patrols, attacking isolated barracks and forcing the soldiers and policemen to abandon them.

It was at this point that the British government brought in a force of Temporary Constables, the Black and Tans, whose nickname came from the colour of the improvised khaki uniforms they initially wore, and the Auxiliary Division, a counter-insurgency unit of the RIC, made up of former British officers. These men became notorious for their brutal attacks on civilians and their name was soon hated throughout the length and breadth of Ireland. In the North, the first cycle of attacks and reprisals broke out in the summer of 1920. On 19 June a week of inter-sectarian rioting and sniping started in Derry, resulting in 18 deaths.

It was not until just before John Henry's return that the troubles reached Dromore. On 17 July 1920, while John Henry was making his way home after at last being demobilized, General Gerald Smyth, who originally came from the nearby town of Banbridge, was assassinated in Cork for his speech encouraging the police force to shoot without fear of punishment. Shortly after his death, some Catholics were shot, by way of reprisal, in Smyth's home town of Banbridge and nearby Dromore.

Rose found it hard to believe. She had known one of the victims well. 'A harmless critter,' as she later told John Henry. A bit of an eedjit, but a man who had been a friend of her older brother, Hughie, since their schooldays. A very different man from his other friend Bernie O'Hagan.

Rose was sitting quietly by the fire one night in late July working on the never ending pile of mending for her brothers and her sister, and wondering when she would see John Henry again, when she became aware of loud noises and threatening voices just outside. Emily was safely in bed, Hughie and Sammy were out somewhere with their mates.

Rose stood up quite slowly and set her mending aside. Whatever was going on, she knew she would be wise not to go out into the middle of it. She crept silently to the nearest window and tried to see out without being seen.

'Come out of there, ye Fenian rats!' shouted a loud hoarse voice.

'Come out, or we'll burn ye out!' screamed another, surely female?

Rose shuddered.

Seconds later a rock crashed through the window where she was crouching, missing her by inches and shattering the glass.

Rose's first thought was for Emily. She must have heard the crash, and would be awake and wondering what was going on. The stairs led up from one corner of the main downstairs room. Rose went up them quickly and slipped into the room which she shared with Emily.

Chapter 33

'Is that you, Rose?' quavered a small, frightened voice. 'Oh, what's going on?'

'Just some eedjits, darlin', don't worry,' Rose reassured her. 'Maybe if we keep quiet they'll think there's no one here, and go home to their beds.'

Emily nodded unhappily. Rose sat down on the bed beside her, and cuddled her in her arms. She thought about what she had heard. It was the threat of fire that worried her most. Would they really go to such extremes? But she hadn't thought they would shoot poor wee Jimmy Fagan. She made up her mind. 'Just in case we need to get out of here, I want you to get dressed as quietly as possible, Emily,' she said.

It didn't take long to get Emily's clothes from the tidy pile at the foot of the bed where she had left them, and to help her get back into them. There was no sign of the noise outside getting any less. She could hear the jeering and shouting and the crash of the repeated throwing of stones. Rose, wearing her slippers as usual in the house, decided that she had better collect her heavy shoes on the way out.

'Just put on your slippers for now, Emily darlin',' she whispered. 'But pick up your shoes and carry them – you'll want them once we're outside.'

It all depended, she realised, on whether the crowd were all at the front of the cottage or whether they had thought of surrounding it.

The two girls made their way downstairs, crossed the floor of the main room, picking up Rose's shoes on the way, and reached the back door which opened out from the scullery. Rose motioned to Emily to wait, and stood by the scullery window listening carefully. As far as she could tell, the roars and the shouting all came from the front.

'I'm going to unbolt the door, Emily,' she whispered. 'I want to take a quick look out first. Then, if all's well, you and I will run as fast as we've ever run, across the field and away, see?'

Emily nodded.

'Right.'

Rose unbolted the door, opened it a fraction, and peered out through the crack. There was no one to be seen.

'Come on, Emily,' she said, and opened the door just wide enough for them to slip through. Rose went first, then Emily. Rose pulled the door carefully shut behind them. Taking her sister by one hand, while each of them held their heavy shoes in the other, she murmured 'Now, run, ye girl ye!' and set off pushing through the hedge and across the barley field behind the cottage, Emily keeping up as well as she could.

They were halfway across the field when Rose heard a shout. 'Look out! There they go! They're getting away!'

Chapter Thirty-Four

There was no time to stop and think. Rose didn't know if they'd been seen by one lone rioter or by the whole bunch, but she knew instinctively that the only hope for her and Emily was to keep going. She had hoped to stop while they fastened on their shoes at an early stage, but there was no chance of that now.

They were running around the outskirts of the field, aware that to trample over the farmer's barley was an unforgivable sin, and even now in their acute need for haste Rose continued to take them by way of the edge. There would be a gate or a stile soon. She thought she remembered a stile from her childhood, though it was years now since she'd played here with her friends.

As she ran, she listened hard. Someone was following them, that at least was clear, but she still couldn't tell if it was the one man who had shouted or a number of people. He or they were still some distance behind. As they reached the second corner and headed along the path, she rejoiced to see the stile which she'd climbed many times as a child not too far away.

One last burst took them to it, and then she was hoisting Emily up and over and climbing after her. For a moment they crouched down in the new field to catch their breath, and Rose told her sister to put on her shoes. 'It's a wonder our feet aren't ripped to pieces already, running in these slippers,' she said breathlessly as she wriggled her sore feet into her own heavy work shoes. 'These will give us a bit more protection.'

As she spoke, she was looking around, deciding which was the best way to go, and where they should aim for ultimately. The Reillys' farm was too far away. Besides, the Reillys were Catholics like Rose's own family, and might be equally under attack. Rose wondered briefly where Hughie and Sammy were, and if they were safe. Then she put the thought out of her mind and offered a brief prayer for her brothers' safety, for the Reillys, and for some idea of where she and Emily should go. It was some minutes now since she had heard the sound of pursuit.

There was no time to waste. Only a few seconds, mostly occupied in putting on their shoes, had passed before Rose had Emily back on her feet and they were crossing the next field. This was rough pasture, so Rose knew there was no need to keep to the sides. Instead they ran straight across, tripping and stumbling on the rocks and hummocks and ankle deep in the long grass. As she prayed, it had become clear to Rose that there was only one place where it would be wise to go, and that was the local police station, in the centre of the village of Dromore. Across this field, Rose realised, they should come to the lane leading into the village. The Flanagans' cottage was no more than half a mile from the rest of Dromore. They could be there in ten minutes or less.

Still running, they reached end of the field where Rose knew they would come out unto the lane. Leaving the field, they began to run along the lane towards the village. But as they ran, Rose began to realise that maybe this wasn't a good idea. This was where matters might become dangerous again. Would the people who had attacked their cottage have given up by now and be heading back to the village along this same lane? Rose had reached it by a roundabout route, trying to avoid pursuit, but there was a much shorter way to the lane from the front of the cottage. She realised that it would be madness to run in the open, now. She stopped, halting Emily, whose hand she still had hold of, at the same time.

'We'd better get behind the hedge and move along there, Emily,' she explained to her sister. 'It'll be safer.' She noticed with compunction that Emily was breathing heavily and had obviously had about enough. She had never been as strong as Rose. A lover of books and study, she had spent more of her free time indoors than Rose ever had, and had missed out on the healthy outdoor exercise that Rose had enjoyed.

'It's all right, darlin',' Rose said quickly. 'We aren't going to run any more. We'll take it easy.' The lack of moonlight made it hard to find a useful break in the hedge where they leave the lane, but presently Rose found one and they scrambled through. Then it was a matter of moving as quickly and quietly as possible while making sure to keep out of sight.

Before long Rose was glad she had taken the precaution. Sounds of a crowd of people singing anti-Catholic songs came to her ears. The rioters were heading along the lane to the village, as she'd guessed they might. She pulled Emily down and they knelt in the shelter of the hedge, as silent and motionless as rabbits in the face of their enemies.

As the sound of the feet came nearer, Rose could make out the voices. 'Nobody there, after all, Tommy,' said one. 'Waste of time. Well, I'm for my bed.'

'If you ask me nicely, I might join you there, Andy,' giggled a woman whose voice sounded vaguely familiar. She might have been the one who not long before had threatened to burn out Rose and anyone else in the cottage.

Joking and boasting of their exploits, the crowd went on its way.

'I think we should be able to go back home now, Emily,' Rose said soberly. She was silent as they made their way back along the lane. It was hard to believe that there were people like this living so near to her. She had recognised one or two or them, people she had always thought of as decent and respectable. They had sounded drunk – probably that was how they had worked themselves up to tonight's attack. She wondered if it would happen again, or if they would feel ashamed in the morning.

Chapter Thirty-Five

Hughie and Sammy came home shortly after Rose and Emily got back. They were astounded and very angry when they heard Rose's story and saw the broken windows.

'I'm just thankful nothing happened to yourselves, boys,' Rose said. 'Sure, you can fix the windows all right, and that'll be the end of it.'

'Aye, but will it?' asked Hughie gloomily. But Rose was right. They had no more trouble. Things in their area settled down. Although the trouble continued throughout the country, and Belfast saw regular outbreaks of violence, little enough happened in the district around Dromore. Some neighbours who had been friendly withdrew from them. But, as Rose sensibly said, if there was nothing worse than that, they could put up with it. People like that weren't worth having as friends in the first place.

It was shortly after this that John Henry, finally demobilised, arrived home in late July1920, to find himself with no job, little prospect of one, and a country torn with passion and violence. Unlike so many of his fellow Irishmen he had survived the war unharmed, and was grateful for that. But otherwise, there was little to rejoice in.

Rose had been concerned that John Henry, unlike herself, might want to get involved in the conflict, but he soon relieved her mind of that particular worry.

'I've seen enough of fighting and killing to last me a lifetime, Rosie,' he told her. 'I hate to have to say it, but you were right. War is no place for a man of my beliefs. I've sworn never to get involved in that sort of thing again.'

This time they saw eye to eye, for Rose, also, had no desire to be involved in the bitterness that was pulling Ireland apart. She had already seen enough of it. Until recently, most of the trouble and fighting had been around Dublin and other places far south of her home in County Down. She had said little enough of it all in her letters, for she hadn't wanted John Henry to be discouraged by what he might come home to.

Among the few things she had mentioned was the execution of the young poet, Joseph Plunkett, after the Easter Rising. They had both loved his poem, *'I See His Blood Upon The Rose'*, which the speaker had quoted at the tent mission where they met. It seemed unbelievable that some-one who could write such beautiful words should be taken out one grey morning and shot to death. What sort of world were they living in? Rose wondered.

The recent attack on the Flanagans' cottage could not be kept from him, however. For Rose, it took away some of the joy of John Henry's home-coming. She sat on the floor at his feet, that first evening, and wept with her face in his lap as she told him of it.

John Henry had come back tired, uncertain of the future, but relieved, in a quiet way, to be free of the fighting and its depressing aftermath. He had seen, as he told Rose, all he wanted to of death and killings. To meet with it here on his own doorstep, and hear of it from Rose, who for him represented everything he had longed to come home to, was a blow.

But the man who had returned from the war was not the boy who had left more than five years ago. He knew how to handle grief, how to turn from it and replace it with the things that meant happiness.

Presently he drew Rose to her feet and wiped her eyes with his hand-kerchief. 'It's a bad state of affairs, Rosie,' he said gently. 'But there's no need for us to be involved in it.'

Then he pulled her down onto his knee. 'Rosie, Rosie, I've been waiting for this for near on six years! Come here, wumman, till I get at you.'

And Rose laughed, and kissed him with a passion that matched his own, until at last John Henry drew back in alarm. 'The sooner we get married, the better, Rosie,' he said. 'For otherwise, it's not going to be easy.'

Rose agreed wholeheartedly.

But John Henry had no job and only a small amount of money from the army. To marry on that was easier said than done. Jobs, he knew, and Rose was able to confirm, were few and far between. John Henry was only one of thousands coming home from the war. Men who had left the army, and were in search of a job and a regular income. He would just have to search, like all the others.

At first he was optimistic. After all, he had the certificates he had gained during his training, qualifications that should surely be worth something.

But it wasn't long before he discovered that their true value was very low.

He also found, as trouble escalated round him, that it wasn't easy to put aside the death and destruction by saying that it had nothing to do with him or Rose.

It rolled over them from all sides.

Chapter 35

About a week after he had heard from Rose about the shooting of her brother's friend, and the attack on the Flanagans' cottage in Dromore, John Henry went to Belfast for the day to explore the possibilities of getting employment.

He was walking down the Short Strand, coming away from a factory where he had been told that they were not taking on workers, when he suddenly found himself in the middle of an uproar.

There were crowds of people shouting and pushing, and a sound that John Henry couldn't believe he was hearing again: snipers' bullets were singing past his head. He'd thought he had left that behind him for good with the signing of the Armistice. Before he could throw himself to the ground he heard a voice in his ear. It was familiar but at first he couldn't place it. 'Keep your head down, mate. Come on! In here!'

A hand seized his arm, and hauled him into a nearby doorway. John Henry looked into a friendly, grinning face. It was Geordie, the young Belfast boy whom he had helped with his letters home.

Chapter Thirty-Six

'Geordie! I th-thought you were killed!' he stuttered.

'Not me!   Got the rest of me eight lives still – a tiger cat, me.' Geordie kicked open the door behind him. 'In here!' he half advised, half ordered, and dragged John Henry into an empty, dusty hallway. 'Upstairs!' Geordie said. They ran upward, their feet clattering on the uncarpeted wooden flights. Geordie pushed open another door, and took John Henry with him into an unfurnished attic room where a man was crouching at an open window, aiming a rifle down the street in the direction of the Albert Bridge Road.

'What's going on?' John Henry asked. 'And, Geordie, how did you get out in one piece? I heard the mine that got you – right beside me, I thought it was.' He was shuddering at the memory.

'Not just in one piece, boyo,' Geordie said. 'Lucky thon auld mine wasn't all that near me, or you'd have been right. But I lost an arm.' John Henry noticed for the first time that one of Geordie's sleeves was pinned across his chest, empty. 'I had a bit of time in hospital, but they reckoned it was a Blighty one, and they sent me home. I wasn't half pleased! Well worth it, I reckon.

'But I got here to find when I got out of the convalescent home that there was just as much fighting needed here as in Flanders.' Geordie's friendly grin was replaced by a momentary scowl. Then he grinned again. 'Hey, Johnny, it's good to see you, me old mucker! But don't go walking down places like Short Strand that way another time. Lucky for you I saw you in time. The papists are shootin' at us right now, and nothin' new in that.'

'Papists?' John Henry repeated. 'I don't remember hearing you talk like that out in the trenches, Geordie. You never spoke like that to young Charlie. I thought he was a good mate of yours.'

'Oh, aye ... Charlie. Nothing wrong with Charlie,' muttered Geordie. 'A dacent wee fella. But Charlie was out there fighting for his king and country, like you and me, Johnny. Not like these scum, trying to destroy the country, with their rebel hearts.'

'They think they're fighting for their country, too, Geordie,' said John Henry gently. 'And since when does a man's religion matter to you, boy? As I remember it, you hadn't much time for religion when I knew you?

Did you get converted? And I may as well say, if you've got converted, it's to a very different sort of religion than mine, if it leads you into this sort of bitterness.'

'Ach, now, Johnny, who said anything about being converted?' Geordie protested, half laughing. He ran his fingers through his fine, bright blond hair. 'You know me, Johnny, that's not in my line. But I can't stand back and see my country destroyed, boy, me that knows as much as I do about handling a firearm.'

There was a lot more John Henry could have said. But before he could speak, the shrill whistle of a bullet woke him up to where he was. Geordie seized him and pushed him back from the line of sight through the window.

As they both crouched near the doorway, they heard a scream and a groan, and the sniper at the window fell back, clutching his shoulder.

John Henry was the first to move. Diving low across the room, he took the man in his arms and dragged him to the safety zone. Then he spoke sharply to Geordie. 'Get moving. You can see rightly that this man's injured. Have you a first-aid kit in the house or, better still, someone who knows a bit about medicine? And give me your hankie, if it's clean enough.'

Geordie, looking dazed, obediently handed over his handkerchief, and said, 'There's a first-aid kit in the next room. I'll get it for you. But you'd be knowing as much as anyone here about wounds, and the way to be dealing with them, Johnny.'

John Henry wasted no time on further words. Tearing the shirt from the sniper's shoulder, he examined the wound. Folding the handkerchief into a pad, he pressed it against the fountain of blood that spurted from it. 'Could be worse,' he grunted, as Geordie returned with the first aid box. He searched in it, and produced some clean lint and bandages – better than Geordie's handkerchief, thank heaven – and a useful-looking ointment. 'Is there any brandy about?' he asked. And then, as Geordie looked blank, 'Any spirits, man? Gin? Whiskey?'

'Aye.' Geordie, suddenly understanding, darted away again, and returned with a glass of whiskey, which he held out to John Henry with a trembling hand. 'I thought you didn't drink, Johnny.'

'It's not for me, eedjit. It's for this poor critter here, to ease his pain a bit while I do what I can for him. What's his name, anyway?'

'Liam McClatchy.'

John Henry gave a snort of amusement at the very Irish name, then controlled himself. Geordie was unlikely to see the joke. 'I don't think the bullet's lodged in him,' he said, 'which is a blessing, for I've little or no experience in getting one out. If it had been, you'd have needed to get him to a surgeon. As it is, I'll do my best to clean and bandage the wound, but you'll still need to get a professional man to look at him as soon as you can, understand me? You don't want to see the wound going septic and yer man here developing gangrene, do you now, Geordie?'

He spoke in as menacing a manner as he could, for he was well aware that it would be against all Geordie's instincts to reveal Liam's activities, and his own, to anyone in authority.

He saw that Liam's eyes were open now, and spoke to him calmly and gently. 'You're going to be fine, Liam, boy. If you let me prop you up a bit and drink this wee drop of *uisque beatha*, you'll feel a lot better for it.'

Then John Henry began to clean and bandage the wound, noticing with satisfaction that Liam McClatchy was oblivious to more than a faint sensation of pain somewhere in the far distance. 'Well, Geordie,' he said briskly, when he was sure he had done everything he could, 'you'll need someone to help you with this fella. Get him away somewhere safe, where there'll be people to look after him. I'll have to be getting on home now, soon as it's safe to leave.'

'You'd better stop a while yet, Johnny,' Geordie urged. 'I'd like you to meet the unit commander, see? He could use a good man like yourself, Johnny.'

'Unit commander?' John Henry asked. 'Are you tellin' me you've got yourselves all set out in units like a real army?'

'Aye, Johnny, sure we have.' Geordie spoke proudly. 'Most of the boys fought in the regulars like you and me. The feeling is, they didn't fight the Germans to come back home and find these fellas destroying our own land, Johnny.'

John Henry felt sick. He wondered for a moment if he was going to throw up. Then he took hold of himself. 'Did you not see enough of fighting and killing out there, Geordie?' he asked. 'Why do you want to bring it back here with you?'

'But it's not us that's bringing it, Johnny!' Geordie protested eagerly. 'It's them auld ...'

But John Henry could take no more. 'I don't want to meet your commander, Geordie,' he said violently. 'And I'm not for joining any unit for any reason. I came home to get away from all that, not to get into more of it. Now, have you got that straight? If so, I'll say goodbye. Would there be a back way out of here?'

Geordie, his mouth still open in disbelief, took him to the door.

A few minutes later, John Henry was making his way down the narrow cobble-stoned alley to the main road and the nearby bus stop that would put him on his way back home.

Chapter Thirty-Seven

The trouble was, if he was to search for a job, John Henry was bound to spend some time, at least, moving round Belfast, as well as looking nearer home. And since so many of his old army mates were involved in this new fighting, the meeting with Geordie was only the first of many such.

He was not often involved in actual shooting incidents, but time after time, when he bumped into an old army comrade, he would find himself, before long, being invited to join what had become known as the Ulster Volunteer Force, a follow-on from the UVF of pre-war days. John Henry found it hard enough to convince his former colleagues that he had done with fighting. That, in fact, it was the very last thing he wanted to think of, or know about.

Rose was a great strength to him. More than happy that he had changed his view of war, she did everything in her power to encourage him to remain firm. She herself had been the object of many attempts to persuade her – indeed, said Rose indignantly, it would be fair to describe those efforts as bullying – to support the Republican side, and even to join the women's group, the *Cumann na mBan*, who had played a crucial role in the Easter Rising, gathering intelligence, trans-porting arms, nursing wounded men, and providing safe houses and support for men in prison.

Although the role of *Cumann na mBan* had been mainly in the South, women in the North had been equally keen to play their part and become involved in the fight for Irish Home Rule. For several years Rose had been subjected to the arguments and the efforts of her friends to persuade her to join with them. Friends since childhood, even schoolmates like Peggy McCracken, her best friend, had tried hard to persuade her to make herself available to give whatever help she could.

'I know you believe Ireland should rule itself, Rose,' Peggy urged, shaking back the lock of red hair which constantly fell down across her white forehead whenever she grew excited. 'Don't I remember well listening to you at school, when you used to preach to us all every lunch time that Ireland is a nation and has the right to run its own affairs?'

'Aye, that may well be, Peggy,' Rose answered firmly. 'But what I said then didn't include shooting and killing our innocent fellow country-men who happen to have different beliefs from us. Sure, you know, Peggy, for I haven't been backward in telling you, that I gave my life to the Lord a few years ago, and you must know, or if you don't I'm telling you now, he told us that those who live by the sword will perish by the sword? And that includes rifles and bombs, girl!'

If she'd known that John Henry was pondering exactly the same words on the battlefield of Passchendaele at much the same time, Rose would have been pleased, but not surprised. In her view, it was natural that she and her Johnny should come to the same conclusions eventually.

She didn't succeed in convincing Peggy. But Rose stuck firmly to her guns – or, rather, her opposition to guns – and had somehow managed to do this without, for the most part, antagonising her friends and neighbours.

The hardest of all was when old Mrs Reilly, the farmer's wife for whom Rose had worked on the friendliest of terms for many years, began to pressure her, along with others less close. Annie Reilly had been a second mother to Rose, especially since the death of Rose's own mother many years ago, long before John Henry went away to the war.

'Sure, Rose,' Annie Reilly said one day, 'I can't understand a good girl like you not wanting to stand up for your country, as is only right.'

Rose tried to speak, but Annie rode over her.

'And you've seen for yourself the savages that these people are, shooting poor young Joe Kilpatrick only the other week, up in Belfast, and him a dacent young fella that never did harm to anyone. I remember wee Joe when he was growing up, went to school with yourself and my Lizzie, and only moved up to the city because he couldn't get the work near here.'

Annie stopped to dab her eyes with the corner of her apron. Rose was indeed upset about Joe's death: like Annie, she remembered him well – he had had untidy fair hair, and a shy smile, and had often offered Rose a bit of his lunch-time piece, when Rose herself had had nothing with her to eat.

But before she could speak, Annie went on, 'Would you not think better of it, and join with the rest of your friends and neighbours and put a stop to all this, for it's plain that if we don't do it ourselves, no one else will?'

'Mrs Reilly, I've thought all I need to about this,' said Rose, firmly. 'I can't see how more killing's going to make things any better.'

But she went home that night and cried herself to sleep, for she could see something very like enmity creeping into Annie Reilly's eyes. It would be so much easier not to struggle any more, to be part of the movement that all their friends were part of. But she knew it would be wrong. And even apart from that, what about John Henry? As a British soldier, he was the natural enemy of these people who wanted her to join them. And yet Rose knew from the depths of her heart that John Henry was a good man, and that anything which brought her into opposition to him could not be other than bad.

By the time John Henry returned from the war, Rose was confident that she had made her position clear, and expected no further bullying about it. But so far from easy was it for either Rose or John Henry to keep out of the bitterness, that even in their churches pressure was heavy on them to go with the crowd.

One particularly black day, John Henry found himself cornered at one side of the churchyard, almost pushed up against the low wooden gate that led into the graveyard, and hearing one after another of the young men, Tommy Maguire, Willie Morgan, Artie Baird and the rest, whom he had thought of as his friends, telling him, first seriously, then angrily, how important it was for him to join them in fighting for their country.

With an inward smile at the irony of it, John Henry heard the voices repeating to him the arguments he had used against Rose when he had decided to enlist. And heard himself using against them the arguments Rose had used to him.

'And what does the Reverend Thornton say about all this?' he asked eventually, finding it hard to believe that a minister would support such opinions.

'Ach, him!'

'Thon one's just scared to speak out the way he should!'

'He thinks the same as us, underneath, you can be sure!'

'Boys, you just don't know the first thing about real fighting,' John Henry told them wearily. 'If you'd been over in Flanders like me, you'd not want to see the misery of it repeated in your own land, I'm telling you!'

But this only made them angrier.

They knew all about fighting, they said, and about fighting for the things that really mattered.

John Henry was glad to slip away in the end without punches being thrown. At one moment Tommy Maguire had lifted his fist, but it had come to nothing, and finally the crowd had given up, turned their backs coldly, and left him to it. Making his way unobtrusively through the low gate and across the graveyard to the path at the far end which led to the road, John Henry decided that before long he would have a word with Mr Thornton.

Chapter Thirty-Eight

The opportunity came about a week later.

John Henry was strolling along at his ease, wandering mostly through fields, with the occasional excursion onto a convenient lane, glad for once not to be tramping round the hot dirty streets of Belfast. As he passed the door of McGilligan's farmhouse, the Reverend William Thornton came out. He had obviously been doing some sick visiting, for as he paused to say goodbye to the woman at the door, John Henry heard his loud, carrying pulpit voice saying he hoped someone would be much better before long.

John Henry waited politely until the minister came out onto the lane, and they walked along together in a friendly way. The Reverend William Thornton was a short, stocky man who nevertheless carried himself with an air. He was proud of his education, and considered himself superior to his parishioners, who indeed for the most part were happy to share his opinion.

'Still looking for a job, McClintock?' asked Mr Thornton, wiping his brow with a clean, folded white handkerchief, for the summer day was hot.

'Aye, sir,' replied John Henry briefly.

The Reverend William Thornton liked to demonstrate his importance in local affairs. He would never have dreamt of taking part in any violent action, but he was proud to think that he had an influence on whatever decisions were made about such matters, and that he knew all the right people: the people, that is, who ordered and carried out those actions. The people who stood up, as Mr Thornton would have said, for their country and their religion.

'If you like, I could put you in touch with a man who knows how to pull a few strings,' he now suggested pleasantly to John Henry. 'I don't think you know him, but I'm sure he could find you a job soon enough, if he thought you were a man he could trust.'

John Henry looked at him. 'And who would that be, sir?' he asked, still trying to sound polite, even though he had an idea of what was coming.

'This man's name is Peter Moore,' the minister said. 'You'll maybe have heard of him, but I hear you haven't met him as yet.'

John Henry flushed. He came to a standstill in the dusty lane. 'I know that name,' he said slowly.

'You'll know him as a respected leader in the community, I suppose. A man who stands up for what's right.'

It was a while since John Henry had been so angry. 'Don't let me mistake you now, Mr Thornton,' he said. In his anger he no longer bothered with, 'sir.' 'The man you're speaking of is the district commander of the UVF, is that right?'

'Well, that's right,' agreed Mr Thornton, beaming. He hadn't yet picked up on John Henry's reaction. 'We don't usually mention that, McClintock. But just between you and me, that's certainly the case. Mr. Moore can get you a job tomorrow, if so be you're prepared to back him in the stance he's taking.'

John Henry's indignation was choking him. When he could speak, he said, 'And do you think it's right, sir, for a minister of the Church like yourself to applaud this man and his comrades? To give at least verbal support to what they're doing?'

Mr. Thornton stiffened.

'I think, as a minister of the Church, I may be in a better position to judge the rights and wrongs of people's actions than yourself, McClintock,' he replied. 'But if my well-meant attempt to help you to a job is going to be received like this, we'll say no more about it. Good day to you, McClintock!'

He strode off down the lane, muttering to himself.

John Henry kicked unhappily at the white dust round his feet. He was more shocked than he had expected to be by the minister's words. If he couldn't find what he was convinced was the right perspective in his own church, where could he find it? And was his only chance of a job to be dependent on going against his deepest beliefs?

There seemed no easy answer.

In the end, John Henry felt obliged to leave the church he had been brought up in, and which he had thrown himself into whole heartedly after the mission. His father was upset by his decision, but was so glad to have his son home again that he said less than he might otherwise have done. John Henry decided instead to join a small group he had heard of who called themselves 'brothers', later known generally as the Plymouth Brethren, who believed, like Rose and now John Henry, that all fighting was wrong.

Chapter 38

John Henry, with his war record, sat awkwardly among them. But the war was in the past, and for the present, he and they were in whole-hearted agreement.

John Henry went on spending his days in the search for work, while Rose worked at the Reilly's and saved what she could.

It was one day some months into this apparently dead end situation that John Henry came home from the nearby town of Lurgan after another fruitless day, and called at Rose's house, to find a frightening state of affairs.

Chapter Thirty-Nine

Knocking on the door, John Henry became aware of voices inside and an atmosphere of worry and indeed panic.

'Hello!' he called. 'Hughie! Emily! Come and answer the door!'

A moment later, the door was thrown open and he was greeted by the white, tear stained face of Rose's sister Emily. 'Oh, Johnny I'm so glad to see you!' she gasped out. 'Come on in, come on in and help us, please! Something's happened to Rose! We don't know where she is!'

'What?' John Henry's pallor echoed Emily's. 'What do you mean, Emily? Where's your brother Hughie?'

'Hughie's gone out to find out what he can and my brother Sammy with him. I'm the only one here. Oh, Johnny, you must be able to help us! We don't know what happened! When I come home from school, Rose is never here, so I wasn't worried at first. And when it got later and there was still no sign of her I just thought she'd gone into the village to buy some food before coming on home, but when Hughie and Sammy came home from the farm she still wasn't back and we all started to get worried about her, Johnny. Hughie went down to the Reillys to ask if she'd been working late, but no, she hadn't, and Mrs Reilly came back with him – oh, I'm sorry, Johnny. This is Mrs Reilly.'

A quiet looking grey haired woman came out of the parlour door and nodded to John Henry.

'The poor girl's upset, and who can blame her?' she said. 'Come in and take a seat, mister. It's John Henry McClintock, that's engaged to Rose, am I right?'

'Aye.'

'Rose went home at the normal time. That's all I can say. She seemed quite as usual, happy and quiet enough. She was talking to me earlier on about how you were looking for work and about how the two of you meant to wed as soon as you could manage it.'

'Aye.' John Henry didn't want to engage in chit chat. 'Mrs. Reilly, you tell me Rosie set out for home at the usual time. When exactly would that have been?'

'About eight o'clock, Johnny.'

'And did you see which way she went?'

'Sure, there's only the one way, Johnny. Down the lane and turn right just before you get to the main road. And then along Miller's Lane towards her own place. Not more than a mile or so, all told. But you know it would have been getting a bit dark by the time she got to Miller's Lane, Johnny.'

'Aye.' John Henry knew well. Usually he waited for Rose outside the Reilly's front gate and walked her home, for he hated to think of her on her own these dark late Autumn evenings, but today he'd been away in Lurgan exploring the possibility of a job in the factory there which he'd been told about. He'd hoped to get back in time to meet Rose, but had realised as he got into the bus home that he would be too late to meet her, so had come on out to Rose's house. There had been no job going as it turned out. And now this had happened. But what exactly was 'this'? What had happened to Rose? And where was she now?

At that same moment Rose, coming back to consciousness, was wondering the same thing. What had happened? And where was she?

Shaking her head in an attempt to clear it, she looked all round her. She was lying on one side with her back against a rough stone wall, and the only light, from a half moon bright enough from time to time but often hidden and invisible behind fleeting clouds, came sluggishly through a small window to her left. She began to raise her right hand to push back the hair which kept falling over her eyes, and it was only then that she realised in horror that her hands were tied to each other at the wrists. It was impossible to raise only one of them. She had to raise both together.

For a moment the shock of this discovery rendered her paralysed. Then strength of mind came flooding back, and she knew that she should find out straightaway if she was bound in any other way or not. She stretched out her legs and found that she could move them freely, first one then the other. No restraints there, then. That was good, anyway.

It came to her that her position, lying on this cold floor with its covering of loose straw, as far as she could tell, added to her feeling of helplessness. It was time she pulled herself together.

Moving carefully, anxious not to bump or otherwise injure herself against the wall or the floor in the semi-darkness, Rose managed to sit up. She propped herself with her back against the wall and found that even this improvement in her position made her feel at once considerably better.

Chapter 39

'Oh, Lord,' prayed Rose, 'I don't know why I'm here like this, but you do. Help me now! Get me safely out of this!'

Chapter Forty

Memory began to return. She recalled leaving Annie Reilly at her usual time.

'A good day's work, Rose,' Annie had said to her as Rose gathered up her shawl and began to wrap it round her. 'It'll be a sorry day for me when you and your man get enough gathered up to wed, and I lose you. Best wee worker I've ever had.'

Rose smiled at her. She was glad to know that Annie Reilly had got over her annoyance with Rose when she had steadfastly refused to join the local support for the Irish Republican Army.

'But, pet, wouldn't you be better to wait awhile for your Johnny? It's a lonely, dark walk back to your cottage at this time of year.'

'Ach, Mrs Reilly, stop your worrying!' Rose said lightly. 'Sure, Hughie and Sammy and Emily expect me home and with their tea made by the time they get there. Well, Emily'll be there by now, of course, and waiting for me. It's lonely for her waiting at home on her own for me to come, when she gets in from school. I just hope she's getting on with her homework and not lounging about doing nothing.'

'It's a mystery to me why you let that girl off with so little housework, Rose,' said Annie Reilly energetically. 'Ach, I know she's a good scholar and you want to encourage her, but a bit more work to help you round the house would do her no harm!'

'She's certainly a good scholar, Mrs. Reilly,' Rose said, flushing. 'And I want to help her stick to that and make something of her life, as she well could, and I'd rather see she was getting on with her homework when I get back than taking up her time washing the spuds or anything like that. She'll be sitting for her scholarship to college soon now and I want to give her every chance to get it.'

'Well, I'll say no more.' Annie Reilly was clearly about to say a lot more. But Rose didn't want someone else, even Mrs Reilly, who spoke only out of kind-ness, telling her how to live her life or how to make her own decisions. She might have waited a bit longer for John Henry, but not if it meant listening to Annie Reilly's well meant advice. Rose wanted better things for Emily than Mrs Reilly could visualise. So wrapping her shawl round her shoulders she stepped out into the gathering dusk.

At first it wasn't too bad. The watery autumn sun still cast its light across the fields and lanes. Rose sang happily to herself. Before long, she'd be home and either then or not much later she'd see her sweetheart again, and maybe he'd have good news about a job.

Sooner or later, she was sure, he'd have such news, and then they'd be married. It would be madness to try to marry before that, for she'd have to leave her job as soon as the wee ones started coming, maybe sooner if they were living at a distance from the Reillys' farm, and how would they live if John Henry wasn't bringing in something, however little?

Rose turned off into the even smaller lane which was a shortcut to her own home. The dusk had passed now, and darkness was rapidly descending. There was no moonlight as yet. A few stars twinkled in the sky, allowing her to see her way along the rutted, muddy lane, overcast by the high hedges, bereft of their summer leaves and now brown and bare and tangled, a thick shield against much of the possible light.

Small animals, rabbits and rats and other such, rustled in the under-growth by the side of the lane. Rose, a country girl by birth and upbringing, thought little of them, except when a particularly loud rustle made her jump a little. She walked on happily, her thoughts a million miles away in the little cottage she and John Henry would live in at some time not too far into the future.

She planned out her living room, working on the assumption that she would have all the money in the world and could buy what she wanted, and had just decided on a matching suite of two armchairs and a sofa in a mixture of blue and green with white and red flowers, with a low coffee table; and an open fire where they could burn both logs and peat and sit side by side on the sofa at nights staring into its depths and reading what-ever they wanted into its flames.

The moon was up by now. Beginning as a faint wisp of white against the still pale sky, it had grown and changed and was now lighting up the difficult path before her feet. Rose was glad of it. She had no desire to trip over an unseen stone or slip onto the muddy roadside. She went on, able to walk faster now.

Suddenly a louder than usual rustle made her stop short and stare instead into the hedge just before her and to her right, from which the noise seemed to come. That was no rabbit. A fox, maybe?

Three huge black shapes emerged from the hedge, looming over her. They began walking towards her.

Chapter Forty-One

It was one of her wildest nightmares come true. Rose stood stock still for just one second too long, then turned and began to run. The feet pounding behind her were the echoes of terror. She ran faster, her shawl falling from her shoulders as she stopped holding it round her and used her arms instead to propel herself forward. Her flying feet churned up the mud beneath them, covering her skirts. Rose didn't even notice it.

She ran even faster, her breath now coming in short pants, her mind unable to think, her heart beating too rapidly in her breast. The footsteps coming up behind her were closer and ever closer. She felt a hot breath on her neck. Then hands were grabbing her, and she just managed to get away from them, pushing herself harder and harder.

But fast as she ran, the pounding feet behind her were faster. Arms stretched out to grasp her. This time there was no avoiding them. She screamed and found herself struggling dementedly against strong hands and arms, while hoarse voices in her ears muttered threats. 'Would ye, now? Traitor! Prod lover! Stop it now or you'll wish you had!'

None of the voices were familiar.

'What do you want with me?' she panted.

'We want a bit of loyalty, girl. We want you to stop planning to marry a Prod and take a dacent Catholic boy, so we do!'

And as the words echoed through Rose's ears, a cloth was pressed round her mouth and she was breathing in, helplessly, unable to resist it, a strange smelling gas – ether, would it be? – which sent her into a mysterious dream land where everything was exotic and sinister and she floated helpless through clouds of wonders and nightmares mixed unbelievably. Then there was nothing but darkness.

And now she was sitting here in the same darkness, but able to breath freely again, her wrists tied but her legs, at least, unfettered.

Time to stand up.

Rose struggled with difficulty to her feet, her hands unable to give her much support, linked together as they were. The next thing was to find a way out of this place. What was it, a barn, a shed? Nothing more civilised, certainly.

She decided that the best thing was to feel her way around the walls, by the little light there was coming through the window. She started off, going to the right, feeling cautiously with her linked hands along the rough stone wall. It wasn't more than a minute before she came to the first corner and then proceeded along the next wall, balancing carefully on her cramped legs, so recently restored to use. Her hands were still nearly numb, tied so tightly at the wrists that they were unable to feel much.

Moving quite slowly, she came eventually to what was clearly a large wooden door. But now what? Rose thought about it. The door was closed. Was it also locked? Alas, a very few minutes exploration told her that it was. There was no way this door was going to open for her. She tried the handle, operating it with great difficulty, then pushed in vain. There was no bolt on the inside, naturally. She hoped there was no bolt on the outside either, for if there was it might well be fastened. But even if there were none, the lock had already defeated her. Was there no way she could open the lock and escape?

There were sounds outside. Rose stiffened. Someone was approaching. Just one person, she thought. She might have more chance against one than against the three or more who had captured her. She hoped so. Was there a lump of wood she could use as a weapon? Something she could bring down on his head as he came through the door? Rose began to search hopefully round. Then she realised that she was too late. The door was already creaking open.

Someone was standing there, his silhouette clear cut against the bright moonlight which streamed down, temporarily free of its covering of cloud. It was all Rose could do not to scream. Her native courage came to her aid and instead she bit hard on her lip and stood her ground, looking at the newcomer.

'Well, Rosie, are you all right?'

In a moment, at the sound of that voice, Rose lost her fear and anger flared instead. Bernie O'Hagan, the man her brother Hughie still called friend, who had tried to rape her while her Johnny was still away at the war.

'I'm fine, Bernie,' she said coolly. 'What, did you come looking for another ding on the head? Are your stitches all healed up now that you feel the need of some more?'

'Ach, now, Rosie, don't be like that!' Bernie protested. 'But, hey, girl, you've got some spirit, so you have! I've always liked that in you, Rosie.'

'So, what's this all about, Bernie O'Hagan? And are you going to untie my hands, I should hope?'

'Ach, well, Rosie,' Bernie sounded sheepish. 'The thing is I promised I wouldn't if they'd let me talk to you on my own.'

'Who did you promise, Bernie O'Hagan? Tell me what's going on this minute!'

Bernie stared at her helplessly. 'I'm not supposed to tell you, Rosie – but I suppose I'll have to.'

'Get on with it!' Rose ordered him grimly.

Bernie took a deep breath and began.

Chapter Forty-Two

'It's the boyos, Rosie. The Fenian Brotherhood, they're called. It's sort of linked to the local regiment of the Irish Republican Army, d'ye see, but it's not quite official? I'm sort of involved with them, Rosie, and when I was telling some of my mates about you turning me down to marry a Prod, and a soldier at that, they were right and angry. It was wee Vincie's idea – he's the boss, see? He said he'd send along some of the boys to teach you a lesson and make you change your mind. But I said I wasn't having you hurt, Rosie, I insisted on that, girl, I wouldn't harm you for the world, Rosie! So all you have to do is say you'll marry me after all instead of that McClintock fella and it'll be all right. They'll let you go, easy enough.'

'I can't believe you could ha' been such a fool Bernie O'Hagan!' Rose flared. 'Marry you, is it? Forget it! There's no way you can make me agree to that, you eedjit!'

'Ach, Rosie –'

'And do you realise what you've done, Bernie O'Hagan? You've got me taken by these dangerous men and how do you think you can get me out of this without they torture me or even kill me?'

'No, no, Rosie, you've got them wrong, they wouldn't go as far as that –'

'Oh, wouldn't they? It was them shot young Tommy McMurdy a month ago, wasn't it? That's what I heard, anyway! Just because he was a policeman in the Royal Irish Constabulary. The poor wee fella. A dacant man, Tommy was.' Rose paused, a catch in her voice as she remembered the solid, kind young policeman she'd known as he bicycled round his country beat. He'd moved up to Banbridge – a promotion – and the next they heard, he was dead, shot by the 'Fenian Brotherhood', as they called themselves. It horrified her to think she was talking to someone who called these people his 'mates,' and to think that she herself was in their hands.

'Ach, Bernie, what were you thinking of to start this business?' she burst out, almost wailing. But she was determined not to break down, and a moment later she had herself well under control again.

'What would our Hughie think of you if he knew what you'd been up to?' she asked him. 'I thought you and he were supposed to be best mates? Or am I wrong?'

'Ach, well, Rosie, to tell you the truth, Hughie and me haven't been that friendly since that night you and I – you know –'

'I know,' Rose said grimly. He was talking about his attempted rape of her, but was clearly squeamish about putting that into words.

'I always wondered if you'd said anything to him about it?'

'No, I didn't, Bernie.'

'Well, I wasn't just sure, so it made me a bit wary of talking to him, see? And when your Johnny came back, it was even worse, because he knew I fancied you, Rosie, Hughie did, and he knew you were for marrying Johnny McClintock, and he knew I thought you didn't ought to marry a Prod. I'd told him I was sort of partly in the Fenian Brotherhood, too, and he didn't much like that, either. So what with one thing and another, we haven't been that close lately, Rosie. Not by my choice, now.'

'No, Hughie wouldn't be the sort of man who'd get involved with people who shoot other people just because they believe something different, Bernie O'Hagan, and thank goodness for that. And I'm surprised that you should be in on this sort of thing, I must say – I'd thought better of you.'

'I'm fighting for my country, Rosie!' O'Hagan protested. 'And I didn't think you'd have been so disloyal as to get engaged to one of these soldiers, and a Protestant one at that, when our country's in the state it is, just on the verge of freedom but still needing every loyal Irishman to fight for it.'

'I'm a loyal Irishwoman, Bernie O'Hagan,' said Rosie fiercely, 'and I'll fight for my country in my own way. But I don't think all this violence is getting us anywhere.'

'If it was up to me,' Bernie said angrily, 'I'd shoot every one of these Protestant soldiers!'

'And if you dared to lay a finger on my Johnny,' Rose flashed out, 'I'd come after you with a pickaxe, Bernie O'Hagan, and you wouldn't know what hit you!'

This from Rose, the ardent pacifist who had tried to argue John Henry out of joining up. But circumstances alter opinions. So fierce did she sound, her eyes glittering in the moonlight and her bound hands raised as though they already held a pickaxe, that Bernie backed hastily away.

'Now, Rosie! There now, Rosie,' he implored her. 'Calm down, for the love of all the saints, will ye! No one's said anything about hurting your Johnny. Sure, for all I know he's a good enough lad. Sure, I've nothing against him if it were just that you weren't going to marry the man.'

'Well, you can be sure of one thing, Bernie O'Hagan,' said Rose in the same fierce voice, 'and that is that Johnny and I will be wed just as soon as he gets himself a job. And that'll be soon enough, the clever boy that he is.' She glared at the cringing young man before her, and followed up her advantage. 'So, will you for any sake untie this stupid rope round my wrists and let me go free?'

'Rosie, Rosie, I daren't!' Bernie moaned. 'You don't know these boyos! If I let you go they'd be that angry they'd come after me instead. Ach, I wish now I'd said nothing to them, but I was so upset about you, Rosie, wanting to wed you myself, as you well know, that it was out of my mouth one night before I knew it.'

'Aye, when you'd been drinking!' Rose said contemptuously.

'I might have had a wee sup,' Bernie admitted, 'but not that much, Rosie. Sure, I'm really sorry to see you in this state, girl! It wasn't my intention, at all at all!'

'Aye, and you'll be sorrier yet when my Johnny finds out what you've done, Bernie O'Hagan. If I wasn't so angry with you I might even be sorry for you myself, with what's coming to you!'

O'Hagan staggered away from her and sank to the ground with his head in his hands. He was truly in despair, for it seemed that he had lost Rosie, whatever happened. She would never marry him now.

His eye, roving desperately round for any chance of relief, caught something shining in the moonlight over to his left. Moving his left hand cautiously, he managed to slide his fingers over it without Rose noticing anything. It felt like a ring. Was it hers? Yes, surely it must be. There'd been no other woman in this barn, he was sure enough of that. If it was ... A plan came into Bernie O'Hagan's head. It was a stupid plan, and not thoroughly worked out. A plan that might cause him more trouble than he bargained for. But then Bernie O'Hagan had never been noted for his intelligence.

He scrambled to his feet, the ring clenched in his left hand, and darted over to the door. Before Rose realised what was happening, he was through it and had slammed it in her face. She heard the heavy bolt slamming into place, and almost shouted with the pain of her despair. Why, oh, why, had she not run for it while she could, while the door lay open and Bernie was sitting with his head in his hands?

But the truth was, she told herself, that she'd been much too confident in her power over him, had been sure she was winning him over, and that in a few more minutes of persuasion he would have been ready to release her and give up this foolish idea of forcing her into marriage – such a stupid plan! Like one of the melodramatic magazine stories she'd read occasionally and had thrown aside, despising them. But once someone got involved with people like this Fenian Brotherhood, she realised, melodrama came bursting into real life.

She recognised now that O'Hagan's fear of his unknown comrades was greater than any imagined love he believed he had for her. With a groan of dismay, Rose sank back against the wall. She hadn't given up. In a short while, when she had pulled herself together, she would try to undo her fetters herself. Maybe she could climb out of the window if she could only get her hands free. Clearly the bolt on the outside of the door made it beyond her capacity to open. But she wasn't ready to try anything for a moment or two. She needed to wait until she had built up her courage again.

Chapter Forty-Three

John Henry, despair in his heart, throwing all his hope and his cares on his God, trudged unhappily along the lane in the direction Rose must have taken ages ago. He had no real plan in his head, no idea as to how he could find her. But there must be a way. He wasn't going to give up as long as there was something he could do.

He had left instructions with the Reillys to contact the local police and see that a search party for Rose was set up, and he knew that, in spite of their native Catholic distrust of the police, they cared enough about his Rosie to do as he had asked. But he needed to do anything he could himself, without waiting for the police. Maybe if he covered the same ground that she must have covered, he would find something, some clue as they said in the mystery stories in the magazines. Sherlock Holmes, if he were here, could soon discover what had happened to Rosie.

John Henry knew that he was more of a Dr Watson than a Sherlock Holmes, much as he loved the stories he'd read in the *Strand Magazine*, for this wasn't a story with himself as the all knowing hero. This was real life. He didn't have Holmes's knowledge of footprints and different types of earth or cigarette ash. He could only keep his eyes on the ground and hope to see something which would have a meaning. Something which would show him what had happened to Rosie.

And indeed, there came a point when he could see, from the scuffling marks on the ground, still wet and muddy from the recent rain and able to show up footmarks, signs of what he thought looked as if there had been a struggle.

The moon disappeared behind a cloud. There was little or nothing John Henry could do in the weak starlight which remained. Impossible to tell what the marks of the struggle meant unless he could see them clearly. There was nothing to do but wait until the white enveloping cloud moved away and left the moon to do its work again of providing light in the darkness of the night.

John Henry waited.

At last he could see a moonbeam striking the edge of the lane. Then there was more and more light, and finally the marks on the lane were lit up as if by a floodlight in a theatre. John Henry knelt down, being careful not to obliterate any of the prints, and examined them carefully.

There were the prints of three men, two of them made by large feet and deeply impressed on the mud as if their owners were large heavy men who matched their feet, the third marks much smaller and more lightly impressed. John Henry thought Sherlock Holmes would have deduced that these footprints had been made by a smaller man. The marks of this third man were mostly on the outskirts of the confusion, and John Henry pictured him, a small, thin man, dancing around on the edge of the conflict shouting orders to his two bigger and stronger subordinates.

The fourth person present, represented by a small foot which could only belong to a woman, must, he was sure, have been Rose, and at the sight of it and his recognition of her helplessness in the grasp of these three opponents John Henry felt his heart thump and the blood surge up into his head. His ears throbbed, his cheeks flamed, his brain felt as it if had turned to liquid.

It took him a moment to recover sufficiently to search further. The next question was, where had these men taken his Rosie?

John Henry, anxious to make use of the moonlight before another hurrying cloud overtook it and covered up the light, would not allow himself time to mourn. Instead, he sent his eyes searching over the ground, and soon identified the footprints of all four combatants moving across to the hedge at the side of the lane. The broken branches were the next obvious clue. They had forced their way through the hedge – and what then?

John Henry followed slowly and carefully in their wake.

On the other side of the hedge was a field of kale. No one had struck across it. If they had done so they would have left signs of bruised and crushed kale leaves, damaged by their feet, which would have been unmistakeable. There would have been a track left by the damage stretching clearly across the crop, and in fact there was nothing. They must have gone round the edge of the field on the narrow path left by the farmer and his farm labourers, close along the hedges which ran not only beside the lane but on the other three sides of the field also.

But here John Henry met with a hitch. The path was sheltered by the hedge and, unlike the lane outside, it had been kept dry from the rain. The surface had taken no marks from the people who had passed along it. So had they gone left or right?

John Henry decided to try right, first of all. Presently he was confirmed in his guess. A scrap of cloth, thin wool fringing from the edge of a dress, such as Rose might have worn, was caught in a branch of the hedge not too far along. A few yards further, someone had spat out a lump of tobacco, clearly chewed for long enough to be past giving pleasure.

As John made his way along and presently reached the corner of the field and turned at right angles, still following the little path, he saw other signs, small enough but sufficient to indicate that a party had pushed along in this direction – the occasional broken branch, or a footstep planted by accident in the kale where the path had been too constricted for its burly users.

John Henry hurried on, convinced now that he was on the right track and unwilling to waste much time on unnecessary care. But it must have been over an hour since Rosie and her captors had come this way.

Was he already too late? Was he heading only towards the discovery of her dead body?

'Please, no, Lord!' John Henry prayed desperately.

Then he took comfort from the thought that plainly Rose had been carried off. If these men had intended to kill her, why had they not done so in the lane when they had set upon her? It would surely be pointless of them to take her with them by force, unless they had some other purpose in mind than her murder?

Moving on, John Henry came to a second corner and made his way along the far edge of the field. He was still walking in bright moonlight. And that was why he suddenly realised that he could see the silhouette of a man not far away from him, climbing the stile which he could see breaking the hedge about halfway along the field.

Chapter Forty-Four

John Henry stiffened. He stood motionless for a short space of time, just long enough to wonder if this could be one of Rose's attackers. But maybe it was a harmless passerby, making his way home from some social happening.

John Henry stood for a moment against the hedge, holding himself so quietly that no one could have known he was there, while the man reached the top of the stile and stood balanced there with one leg over. Then he stepped forward. The man gave a loud gasp and almost screamed before recovering himself.

'Hey, boyo, you gave me a right shock there!' he exclaimed.

John Henry peered into what he could see of the man's features. 'Bernie O'Hagan, isn't it?' he said slowly. 'You'd be a friend of Hughie Flanagan, am I right?'

'Yes, indeed you are right,' Bernie said eagerly. 'You know Hughie, do you?' He peered at John Henry's face in turn. 'Why, it's John Henry McClintock, isn't that so?'

'Aye.'

'John Henry, you're the very man I was looking for!' Bernie said bluffly. 'I hear from Hughie that you and his sister Rosie are walking out.'

'Aye.'

John Henry was remembering things he had heard about Bernie O'Hagan, and none of them were good. As it happened, Rose had never told him of her unpleasant experience with O'Hagan, for she saw no reason to upset him, but when she had mentioned her brother's friend occasionally it had been in tones which had left John Henry in no doubt about her opinion of the man. This, added to the other things he had heard, made John Henry reluctant to trust this Bernie O'Hagan an inch. What was he doing out here, on the path Rose's attackers had taken?

Bernie O'Hagan was at that moment wondering much the same thing. His plan hadn't included being caught with Rose's ring so near to the barn where she was hidden. He had meant to call with John Henry McClintock the next morning, explain that he'd found the ring, and give a location for its finding many miles away. Put them all on the wrong track, he thought. Pride in his own cunning filled his mind. But now he didn't know whether to mention the ring or not. He had his hand clutched round it in his pocket.

Without thinking he took his hand out of the pocket to steady himself as he jumped down from the stile, and the ring came too. It fell with a tinkling sound against an empty bottle lying at the foot of the stile, discarded by some passing workman. Bernie O'Hagan heard the sound, realised what he had done, and began to panic.

'You've dropped something,' said John Henry. He moved forward and bent to pick up whatever had made the noise. Then he stiffened.

Standing up quite slowly, he opened his hand and stretched it out for O'Hagan to see the small object which now lay in his palm. The ring which John Henry had given to Rose before he went to the war shone in the moonlight, its large amethyst gleaming softly purple, and the tiny diamond chips on either side of the central stone sparkling. It had cost John Henry a week's wages and he would have recognised it anywhere.

'Well, O'Hagan?' he asked softly. 'Can you explain to me where you got this?'

Bernie O'Hagan's jaw dropped. 'Ach, Johnny, do you recognise it then? I thought it looked like one I'd seen on Rosie's finger,' he babbled. 'Sure, I picked it up a good distance from here, away along the main road.'

He scrambled down from the stile and then wished he hadn't as he saw how John Henry loomed over him.

'Johnny, you don't think I took it off her? No, no, you can't think such a thing! Sure, I'm fond of Rosie, I've been worrying myself sick about her, wondering what happened to her –'

'What happened to her?' John Henry said. 'And how did you know, O'Hagan, that anything had happened to her? It hasn't been broadcast until just now, boyo, when I told the Reillys to get in touch with the police and start a search. So how did you know anything about it?'

O'Hagan panicked. 'Ach, I heard them discussing it in the village not more than twenty minutes ago!'

'So, why did you not turn over the ring to the police and tell them where you found it?'

'Because – because – '

'You've no answer, have you, Bernie?' John Henry's tone was scathing. Springing forward, he seized O'Hagan by the throat. 'You know where my Rosie is, you villain. Take me to her right now or I swear to God I'll murder you!'

All his promises made in the horror of war never again, if he came safely home, to try to solve a problem by the use of force had vanished like smoke.

'Johnny, Johnny, I daresn't! The brotherhood would have me dead at their feet if I let on to anyone about where she is or what they've done!'

'And I'll have you dead at my feet if you don't take me there this minute, O'Hagan. So which would you rather? Certain death right now or a chance that your fine brotherhood won't find out what you've done?' As he spoke, his grip on Bernie O'Hagan's throat tightened until the man could hardly breathe. John Henry pulled himself together as he heard O'Hagan's painful exhalations, his breaths coming with hard effort. It wouldn't serve his purpose to kill O'Hagan without finding out from him where Rose was being held.

'Take me to her, O'Hagan, if you want to go on living!' John Henry commanded.

He released his grip on O'Hagan's neck enough to allow the man to stand upright and breathe in.

'Johnny, suppose the Fenian Brotherhood are there when I take you to her?'

'Then, Bernie my boy, it'll be an unhappy time for them,' John Henry said grimly.

'Do you have a gun, Johnny?'

'No gun. But I have my fists and I have my hatred of anyone who harms my Rosie. And let me tell you, Bernie O'Hagan, if I find when we get there that Rosie's been hurt in any way, it will go hard with you and your brotherhood. I'll kill every last one of you if it takes me a lifetime.'

Chapter Forty-Five

He dragged the man round to face away from him, grabbed his right arm and twisted it up his back. Bernie O'Hagan gave a shriek of pain and tried to force himself into a slightly more comfortable position. 'Start moving!' John Henry ordered. 'I don't think she's too far away. But even if it's miles, you're going to lead me there if you don't want your arm broken from your body.'

'All right, Johnny, all right, Johnny. For any sake don't twist my arm so hard! And we'll need to start by getting over this stile, Johnny, and I can't do it without the use of both arms, now!'

'I'll let you go until you're over it,' John Henry said. He marched O'Hagan up to the stile and released him for long enough to scramble over it. He himself was on the man's heels. Nevertheless, O'Hagan had no sooner reached the ground than he took off with the speed of light across the rough pasture which lay on the other side of the stile, hoping to escape from his captor. But John Henry was after him in a flash and threw him to the ground without a second's thought the moment he caught up with him.

Bruised from the rough ground, stung by high nettles and pricked by thistles, Bernie O'Hagan could do nothing at first but lie where he was and groan.

'Ach, Johnny, you've broke my ankle! I can't move now.'

'Rubbish, man! Get up and start moving.'

'You'll have to help me, Johnny.'

John Henry seized him impatiently, dragged him to his feet, and began to propel him forward. 'Are we heading in the right direction?'

'Yes, on across there. But, Johnny, I'm lamed, I can't do it!'

'You can do it all right, boy, unless you want a beating.'

'Johnny, you'll have to help me.'

John Henry frowned angrily. 'I'll let you lean on me if you have to, O'Hagan, but it's time we were moving on. I can't bear to have my Rosie frightened and held prisoner any longer, do you see?'

'Ach, Johnny, frightened? Not Rosie, I'm telling you! She's a brave lass, don't you know? It'd take more than this to frighten Rosie Flanagan!'

In spite of himself, John Henry couldn't help being pleased by the admiration shining out of Bernie O'Hagan as he spoke of Rose. Maybe she was managing better than he had feared.

They stumbled across the rough pasture ground, Bernie O'Hagan limping and clinging on to John Henry's arm with all his might, and after what seemed a long time John Henry saw a dark shape which might have been a barn looming in the distance.

'Is that the place, O'Hagan?'

'Aye, it is, Johnny, but listen, maybe wee Vincie and the other two boyos are there – you'd better be careful how close you go.'

'How close I go, Bernie? Why, boy, I thought you were the one who's going to the door? But now, don't you worry, I'll be right behind you.' He gave O'Hagan's arm a playful shake and the man gasped in pain. 'You open the door and see if anyone's there apart from Rosie. And you don't warn them that I'm just outside waiting or you'll be very sorry, d'ye understand?'

'Y – yes, Johnny, yes, I do!'

'Keep going, then.'

The two men moved quietly nearer to the barn. When they were only a few feet away, John Henry let go of O'Hagan's arm and gave him a light shove towards the shut door. 'Go on, Bernie. Open it up – carefully, mind.'

Bernie O'Hagan went up to the door and began to undo the huge bolt which held it shut. John Henry said nothing, but he had realised as soon as he saw the bolt that there was not likely to be anyone else there but the prisoner. Unless one man had been left behind on purpose to guard her, and the others in leaving had secured the door for safety. That was always possible. But in that case surely he would have lit a lamp or a candle, and there was no chink of light coming through the cracks in the door. John Henry positioned himself carefully against the wall beside the door, on the side where it opened. He could see O'Hagan, and O'Hagan could see him. But no one inside could see him when the door opened.

'There's no one here, Johnny,' he heard O'Hagan say.

'Except Rose, you mean.'

'No, Johnny, Rosie's not here either.'

Chapter 45

'What?' John Henry pushed savagely past O'Hagan and peered anxiously round the huge interior of the barn. There was nothing to be seen but clumps of straw and a tattered piece of rope. There was no one there.

Chapter Forty-Six

Rose, left alone by Bernie O'Hagan some time ago, had not taken long to recover her nerve. The important thing was to get rid of her fetters first, then to try by some means or other to scramble out through the window, if only there was room. It was a small window but not, she thought hopefully, attempting to estimate its dimensions by appearance alone, too small for someone of her size.

The rope twisted round her wrists was thick and coarse, and it was tightly bound round her. It would be hard to wriggle free from. She began the attempt, however, straining her wrists apart and striving to slip the rope down over her hands. A considerable time went past before she had to concede that she was achieving very little, and was hurting her wrists badly. There had to be some other solution.

For a moment or two, panting hard as she tried to regain her breath and recover her strength, Rose sat back, propped against the wall for support, and tried to think.

This was a barn. Might there be some sharp farming implement left about? If she could manage to rub the ropes against a rough edge she might eventually be able to fray the bonds sufficiently to break free from them. It had to be worth the attempt.

She stood up with some difficulty, for the strenuous work she had put in trying to twist the rope off her wrists had left her exhausted, and the cold in which she had been kept for so long now was making her stiff and sore.

The floor was fairly well covered in straw, some of it piled up against the various walls in damp heaps. This barn, Rose decided, had not been used for some time, from the look of things. It was still dark outside, with only occasional moonlight as the clouds pulled back at times and allowed the moon to shine through the gaps they left, but Rose's eyes were becoming more and more acclimatised to the darkness and she could see around her well enough for her purpose.

Aha! Over against the left hand wall, just under the window, surely that was something iron poking out from beneath the straw pile?

Rose darted over, pushed aside the straw awkwardly with her tied hands, and looked at her discovery.

It was a worn, rusted plough share, with one sharp edge. Surely it would serve her purpose? She began eagerly to haul it out and prop it up in a position where she could get at it, and started rubbing the rope around her wrists against it.

Alas, within a few minutes the plough share began to crumble under the rough usage and to fall apart. There was no longer any piece of it sharp enough to cut anything or even to rub against anything to any great effect. Rose sank back from it with a sigh. Useless. But might there be something else? She traversed the barn, kicking straw aside, feeling beneath the piles, hoping against hope to find something else.

Suddenly her hope flared. There was something beneath this last pile. She worked at it eagerly and at last exposed something which she was sure she could use.

It was a scythe, an instrument for cutting hay or tall grass, and to Rose's experienced eye, the eye of someone who had worked on a farm for some years now, albeit in the kitchen, it wasn't so far gone in rust as the plough share she had unearthed previously. Rose had seen scythes around the Reilly's farm in not much worse condition, still able to be used when needed. It might do the job. It had to.

Kneeling down beside it, she began sawing at her ropes again, and this time her efforts seemed not to be in vain. The scythe might need sharpened before it would be ready for use in the fields, but she was sure she could feel it working on the ropes around her wrists. They weren't cut yet, but nearly. Yes, nearly.

Rose was gasping with the effort, longing to give up, but determined not to actually do so, when at last she felt the rope round her right wrist begin to yield. She had been concentrating on it, believing that if her right hand was free she could manage the window even if the remnants of the rope still hung round her left wrist.

Breathing a prayer of thanks, she sprang to her feet, full of renewed vigour, as the final strands fell away from her hand. Now for the window.

But as she reached up to it, feeling for a way to open it, she heard a sound behind her which stunned her and suddenly rendered her helpless. Someone was working at the bolt on the barn door. She had heard Bernie O'Hagan doing this some time ago before he came in. It was the same noise. Was it only Bernie again? She had no doubt about her ability to deal with Bernie if it that was who it was. But suppose it was someone else? One of Bernie's 'mates' from the Fenian Brotherhood?

Rose felt herself shiver, and immediately refused to be frightened. She pulled herself together. She definitely would not respond in such a feeble way. Why should she be afraid? They were only men. She remembered the 13th chapter of Hebrews, *'The Lord is my helper. I will not fear. What can man do unto me?'*

There was no time to try to scramble out of the window, even if she had been able to open it. At least her hands were free. That gave her a better feeling.

Standing up straight, she faced whatever was coming to her.

The barn door swung open. Two men, one of them holding a lamp, came through it. One was small, the other to Rose's eyes was a giant. It was clearly the smaller of the two who was in charge.

'So, Rosie Flanagan,' he said in a soft, greasy voice, 'you've managed to untie your wrists? What a clever girl you are.'

'My name is Rose,' Rose said coldly. 'No one gave you permission to call me Rosie.'

The small man burst out laughing. 'Ah, it's the brave girl you are, Miss Flanagan! I picked up the name from your future husband – forgive me for presuming! I can see that something which is fine for your lover isn't so fine from all and sundry.'

'My future husband?' Rose asked. Surely he couldn't mean Johnny!

'Bernie O'Hagan – and a fine broth of a boy he is. You're a lucky girl, Miss Flanagan, to have such a great boy wanting you. But enough of that. Time we got you out of here before someone tracks you down. The marks on the ground are clear enough. We want to take you to a much safer place, an ordinary place, where the priest can come without worrying too much about it seeming strange and unnatural, not like this barn which you'd have to call an unconventional spot for the purpose. A place where he can marry you and Bernie before the morning.'

'I've no intention of marrying Bernie O'Hagan,' said Rose firmly. 'The only man I'll ever marry is John Henry McClintock. He and me have been hand fast since before he went away to the war, and now he's back we're only waiting till he gets him a job – and that won't be long, because he's a clever man anyone would be glad to employ.'

'We'll see about that,' said the little man. 'Are you wondering why I brought you here in the first place and left you, just to come back and take you some place else? Why, I've been arranging your wedding for you, Rosie! I had to wait until I was sure I had you. But when I left you here safe, I went to call on Father O'Sullivan to ask him to call round to my house later and perform a wedding for two loving hearts who wanted a private ceremony. That's you and Bernie, Rosie. So now I have to get you there before the priest arrives, d'ye see?'

Then he suddenly changed his attitude, and his anger leapt forth. 'Marry a Prod soldier, would you, and you a good Catholic girl? And a good Catholic boy waiting for you? You'll not do that Rose Flanagan, if I have any say in the matter!'

'Catholics and Protestants, what has that got to do with anything?' Rose hurled at him. 'Do you believe anything yourself, you who want to rule things your own way without regard for what God says is right or wrong? Johnny and me believe the same things, and neither of us care whether we're Protestant or Catholic – we only care that we believe in Jesus, both of us!'

But her words only angered the small man even more. 'Aidan!' he screamed. 'Grab hold of the bitch and drag her out if you have to! We'll take her, willing or not! It'll be for O'Hagan to tame her once they're safely tied together!'

Approaching Rose stealthily, he drew a sharp knife from his pocket and flourished it within inches of her face.

'Would you like a little souvenir of this occasion?' he hissed. 'A mark or two to spoil your beautiful complexion, wee Rosie? Do you think your Proddy soldier Johnny would be just so keen to marry you then?'

Rose flinched back from the knife. Then she held herself together and refused to allow the little man to intimidate her, knife or not.

'Yes,' she said calmly. 'I know he would. "For Man looks on the outward appearance, but God looks on the heart." Johnny and I know each other's hearts, and that's what matters to us.'

The little man screeched again. Then he waved frantically at big Aidan, and a moment later Rose felt the huge man's hands seizing her arms and knew as she was dragged out of the barn that there was nothing else she could do right then.

Chapter Forty-Seven

For a moment John Henry, discovering Rose's absence, felt his heart fill up with despair. What had happened? Where was Rose now?

He took hold of himself and refused to panic. 'You know where she is, Lord,' he prayed silently, 'so please keep her safe and go on helping me to find her.' Then he cleared his mind and began to think.

There were only two options as far as he could see. Rose might have escaped. Not through the door which was bolted on the outside when he and O'Hagan reached it, but maybe through the window. Or else Bernie O'Hagan's companions from the Fenian Brotherhood had come back and taken her somewhere else.

If Rose had escaped she would have gone straight home, wouldn't she? So that was the first place to look. But if not – John Henry's face became grim, and he renewed his grasp on O'Hagan's arm. If not, Bernie O'Hagan must have a fairly good idea of the places she might have been taken to, and John Henry didn't intend to let the man out of his sight until he'd found Rose one way or the other.

The window – it would probably show signs of having been opened if Rose had scrambled through it. John Henry, dragging the protesting O'Hagan with him, went over to examine the window at close quarters. But, alas, it showed no sign of having been opened, in fact it looked as if it had been jammed shut for years. A thick spider's web which was stretched across one filthy corner settled the matter. No one had even opened this window, let alone climbed through it.

There still remained the possibility, John Henry realised, that Rose had got away through the door which someone had left open, and that it had been bolted again after her escape. It was still worth checking if she had come home during his own absence.

'Come on, you.'

O'Hagan shrieked as John Henry tightened his grip on the man's arm and pushed him towards the door, propelling him through it. He paid no attention to O'Hagan's groans as they retraced their footsteps back to the lane where the muddy footprints had told John Henry the story of Rose's abduction.

It didn't take them long, moving as quickly as John Henry could drive his captive, to reach the Flanagan's house again. But Rose was not there, and Emily had seen no sign of her since John Henry had left to go to the Reillys' farm in search of her.

John Henry had no desire to frighten Emily even further by telling her what had happened.

'Well, I've a fair idea where she is then,' he said. 'I just wanted to check first that she hadn't just arrived home.' He gave Bernie O'Hagan's arm a shake and said, 'O'Hagan here knows where she was going, don't you, Bernie?' The smile he offered his prisoner, teeth clenched and no gleam of warmth in his eye, was enough to scare O'Hagan into complete submission.

'Ach, yes, Emily, I've a fair idea where she is,' he mumbled. 'Johnny, you're hurting my arm!'

'Ach, am I, Bernie?' John Henry said, tightening his grip. 'I'm sure you'd like me to be more careful. Bernie hurt his arm as we were going along through the fields. He tripped and gave his ankle a right bang, too. He needs my helping hand now to keep him going, Emily. Well, we'll be on our way now, and you can expect to see Rose back safe and sound before long, isn't that right, Bernie?'

'Yes, yes, that's right, Johnny! Ach, Johnny!' O'Hagan stumbled off down the cottage path with John Henry's grip on his arm even tighter.

'Which way, O'Hagan?' John Henry kept his voice soft to prevent Emily hearing and wondering.

'Left, Johnny, away from the village.'

Without a word John Henry propelled his reluctant guide in the direction given.

For what he reckoned was at least three miles they trudged on through the fitful moonlight, John Henry trying to thrust his captive on ever faster and faster, and O'Hagan pulling back and slowing them both down as much as he dared.

It was much darker now. The moon showed its face seldom, sulking behind a heavy veil of clouds. The way led along a rough lane, dried mud overgrown in the centre with patches of grass and weeds. It was like most of the lanes they had walked along all their lives, but the urgency of the venture and the speed which John Henry tried to maintain combined with the darkness to make their journey hard.

From time to time an owl screeched or a small animal, a mouse or a rabbit perhaps, made scuffling noises along the verge of the lane or in one of the hedges. Bernie O'Hagan jumped and cried out as a fox shot across their path not ten yards away, appearing from one hedge and disappearing into the other, leaving a trail of feathers from whatever he carried in his mouth.

'It's time you told me where you're taking me, O'Hagan,' John Henry said, shaking the man back from fear of the fox to fear of himself. 'Tell me, now!'

'It's Vincie's house, Johnny. He lives about a couple of miles along this way. He told me I was to come here about ten o'clock. I think we'll be a bit early, but that doesn't matter, does it? If Rosie isn't in the barn any more it'll be because he's taken her there.'

John Henry frowned thoughtfully.

'So your pal Vincie'll be expecting you, you tell me?'

'Well, yes, Johnny, otherwise I wouldn't dare go to his house. But he won't be expecting you, Johnny, see? You could maybe get in by a side door while I'm talking to him, d'ye think?'

John Henry smiled grimly in the darkness, unseen by O'Hagan. He didn't trust this man an inch. If he left him alone to talk to his precious Vincie he'd give John Henry's presence away in the first words he uttered, for sure.

'We'll see what's the best when we get there, O'Hagan,' was all he said.

The next few miles seemed unutterably long. They were walking now alongside a wall which bordered the lane on their left. John Henry knew that on the other side of the wall there must be a demesne, a Big House belonging to a wealthy man. Trees grew inside the wall, tall branches overhanging the lane. He could hear the rustle and murmur of the living wood as he and O'Hagan walked within a yard of it.

The sound of feet, of men marching, sounded in the distance. The noise came from in front of them, from some distance along the lane. O'Hagan stopped walking. The blood drained from his face.

'Johnny, it's the Black and Tans!'

Chapter Forty-Eight

John Henry stared at the man.

'What? How do you know that, O'Hagan? It could be anyone.'

'No, no, Johnny, I know it's them boyos! They patrol out here most nights, Vincie told me. He warned me to look out for them. They don't care what they do to you, those Black and Tans, if they catch you out where they don't expect you.'

John Henry frowned. He'd heard a lot of talk about the Black and Tans since his return home, about their ferocity and their unauthorised attacks on farms and villages, many of which they had burnt, and of their vicious treatment of prisoners. But he'd been given to understand that they were mostly operating in the south of the island. He wondered if O'Hagan was using the name as a generic term for anyone working to oppose the Irish Republican Army. For the Ulster Volunteer Force, even. It seemed likely. He'd heard that done a lot.

'Johnny, Johnny, don't just stand there, we have to get off the road!' O'Hagan was growing desperate. 'They're coming towards us, they'll be on us any minute!'

John Henry made up his mind. 'All right, O'Hagan,' he said briskly. 'We'll climb over the wall before they get here, if it makes you happy.'

'Oh, it does, Johnny, it does!'

Still keeping a firm grip on Bernie O'Hagan's arm, John Henry led him over to the wall and, with a scramble, both men managed to reach the top and drop to the other side, where they crouched among the bushes and undergrowth beneath the tall trees. John Henry, listening carefully, could hear the sound of marching feet drawer closer. As they crouched behind the wall the moon came peering out cautiously from behind its concealment. It was possible all of a sudden to see almost as well as by daylight.

'I'd like to see just who these people are,' John Henry murmured to Bernie O'Hagan. 'Stay still, now, while I have a quick look.'

There was a thick blackthorn bush just beside them. Moving over cautiously until he was directly behind it, John Henry stole a look between its branches. He wasn't worried that Bernie O'Hagan would try to escape from him. Bernie's fear of the Black and Tans, as he called this force, was far too strong for him to make any noise that might give them both away.

John Henry, peering between the almost naked branches, could see the men moving close beside him, separated only by the wall, and, as he had guessed, they weren't the dreaded Black and Tans. They were the local battalion of the Ulster Volunteer Force, and he could put names to at least a dozen of the twenty or so men. There was Tommy Maguire, and behind him Willie Morgan, and further back his small dark haired friend Artie Baird, all of them marching clumsily like new recruits with no training.

John Henry smiled grimly to himself as he remembered the days when he himself had marched as awkwardly and clumsily as these men. So Artie had succeeded at last in his ambition to be a fighting man. Long might he live to enjoy it. John Henry's instinct was to despise the fighting ability of these men, to write them off as amateurs, but he knew that this would be a mistake. The fierce pride of country which motivated both sides in this conflict would spur them on to fight like wild creatures when the time arrived.

John Henry wondered if he should explain to them what had happened and ask for their help. But almost at once he dismissed the idea. He had told Tommy and his friends that he would never get involved in their so-called army – and was he now to run to them, to be seen to have changed his mind, to encourage them in their wrong and dangerous activities? But if it had been the best way to help Rose, John Henry knew that he would have humbled his pride without hesitation.

That wasn't the real reason why he was determined to reject the possibility of help from them. He knew these men. They were reckless and without any idea of caution. They would almost certainly plunge into action with no attempt at cunning or finesse, and what would happen to Rose then? They might even shoot her themselves, not deliberately, but by mistake.

And what would her captors do when they heard the battalion approaching? He dreaded to think. No, he wanted no one else getting involved in this business. He would rescue his Rosie without anyone's blundering help. The risk to her if these men interfered was too great. He saw no reason to fear them, but at the same time he was glad he had avoided them.

He withdrew his head, and as he did so there was a crackling noise as Bernie O'Hagan, too frightened to be wise, stumbled over a mixed pile of leaves and sticks and tumbled to the ground. John Henry froze. Would the battalion hear them?

But all was well. The noise which had sounded so loud to John Henry, right beside it, hadn't penetrated across the thick stone wall. Or if it had, it had been attributed to one of the animals who roamed the wood by night, a fox, a cat, any of the midnight hunters searching for their prey. The men continued to march without any hesitation, and before long they had passed and were well away, on down the lane, marching in the opposite direction from where Bernie was taking John Henry and himself.

The moon, having helpfully stayed around long enough to allow John Henry to see and identify the marching men, disappeared again behind a thick bank of cloud. The two men scrambled back over the wall and continued on their way.

They must have covered another mile when O'Hagan stopped, and a momentary ribbon of moonlight showed his pointing finger indicating a short path off to the left. At the end of this path the lights of a big house shone over the fields towards them.

'This is Vincie's house, Johnny. The path takes you right up to his front door.'

John Henry was startled. This Vincie was apparently a rich man, from the look of things.

'What's your friend Vincie's full name, Bernie?' he asked casually.

'Sure, everyone knows that,' Bernie said, apparently seeing no reason to keep the name of the leader of the Fenian Brotherhood a secret. John Henry couldn't help being amused. He wondered just what Vincie would think of his supporter and his loose tongue. 'He's Vincent O'Hara. His people own the big house over there, they've lived there for centuries. The O'Haras used to be part of the Ascendancy, Johnny, sure you must know that, but just before the Rising a few years ago, in 1916, Vincie went over to our side. When his father died he got the house and the land, and he swore he'd see to it that Ireland would be free again. Ach, he's a great man, Johnny.'

John Henry had every sympathy with the brave Irishmen who had fought in the 1916 Rising. But things had moved on since then. This Vincent O'Hara was using means which made John Henry angry, however good his cause might have been originally. He was no better than the men of the Ulster Volunteer Force. Both sides had descended into the sort of violence and ferocity which John Henry's experience during the war had taught him to despise.

He said nothing of this, however, to his companion. 'Right, Bernie,' he said briskly instead, 'this is where we plan our approach carefully. I'm afraid your idea of going to the front door while I try the back or the side isn't going to work. We'll stay together, boyo, unless you want me to break your arm?' He bared his teeth in something which might have been a cheerful grin, or might have been the sort of expression to be seen on the face of a wolf about to tear its prey to pieces.

'Yes, Johnny, whatever you say, Johnny!' Bernie O'Hagan quavered.

'So, let's begin by getting round to the side, Bernie. We might be able to look in through a window and maybe see where Vincie and his boys are right now. Or better still, Rosie.'

'We'd be best going this way, then, Johnny.' Bernie moved over to the right where another less important path led up through the grounds surrounding the house. They began to move along it.

Chapter Forty-Nine

Vincent O'Hara's family home was even more impressive close to. In front, on either side of the drive which would have taken them to the main entrance, there were smooth lawns, dotted with trees, oaks, ashes, sycamores, and beeches, trees which had probably grown there for hundreds of years. Thick clumps of rhododendrons were massed along the side of the house, and must have been a blaze of colour in Spring.

John Henry, by instinct a lover of flowers and plants and all nature, hardly noticed them tonight. He saw only useful cover which might take him in safe concealment to the house where Rose was imprisoned: that was, if he could trust Bernie O'Hagan's word. A question, that. John Henry put it aside. Either she was here or she wasn't. He would find out.

Slipping from bush to bush, still dragging his reluctant companion with him, John Henry made his way through the shrubbery until at last he could see the side of the house directly in front of him. Here there were flowerbeds and a massive rockery full of cacti and Alpine plants. By-passing these, John Henry pushed Bernie towards the house.

The light blazed out from tall windows which stretched from over six feet high down to the ground. French windows, John Henry thought they were called. He had read about them, although he had seen nothing like them in France or Belgium while he was fighting there. John Henry moved closer until he could see clearly into the house.

He was looking into a large, impressive room, at least twenty feet long and probably wider, although it wasn't possible to see that sort of detail from where he was standing. It was brightly lit with many candles and the new gas fittings as well, to John Henry's astonishment. The walls were lined with bookshelves, mirrors and paintings which looked as if they had been there for generations. The bookshelves were made of rich, dark mahogany.

A long table in the same wood could be seen further back, where a tall silver candelabra held what seemed like hundreds of candles. The table was surrounded by matching chairs with backs decorated in a fine pattern of flowers, and there were a number of other, more comfortable chairs covered in red velvet. A matching red velvet couch was set against the nearby wall in front of one of the tall bookcases. It was evident that the room had been furnished by a wealthy family who liked to demonstrate their good taste.

John Henry thought that this man Vincie must be very rich, even more so than he had realised. What was he doing mixing with poor men like Bernie O'Hagan, mixing himself up in their affairs? But then he remembered that in the cause of Irish freedom both rich and poor were working alongside each other. The rich were usually the leaders. Nothing unusual about that, John Henry reflected realistically. It reminded him of his experience in the army where the rich were always in charge. But the rank and file were needed, too, and that was where Bernie and his like came into the picture. He pulled himself together, stopped marvelling at the richness of the room, and looked at it with a view to action.

His first impression was that, in spite of its size, the room was crowded with people. Second thoughts, however, allowed him to see that there were four men and one woman. And – oh, joy! – the woman was Rose. It was all John Henry could do to bite his tongue and refrain from exclaiming out loud. Instead, he examined the others.

One of them was a small red haired man, who was walking angrily about the room, his hands thrust behind him and a grim expression on his thin, sallow face. Something about him told John Henry straightaway that this was the leader, the 'Vincie' that O'Hagan had talked about. It wasn't just that his clothes stood out as more expensive than those of the other men, or than John Henry's own for that matter. It was more to do with the air of command that emanated from him.

Two of the other men were remarkably similar. They were bigger than average, not just by contrast with Vincie. They both had dark, curly hair, beginning to retreat from the centre of their heads, red faces, and well muscled arms and chests. John Henry thought that they might well be brothers.

The fourth man was a priest.

John Henry dragged Bernie O'Hagan away from the window to a safe distance. There were things he needed to ask him.

When they were hidden again behind the rhododendrons a good way from the house, John Henry spoke in a low voice.

'Which of those men is Vincie? The small, red haired one?'

'Yes, Johnny.' O'Hagan had begun to shiver, not with cold. The reality of his position was beginning to come home to him, at the sight of Vincie, it seemed. John Henry could see that this man's power over his followers must be based mainly on their fear of him.

'And the two big men?'

Chapter 49

'Them's the Miller twins – Aidan and Cathal. You don't want to mess with them. And they'll do anything Vincie tells them, so they will.'

'All right. Now – why is there a priest here?'

Bernie gulped. 'Ach, now, Johnny, you're going to be mad at me. But it wasn't my idea – it was all Vincie. I told him I wanted to marry Rosie but she was promised to a British soldier, a Prod, and he got right an' angry. You should have seen him, Johnny. There wasn't nothing I could do to stop him! He said a good Catholic boy like me shouldn't be done out of his rights to his sweetheart by any Proddy soldier, and a wee Catholic girl like Rosie had no right to act like that.

And he said he'd get Rosie and bring her here with a priest to marry us and I was to come along around ten o'clock. And, oh, Johnny, it must be long after that now, what with having to hide from the Black and Tans and all! He's walking up and down waiting for me and getting angrier than ever! What'll I do, Johnny?'

'You'll do nothing, Bernie,' said John Henry. He no longer sounded grim, simply cold and collected. 'But I don't trust you, see? So I'm going to tie you up and leave you here with a gag in your mouth to stop you letting out a shout to warn your pal Vincie. I'll need to find some rope, so you'll come with me to look for a shed where stuff like rope or cord would be kept, unless you'd rather I broke your arm now? No, I thought not. Come on.'

He gave O'Hagan a savage jerk, and propelled him across the grounds, keeping behind the shrubbery until they had passed the corner of the house and could see that they were nearing the kitchen gardens. A row of glasshouses contained exotic fruits as well as the more normal tomatoes and cucumbers. Before long they came in sight of a shed where the gardener probably kept his tools. The door was shut and bolted, but not locked. John Henry soon had it open.

Inside he could see a wheelbarrow, rakes and hoes and hedge clippers, flower pots, and a number of shelves with odds and ends lying on them. One of the shelves contained balls of cord. That would do. John Henry used the hedge clippers to cut several lengths of the cord, and began to tie O'Hagan into a secure bundle. Looking around, he saw some rags in one corner. He stuffed some of them into O'Hagan's mouth and used another piece to tie the makeshift gag into place, winding it round and round O'Hagan's head before fastening it with a secure knot.

'There you are, now, Bernie,' he said cheerfully. 'You can always lie your way out of your problem. Tell Vincie the Black and Tans jumped out on you as you were coming here in good time. You could say they caught you in the lane – they nearly did, after all! – and they tied you up and dumped you in here for Vincie to find. Leave me out of it, if you don't want me coming after you again, boy. If I were you I'd stick to that story, but it doesn't matter to me one way or another. I hope they find you before too long.'

Ignoring the man's struggles and efforts to speak, John Henry made his way back to the house.

Chapter Fifty

The question now was, if he simply walked into the big library, could he rely on the priest to support his demand that they allow Rose to leave with him? How much did the priest know about the situation? Did he believe Rose was there by her own free will? But John Henry knew that Rose wouldn't leave the priest or anyone else for long in doubt about the truth. It wouldn't be his Rosie if she didn't speak out exactly what she thought.

He smiled reminiscently as he remembered how she had come straight out and told his father she was a Catholic, regardless of the consequences. She would certainly refuse to be bullied into marriage with Bernie O'Hagan. So was the priest, like Vincie's other supporters, ready to do anything Vincie wanted, no matter what it was? Willing to carry out a 'marriage' with an unwilling bride?

John Henry realised that he couldn't be sure one way or the other. He couldn't risk it. It would be too dangerous to simply walk in and demand Rose's release. There had to be another way.

John Henry stood silently for a few moments, thinking. He was remembering a trick his friend Paddy O'Connor, always ready for a laugh and a joke, had played on Sergeant Major Hanna in the early days of their unit's training, to give the sergeant major a shock as he went on his rounds of the huts. Making his way back to the shed, John Henry collected the rest of the ball of string – there was still plenty of it, he was glad to see – and a wooden plank which he had noticed propped against one wall.

'Just you lie still, Bernie,' he told the frantically wriggling man. 'I haven't come to do you any harm. Your friends will be coming for you sooner than you expected.'

There was one more thing he needed, and he found it in the nearby rockery. Then he went back to the glasshouses he had noticed earlier.

Inside the brilliantly lit room, Rose had been silent for some time. The disappointment of having her attempt to escape halted at the last moment by the arrival of the man addressed as Vincie had knocked her back. One good thing was that Vincie had cut the rest of the rope from her wrists just before they arrived at the house.

'Don't want the good Father wondering why we have you tied up, do we, Rosie?' he had grinned sardonically at her. Rose said nothing and allowed him to lead her inside.

She stood in the big room examining the priest and her three captors, trying quietly to pull herself together, reaching out to her Lord for peace and help. Finally she felt able to speak.

She addressed herself first to the priest. He was an elderly man, not very tall and with wispy white hair above a round wrinkled face which showed signs of worry at the unconventional position in which he had been placed.

'I don't believe I know you, Father?'

'No, my child, you are not of my parish. I am Father O'Sullivan and I've been the parish priest to the O'Hara family and their demesne for a many a year now. But I think you must live outside my parish, for I don't recognise you.'

'I'm Rose Flanagan, Father.'

'I'm glad to know you, Rose, and to bless you by officiating at your wedding, daughter.'

'But I've no intention of getting married tonight, Father.'

'I don't understand.' The old priest looked nervous. He shot a questioning glance at Vincie. 'I was told I was brought here to marry two young Catholic people who were eager to wed but were afraid of trouble from some Protestant suitor?'

'They've been lying to you, Father. It's just the other way round. I'm promised to John Henry McClintock, and the fact that he's a Protestant is neither here nor there. We both believe in the same God. And I've no intention of marrying this Catholic man they've found for me. I'll be saying, "No!" all through the service, I'll not be taking the wedding mass, and I'll not be signing anything. So where does that leave you?'

The old priest looked flabbergasted. 'I couldn't marry you in those circumstances, my child. But are you sure?'

'I'm sure.'

It was then that Vincie, recovering himself, produced a revolver from the pouch attached to his belt at the rear.

'The marriage is going to take place all the same, Father,' he said in an icy, frightening tone. 'I'd hate to shoot a priest, but if you refuse to marry these two Catholic people and leave the woman free to marry a Protestant then you're no true priest at all and you'd deserve to die!

And as for you, Rosie, you'll either marry Bernie O'Hagan or your next experience of a service of the church will be your own funeral. So make your choice! Which would your Proddy soldier prefer, d'ye think?'

The two huge men, so alike with their dark, curly, receding hair and red faces and their strong bodies, had been standing just behind Rose. They made no sound but Rose was aware that they had moved closer to her. She had no doubt that they would seize her at a word from Vincie.

The old priest's voice quavered. 'Vincent O'Hara, I held you in my arms as an infant when I baptised you. Do you tell me that if I refuse to carry out this mockery of the Christian sacrament of marriage you'll shoot me?'

'That's just what I do tell you, Father O'Sullivan. And so perish all traitors!'

The priest's face crumbled. Rose felt a surge of sympathy for the old man. She moved forward and put her arms round him, leading him to a nearby chair. 'It'll not come to that, Father, I know it won't,' she whispered in his ear.

It was at that moment that a terrifying, penetrating shriek sounded outside the French windows from the garden.

'Vincie! Help! Help!'

An enormous crash sounded from the far side of the grounds.

Chapter Fifty-One

Vincie froze. Then with a snap reaction, he called out to the Miller brothers, 'It must be Bernie! Someone's jumped him! Come on, boys!' Turning to Father O'Sullivan he ordered, 'Make sure yer woman doesn't try to get away, see? I'll not be far away!'

Seconds later, all three of them were out through the French windows. Rose an Father O'Sullivan were left staring at each other. Only for a moment, however. No sooner were Vincie and his boys out of sight than a figure stepped quietly through the windows.

'Johnny!' cried Rose unbelievingly. Running to him, she threw her arms around his neck. John Henry hugged her fiercely for a second, then he gently disengaged himself.

'No time for that right now, Rosie,' he said. 'We need to go.'

'Can I come with you?' asked Father O'Sullivan eagerly.

'If you like. We'll go through the house and slip out by the front door,' John Henry said. 'Don't want to run into those lads in the back garden.'

Taking Rose's hand he led her at a brisk trot to the door of the library and through it to the hall which ran parallel to the room towards the front of the house, Father O'Sullivan following on their heels.

John Henry's main concern was that a servant might come upon them as they made their way out, but he thought it was less of a risk than meeting Vincie coming back from the vain pursuit of Bernie. The huge rock, lifted from the rock garden, which John Henry had balanced on the frame of the greenhouse, had fallen on the glass just as planned when he pulled the string tied to the wooden plank which he had used to prop the rock in place.

The resulting crash – coming from a good distance away from where John Henry stood out of sight against the wall by the French windows, holding the string until the right moment to pull it – had been very satisfactory. So had Vincie's reaction to John Henry's loud cry. Without pausing to consider if it had really been Bernie's voice he had heard, Vincie had gone plunging out into the night, leaving Rose un-guarded except for the old priest.

John Henry was glad the priest had shown no signs of fight. Not, of course, that he would have had any problem in overcoming the old man, but he was relieved that the question didn't arise.

Moving silently along the hall they reached the front door, and John Henry undid the bolt as quietly as possible and pulled the door carefully ajar. There was no sound of creaking. The door was kept well oiled. Moments later the three had slipped through and out unto the front drive. Here John Henry led his companions to one side to take cover in the flowering shrubs which lined the pathway, and hurried them along until they reached the main road.

Even then they were far from safe. It wasn't until they had covered the first mile on the route back to Rose's home that John Henry paused.

'We aren't safe just yet,' he said, 'but I hope Vincie and the boys will be too busy searching for Bernie O'Hagan for a bit yet. And when they find him where I left him, tied up in the gardener's shed, it'll take them some time to get the knots untied. All the same, we need to get a move on.'

'Suppose they come after us, Johnny?' Rose asked anxiously.

'I don't really think they will, Rosie. But I'll be happier when you're safe at home with your brothers.'

Privately he thought that Vincent O'Hara would be too busy thinking about how to avoid the Black and Tans to bother any more about Bernie O'Hagan's desire to marry Rose. He would be concerned that they knew who he was and had dared to come into his grounds and attack one of his men. He would be worried, too, about what Bernie might have told them about him. John Henry was reasonably sure Bernie would use the Black and Tans story he had fed him. He wouldn't want to admit that he'd allowed himself to be caught by John Henry, still less that he'd brought John Henry to Vincie's very door.

'It's John Henry McClintock, is it?' Father O'Sullivan asked. He had been keeping up with them well in spite of his age, but was glad of the break to get his breath back. 'The man Rose tells me she's promised to marry?'

'Aye, that's me, Father.'

'I'd like you to believe I had nothing to do with this, McClintock,' said Father O'Sullivan earnestly. 'Vincent told me there were two young Catholics wanting a priest to marry them in private to save a lot of trouble from yourself. I didn't know he was trying to force the wee girl into it. But when Rose put me right on that, I hope she'll confirm to you that I refused to have anything to do with carrying out a mockery of the sacrament of marriage.'

'That's true enough, Johnny. Father O'Sullivan stood up to Vincie very bravely.'

'Though, you mustn't think I'm in favour of a mixed marriage like you two are intending. I don't think it's right, and I don't think it'll work. You'll have too many problems. But what Vincie tried to do was even worse, in my view.'

'Well, thank you, Father. And now if you're both feeling a bit rested, we ought to move on, Rose. We're nearly at the turn off.'

'And if it's all the same to you, I'll leave you there and head back to my own parish.' The old priest wiped his forehead with a large white handkerchief and sighed. 'It's been a hard night, and I'll be glad to see my own bed as soon as possible.'

They trudged on until they came to the turning, and there Father O'Sullivan sketched a blessing for them and scurried off as fast as his old legs would carry him.

'I hope Vincie won't cause him any more trouble,' Rose said anxiously.

'I don't think he will, Rosie,' said John Henry. He took her arm and they strolled on along the country lane which would take them eventually to Rose's home. 'Vincent O'Hara knows most of his followers would be horrified if he did cause any harm to a priest. And now, Rosie, you can start by telling me just what happened to you.'

'I'll tell you all about it, Johnny. And then I want to hear your side of the story, boyo,' said Rose firmly. 'And how it was that you turned up at Vincie's just in time.'

They were almost at Rose's cottage by the time they had both finished talking and had answered all the questions which they had for each other.

John Henry sighed. 'It'll be hard enough to keep out of more trouble like this, Rosie. We must just be very careful. I wish I had you safely married and maybe moved away from this part of the country.'

'If only you could get a job, Johnny. Any job at all would do to start with.'

They had both given up hope of a job to suit John Henry's qualifications. Clearly that wasn't going to happen. But it was hard that they couldn't get married until some job came along.

'I'll keep looking, Rosie,' said John Henry. 'Looking and praying. That's about all I can do.'

Chapter Fifty-Two

During the years while he had been away at the war John Henry's father Douglas had been very lonely. His two daughters had married, first Martha who had moved to Country Antrim many miles away, and then young Peggy who, even worse, had emigrated with her new husband to Australia.

It was hard for Douglas to realise that Peggy, his baby, was old enough to marry, but he had to accept that it was a fact. The final blow came when the older of his two sons – Wee Dougie as he was called, having been christened Douglas after his father – had decided to emigrate to America.

'I'm sorry to leave you, Da,' he said to Big Douglas, one evening not long before John Henry came home, 'but I can't take much more of the upheaval in this country and the shortage of jobs. It wasn't so bad before the linen factory closed down, but that was months ago and I've been looking for something else ever since, and finding nothing as you well know. They say there are hundreds of jobs in America, and well paid ones too.'

'Could you not give it a wee while longer, son?' Douglas asked.

'Da, I've given it far too long already. My mate Steven McBride is sailing next month, and if I haven't got anything by then, I've made up my mind to go with him. It'll be best to have some company while I'm settling in.'

Douglas said no more. His pride wouldn't allow him to beg Dougie to stay. He could have said, perhaps, that it might not be for long, for Douglas was well aware that the days of his heavy drinking had played havoc with his health, and a recent visit to the doctor had left him with the knowledge that his heart might not last much longer. Doctor Miller had shaken his head and looked grave, and he had warned Douglas to take things easy as much as he could.

But Douglas had said nothing to his elder son about this. He was a man brought up to keep his feelings to himself, and he had found it too difficult to speak about it to Dougie, who had never been as close to him as John Henry. Douglas McClintock had cut down drastically on his drinking since the promise he had made to John Henry, but he knew that the damage had already been done. He was a man old before his time. If John Henry had only been here, he knew, he could have poured out his fears to him.

The month's grace went in, and still Dougie had found no sign of a job. He was due to leave in a few more days when to Douglas's delight his younger son arrived home.

'Johnny, Johnny, you're a sight for sore eyes!' he greeted him, and could hardly hold back the tears. Dougie's intended departure no longer mattered quite so much.

John Henry was glad that he had come home in time to see his brother before he sailed for America, little though they had ever had in common. He knew how much it meant to his father that he would not be left alone, and in particular that it was John Henry who would be with him during his last years. To tell the truth, John Henry was horrified to see his father looking so old and weak. He was glad, even more, that he had come home in time to be a comfort to Douglas, now that both his daughters had moved away and his other son was soon going.

The thought crossed John Henry's mind that he and Rose might live with Douglas McClintock when they married, but he was unhappy with that idea. He still didn't trust his father to behave well to Rose, the more so when he learned that there had been little or no contact between the two during his long years of absence. He didn't want to know whose fault that had mainly been. But he knew that living in the same house would be hard for both of them, and possibly even more so when the children began coming. No, the only real solution was for John Henry to find himself a job and get somewhere to live, if possible near enough to his father to allow them to spend time with each other regularly.

In the end, the solution came easily enough. It was after the uneasy truce in July 1921. It was to be more than another year, after the assassination of Michael Collins, and the end of the civil war in the south, before the killings in the north of the country could be said to have ended. During this time there were, if anything, more shootings than there had been in the previous year.

John Henry was trudging through Belfast one day, wondering if things would ever be any different, and reflecting that, truce or no truce, the danger of walking through certain streets in Belfast had not changed, when he was hailed by an old army comrade, Jamie Patterson. Jamie, although a sergeant, had always, off duty, treated John Henry as an equal; he had a great respect for John Henry's intelligence and book-learning.

'John Henry McClintock! It's yourself!' Striding heartily over to John Henry, he clapped him on the back with one hand, seized John Henry's hand with the other and shook it vigorously. 'Ye auld rascal! Hey, it's great to see you, boyo!'

John Henry responded cautiously. Too many encounters like this had led within a few sentences to invitations to join the UVF.

'And what are you doin' with yerself these days, me auld mucker?' asked Jamie Patterson.

'Not a lot,' admitted John Henry. 'Mostly looking for a job, like the rest of us. What about yourself?'

'Looking for a job? And you with your certificates and book-learning?' Jamie sounded incredulous. He pulled off his cap and scratched his balding head. 'Well, now, I could offer you something, but it's not a job that's fitted to someone as smart as yourself, Johnny. But, maybe, I don't know, might it do to be goin' on with, like, till you come up with something better?' He wore an anxious look on his round, red face. Afraid, John Henry could see, of insulting his old comrade by a degrading offer.

'Jamie, if it's cleaning the streets, I'd be glad of it!' John Henry told him, and Jamie's face cleared.

'Ah, well, in that case, and seeing as how you've a bit of experience in this line, as you once told me, would you be interested in a job in my family's linen factory?'

John Henry's sense of humour was tickled. He had spent more than five nightmare years in the army, followed by another year, now, of unemployment, mainly because he'd wanted so badly to get away from the linen factory where he had worked in his early youth. Now the wheel seemed to have turned full circle, and he was being offered the chance to go back.

He controlled his amusement, and clinched with Jamie Patterson's offer gratefully.

The best thing about it, to John Henry's mind, was that the factory was not in Belfast. In fact, it was in Lurgan, not many miles from his home in Kilmacartan, although a lot further from Rose's home in Dromore. With the job in the linen factory for security, John Henry and Rose decided to marry. They had known each other for more than seven years by now, and although it would not have been uncommon, in those days of poverty, for a couple to wait for much longer, no one could have accused them of rushing into it.

'Rosie, I can hardly believe this is happening for us at last,' John Henry said, holding her in his arms.

'I know, Johnny. It seems like a dream come true.'

'I'll do my best to make you happy, Rosie.'

'You won't have to try hard, Johnny,' Rose told him, half laughing and half crying. 'Just being with you will be enough for me.'

Chapter Fifty-Three

Douglas McClintock, his spirits lifted by his son's safe return, had lasted much longer than Doctor Miller had expected, but his survival couldn't go on forever. A week after John Henry had clinched happily with his friend Jamie Patterson's offer of a job, he came home from visiting Rose one night and was surprised not to see his father sitting in his front garden enjoying the warm evening air and the smell of the roses.

Douglas had his own favourite chair where he liked to sit of an evening, and to see him there had become such a familiar sight to John Henry that at first he could hardly believe his father was not sitting there. The chair was out in the garden, placed to catch the last of the evening sun as usual, but there was no one in it. John Henry looked all round, expecting to see his father over pulling up a weed or bending to smell a flower.

Deciding that Douglas must have gone indoors for something, John Henry pushed open the huge front door and called out. 'Are you there, Da? It's me, Johnny.'

A feeble voice answered him from the direction of the front room, and John Henry went in there. His father was lying stretched out on the sofa. This was something John Henry had never seen before. For as long as he could remember, the kitchen had been the place where Douglas McClintock went to sit. And John Henry had never seen his father lying down. He was a man who sat upright by choice and habit.

'Daddy, are you all right?'

'I don't feel just too good, Johnny. Maybe you'd fetch Doctor Miller to me?'

'I'll go straightaway, Daddy. Would you like me to get you as glass of water or anything first?'

'No, no, Johnny. You're a good boy. Just get me the doctor.'

John Henry could hear that his father's breathing was laboured, and his heart seemed to be beating with an irregular rhythm which worried John Henry more than anything else.

Doctor Miller lived at the opposite end of the village. John Henry, still fit enough from his army training, ran the length of the sunny, dusty road at top speed. Doctor Miller was just finishing his tea, but he picked up his black bag and came at once when his housekeeper gave him John Henry's message.

'His breathing seems bad, doctor,' John Henry said as they made their way back. 'Have you any idea what's wrong?'

'It's his heart, Johnny,' Doctor Miller said. 'I've been concerned about it for some time. Didn't he tell you?'

'No,' said John Henry. 'He's never been a man for talking much about himself, and especially about his health. I wish I'd known.'

The journey back to Douglas's house took longer, of necessity, for Doctor Miller was not as young and fit as John Henry, but when they arrived no time was wasted. Douglas was lying on the sofa where John Henry had left him, his eyes shut and his face pale and tired. When John Henry brought the doctor in, Douglas half opened his eyes and seemed to be trying to speak, but the only sound he made was a long sigh.

'I'd like to get him into his bed straightaway, Johnny,' said Doctor Miller briskly. 'You'll have to help me to carry him. But first of all I'm going to give him an injection of a very small dose of strychnine to stimulate his heart.'

The doctor prepared the syringe, then he rolled up Douglas's sleeve and cleaned an area round the vein in his right arm. The injection was quickly given. Its effects could be seen in quite a short time. Douglas regained some of his colour and his heart began to beat more steadily. As soon as Doctor Miller thought it was safe, he and John Henry lifted Douglas, John Henry taking him under the arms and Doctor Miller taking his feet, and carried him upstairs. Settled in his own bed, Douglas seemed more comfortable.

'Stay with me, Johnny,' he whispered.

'Aye,' said John Henry. He sat down beside the bed and held his father's hand in his. Doctor Miller went downstairs to wash his hands.

'Call me if you need me Johnny,' he said as he went out of the room.

Douglas made the effort to speak to his son. 'Would you read a bit of Scripture to me, Johnny? I feel it might help me.'

John Henry took out his pocket New Testament and turned to Matthew's Gospel. He soon found the part he was looking for, at the end of chapter eleven.

> *Come to me, all you who labour and are heavy laden, and I will give you rest. Take my yoke upon you and learn from me,*

*for I am gentle and lowly in heart, and you will find rest for
your souls. For my yoke is easy and my burden is light.*

Douglas smiled at him.

'Do you remember reading that to us years ago, Daddy? I must have
been about four or five.'

'Aye. Before I started the drinking. Before your mammy died having
Peggy.'

'It's still true, Daddy.'

'I know it is, son.'

'If you've never done it before, now's the time, Daddy.'

'I'd like to, son.'

'Well, it's a thing you have to do yourself. I can't do it for you. Tell the
Lord you want to cast everything on him, Daddy. If you want to.'

So Douglas McClintock, for the first time in many years, prayed. And
presently his face softened, his eyes remained closed, and his breathing
came more slowly and quietly.

'Doctor Miller!' called John Henry. He tried to make it loud enough
for the doctor to hear, but not so loud that it would wake his father, who
seemed to him to be peacefully sleeping. Doctor Miller came back upstairs.

'He's sleeping, doctor,' John Henry said. 'Is he getting better, do you
think?'

Doctor Miller came over to his patient and took his wrist, checking
his pulse. He looked at John Henry very kindly. 'I'm afraid not, Johnny,'
he said. 'He's slipping away. It can't be much longer now.'

John Henry sat by his father's side until presently the doctor, still
speaking gently, told him that Douglas had gone. Then he rested his head
on his father's breast and wept silently for a long time.

Chapter Fifty-Four

Douglas McClintock's funeral drew a large crowd. As was usual in country districts, everyone who knew him and everyone who belonged to the same church came. His elder daughter Martha and her husband Glen travelled down from their sheep farm in the north of County Antrim. But for Peggy, in Australia, and Wee Dougie, in America, the journey was too long and too expensive to be possible.

John Henry was glad of Martha's support, but gladder still to have Rose standing beside him as he greeted the guests and thanked them for their condolences. Refreshments, buns and sandwiches and tea, were being served after the burial service was over in the church hall to anyone who chose to come, and that seemed to be everyone John Henry had ever known. And before drinking their tea and eating freely, the guests lined up to shake hands with John Henry and Martha and to express their sorrow.

There was one face which he had not seen for more than a dozen years, although he recognised its owner at once. It was Michael Fyfe, the young schoolmaster who had tried to persuade Douglas McClintock to allow John Henry to stay on at school. John Henry had not been present when Michael called at their house, but he had heard plenty about it from an angry Douglas for some time afterwards. He had always retained a feeling of gratitude to Michael Fyfe, even though his attempt to help John Henry carry on his education had been so unsuccessful.

'Mr Fyfe!' he exclaimed, shaking the schoolmaster's hand warmly. 'I'm happy to see you.'

'You can call me Michael now, Johnny – I haven't been your teacher for quite a long time now,' Michael Fyfe said, smiling. 'I'm sorry for your loss, Johnny.'

'Thank you, Michael.'

'I've something to say to you afterwards, if you can give me five minutes or so,' Michael said. 'I'll not hold up the queue now.'

'I'd be very glad to have a chat with you, Michael,' John Henry said, not really able to take in properly what Michael had said. The queue moved on. John Henry was ready to collapse with exhaustion by the time the last person had greeted him and Martha. Rose went over quietly to the nearest table and brought him a cup of tea, then gently urged him over to a seat and stood between him and anyone else who wanted to shake his hand, for a short time. But inevitably the numbers of people coming over and trying to be kind continued even after John Henry had taken a seat.

He noticed that Martha was exhibiting a lot more stamina, and seemed able to continue to talk to people long after he had reached the stage of longing for it all to be over. What with having to organise the funeral arrangements and now going through this exhausting day, John Henry had had little time to miss his father. He knew that once everyone had gone, the pain was going to hit him again. He was overwhelmingly grateful for Rose.

The time came at last when he was able to sit quietly in the house where he had grown up and to think about his father. Douglas had been a good father to him for the first part of his childhood. Then had come the death of John Henry's mother, and the start of the heavy drinking. Those were not such good memories. But since the day John Henry had spoken so firmly to him about his treatment of Rose and the drinking which made him lose control, he had improved. And for this last year, since John Henry came home from the war, he had been more like the father he remembered as a child, except that they could talk together as adults. John Henry sincerely mourned him.

Martha and Glen had retired early to the room where they were staying for the night. At daybreak the next day they would leave, for the farm couldn't be left to run itself, and the neighbour who had kindly stepped in to look after the animals for the two days absence necessary to allow them to travel down for the funeral would be glad to see them back. Rose, too, had gone. She had, as always, her brothers and her sister to feed. John Henry continued to relax and to remember his father at his best.

A loud knock came on the door.

Hoping this wasn't yet another acquaintance coming to express their sympathy, John Henry got to his feet with a sigh and went to see. Opening the door, he was taken aback for a moment to see Michael Fyfe standing there, his hat in his hands.

'I hope this is all right, Johnny. You remember I said I had something to say to you? I won't keep you long. I'm sure you're eager to get to your bed after the day you've had.'

'No. No. Come away in, Michael. I'm glad to see you,' John Henry said, although to tell the truth he wished Michael had come tomorrow instead.

'That's a better welcome than I got the last time I was here,' Michael said with a smile.

'Ach, my father wasn't himself that time, Michael. I'm sorry you suffered from his temper. He was a good man when he was himself.'

John Henry drew Michael Fyfe into the kitchen, offered him a chair, and took his hat. 'I'll put the kettle on,' he began, but Michael interrupted him.

'No need, no need. I'm fine as I am. Johnny, I don't want to keep you up, so I'll come straight to the point.' He leaned back in his kitchen chair. 'I heard you were home and looking for a job, Johnny.'

'Well, and so I was, Michael, but an army mate has offered me work in his father's linen factory, so I'm sorted now.'

'And are you satisfied with that?'

'To tell you the truth, Michael, it's the last sort of job I wanted. I spent nearly six years overseas and got some qualifications, and I'd hoped for better. But any job's a blessing at the moment, the way things are.'

'Well, Johnny, that's just what I'd hoped to hear you say. I'd heard that you'd got some qualifications. That makes it all the better. Now, what I have to say to you is this. I've been offered a better teaching job at a big school up in Belfast. I wondered if you'd be interested in taking over the village school here? You'd have to sit for your teacher's certificate, but I'd be happy to help you with that and I can't see you having any difficulty with it. I won't be leaving until after Christmas. If you'd like to take the position on, I'll recommend you to the Board, and I think I can say they'll take my recommendation. So, what do you say?'

John Henry opened his mouth and then shut it again. He was at a loss for words. Suddenly he was being offered something he'd wanted for most of his life – a job which would be fulfilling and interesting, and which he knew he could do well. He was awestruck.

'I say yes, Michael,' he managed at last. 'I can hardly believe this is happening, but if I'm not dreaming, then I say yes! And thank you!'

Michael laughed half in embarrassment and half in delight. 'Well, Johnny, it'll be a real pleasure to me, too, to see you in the sort of job you deserve. It'll make up for having to let you leave all those years ago.'

'I'll have to work at the linen factory in the meantime, Michael,' John Henry felt he had to explain. 'Me and Rose Flanagan are getting wed, and I'll need an income.'

'That's all right, Johnny. If it suits you, I'll come round a couple of evenings during the week and take you through the things you'll need to learn to pass the teaching certificate. I'm very glad to hear you're getting married. I hope you'll be very happy.'

'I know I will,' said John Henry simply. 'I don't think there's ever been a man so blessed as me, what with Rose, and now this!'

Chapter Fifty-Five

The death of John Henry's father left him with possession of the family house. Martha told him, before she and Glen left the next morning, that as far as she was concerned it was his. She had no need of it. 'And you can be sure that Peggy isn't coming back from Australia, nor yet Dougie from America, to put in a claim,' she added.

Peggy's husband had a secure job as an electrician in Australia, and report had it that Dougie, too, was doing well in his new country. And indeed, the letters which came in reply to those sent by John Henry telling them of Douglas McClintock's death confirmed Martha's words. Neither of them put in any claim to the house. It was a place, therefore, where John Henry and Rose could set up life together as a married couple.

Rose was glad to be moving away from Dromore. She had lived there since her parents moved up from Monaghan, and for most of that time she had been happy. But the last couple of years hadn't been so good. There had been a growing coldness that blew into her face like a freezing north wind from her former friends and her neighbours. There had even been a time, past now, when she had almost expected to be asked by the Reillys to leave her job at their farm.

It hadn't come to that, but even her best friends, people like Peggy McCracken, had spoken coolly to her at times.

There had been one dreadful morning only two months ago, after a restless night during which Rose had several times been wakened by voices whispering just outside her bedroom window and more than one set of footsteps moving about, when she had woken to find that someone had painted on the wall, by the front door of the cottage, the words 'Kill the Prod lovers'.

The paint was bright scarlet, and it had dried leaving trickles like blood from the bottom of some of the letters.

Rose stood by the open door looking at it, shocked almost to tears. She had risen early, and was ready to leave before six o'clock, to walk the mile to the Reillys' farm and start her day's work. But in spite of the early hour, the scarlet letters stood out only too plain to see, in the slowly growing light of the summer dawn.

There was no time to do anything about it now. She must hurry on to begin her work at the farm. But she knew, without needing to be told, that her family, especially her sister Emily who shared her room, would be even more worried than before. After the recent attack from the other side they had hoped things had settled down and there would be nothing more, but it seemed that it was hard to get rid of hatred or one sort or another.

That evening she scrubbed hard at the lettering when she came home, but found it difficult to remove. For weeks after, the faint pink remnants accused her every time she left the house.

She never did find out who had written the message. There were plenty who might have been responsible. Rose would be glad to get away from the lot of them, and move to somewhere where no one knew her or cared about her opinions. She was glad that Emily, who had won her scholarship, would be moving away also when she went up to Belfast to the teacher training college.

Michael Fyfe kept his promise to John Henry. Regularly twice a week in the evenings after the day's work he called round and took John Henry through the syllabus for the Teacher Training certificate. He found, with no surprise, that not only was John Henry the apt pupil he had remembered him as, but that the qualifications he had worked for in the army, English Language, Mathematics, French and German, meant that John Henry already knew most of what he needed to learn. Before long, Michael was convinced that his pupil had only to sit the exam to sail through it with flying colours. He put down John Henry's name as a candidate for the next occasion when the exam would be held.

Convincing the School Board that John Henry was the ideal replacement for himself proved to be harder than he had expected. The school had been founded by the local Church of Ireland, and the minister, William Thornton, had considerable influence in the choice of teacher. When John Henry heard this, he warned Michael that he had clashed with Thornton over his refusal to join the UVF, and was sure that the man would reject him without hesitation.

However, Michael had friends on the board, among them Doctor Miller, and he sensibly approached them first and made sure of their support. It was only then that he approached Mr Thornton.

'You'll never get a better man for the job,' he argued persuasively. 'McClintock is not only a clever man, but an honest one. You can trust him to do a good day's work and to do his best for the children.'

The Reverend William Thornton wasn't so sure of that, but he was aware, for Michael Fyfe had made it clear, that his co members on the board were in favour of John Henry. He could, if he chose, push his own opinion through, but it would make for bad feeling. Moreover, he had spent some time recently with John Henry, arranging Douglas McClintock's funeral, and had found, to his surprise, that John Henry McClintock had impressed his as a good man.

'Well, Mr Fyfe,' he said grudgingly at last, 'I can't say this man would be my own first choice. But since feeling is so strong in his favour, I suppose he'll have to have my vote too.'

And so John Henry, passing his Teacher Training certificate with the ease Michael Fyfe had forecast, found to his delight that the job of his dreams was being offered to him.

The board had also decided that as numbers of children had been growing over the last few years, it was time the school had a junior teacher as well to look after the younger children, and so a Miss Agnes Byrne was duly appointed. She was a stranger to John Henry, but he found her easy to get on with. It seemed that everything was working out perfectly for him and Rose.

Chapter Fifty-Six

The Troubles had not ended yet. But John Henry was glad that they had never come closer to his own home village than the talk and the marching of Tommy Maguire, Willie Morgan, Artie Baird, and others like them.

He was sorry for Artie, who he knew was under the influence of the others, especially Tommy Maguire. He hoped that none of these men, whom he had known as boys, would be more involved in the fighting than they had been so far.

Then one night not long before his wedding day John Henry was wakened by a crashing noise. It sounded as if it had come from his back garden. As he sat up in bed wondering whether he should go and see what had caused it or turn over and go back to sleep again, he heard a loud thud. Something heavy had fallen against his kitchen door.

John Henry sprang out of bed, dragged on his trousers over his night-shirt, and stuck his feet into his boots without stopping to lace them up. A moment later he was hurrying downstairs and making for the kitchen. He unbolted the door which led to the back garden. It opened inwards, and as John Henry pulled it towards him a heavy body came with it. It was a man and he was badly injured. There was so much blood over his face that it took John Henry a minute to recognise him. It was wee Artie Baird, his long time friend.

'Artie!' exclaimed John Henry. Going down on his knees, he examined his friend and saw that he had been shot at least once, in the shoulder. He was unconscious, but still breathing. John Henry took Artie under the arms and began to move him carefully into the kitchen. He laid Artie out on the floor and ran for the first aid box which he kept on one of the kitchen shelves. The first thing was to stop the bleeding. John Henry felt as if he was back on the battlefields of Flanders. He had done this sort of thing so many times before.

With the wound cleaned, and a dressing fixed over it and secured with a bandage, John Henry's next care was to keep Artie warm. The nearest blankets were in his own bedroom, so it was back upstairs at top speed, then he was wrapping Artie closely in his own bedcovers.

Artie was still unconscious, although every now and then a moan escaped from his lips. John Henry would have liked to fetch Doctor Miller, but he was worried about leaving Artie alone while he was still unconscious. While he was trying to make up his mind what was best to do, Artie began muttering.

'Tommy – don't leave me, Tommy – where are you?'

Tommy Maguire, he must mean, John Henry thought.

'Artie. It's me, Johnny. You're safe now.'

'Johnny.' Artie's eyes blinked open and he looked surprised. 'I came to find you, Johnny. I knew you would help me.'

'Artie, what's been happening? How did you get shot?'

'I was out with the boys, Johnny. We were just marching along – we weren't meaning to shoot anyone. But the Fenian Brotherhood ambushed us out along the road and started firing, so Tommy and Willie were firing back. I couldn't fire. We didn't have enough guns to go round us all, so I didn't have one. Then they all started running and I was running too when I felt a pain in my shoulder and I couldn't run any more. I don't know what happened after that. It was all dark and I was lying by myself at the side of the road. It's a wonder the Fenian Brotherhood didn't finish me off. Maybe it was so dark they didn't see me. So I got myself together enough to manage to crawl along the road until I got here.'

'Why didn't you try to get to your own home, Artie?' John Henry couldn't help asking.

'Ach, Johnny, I daresn't let me Da know I was out with the UVF unit! He's a strict, respectable man, he'd kill me if he knew! You won't tell him, will you, Johnny?'

'I won't tell him, Artie. But now you've come to yourself, I'll have to leave you for a short while. I need to fetch Doctor Miller.'

'Johnny, Johnny, suppose he tells the police?'

'He won't do that, Artie. He's a kind man. And you need a proper doctor, boy. There's only so much I can do for you.'

Before Artie could say anything more, John Henry went, moving swiftly along the dark village street until he reached Doctor Miller's house. It was as well the way was so familiar to him, for it was hard to see where he was going, but he managed.

Doctor Miller was asleep, but when his housekeeper woke him up he was willing to come, like the good man he was.

'You think it's just the one wound, in his shoulder, Johnny?' he asked as they hurried back through the sleeping village.

'I'm not sure, doctor. I didn't want to move him about too much. I just did the best I could with the wound I could see and came for you.'

'Well, that was the wisest thing you could do, Johnny. It's best not to move someone before the doctor comes – it might make things much worse. You didn't see if there was an exit wound from the shot?'

'I didn't see it, Doctor. I suppose there probably was. I should have checked and bandaged it, too.'

'No, Johnny, you were better coming for me straightaway and leaving that to me. If there's an exit wound it'll need more than just a simple bandage.'

Artie was still lying on the kitchen floor as John Henry had left him, swathed in blankets. His eyes were closed again, and an ominous red stain was spreading from beneath him over one side of the blanket.

Doctor Miller knelt down beside him and pulled back the blanket gently and examined the injured man. The dressing which John Henry had put over the wound in Artie's shoulder was still doing its job, but blood was out seeping from lower down, beneath Artie's body.

'I'll need to turn him over to see what the problem is here, Johnny,' Doctor Miller said. 'Can you help me?'

Between them they turned Artie onto his side. John Henry could not keep back a gasp of horror. Across Artie's back a dreadful wound gaped open. He realised that it was the exit wound from the shot which had gone through Artie's shoulder, just as Doctor Miller had expected. Artie's clothes, which had been hidden from John Henry until now, were saturated in blood, which gushed out more than ever now that he had been moved and the injury exposed.

'I'm afraid this is a more serious wound than the one in his shoulder, Johnny,' said the doctor. 'It's just as well the poor man is unconscious. I'll see what I can do for him. Can you boil some water so I can sterilise my needle – it'll need stitches.'

He began to clean the wound in Artie's back. But as the blood was wiped away, still more came pouring out and John Henry, returning with a kettle of boiling water, was horrified to see the size of the opening slashed across Artie's body.

'Will he live, Doctor Miller?'

'Who knows, Johnny? He's lost so much blood.'

'I wish I'd noticed it earlier!' John Henry said violently.

'There'd have been nothing you could have done, Johnny. Stop blaming yourself.'

But John Henry found that very hard. He felt as if he'd let Artie down when he came crawling along the road to him for help.

In spite of all Doctor Miller's efforts, it was not much later before Artie began to sigh heavily. His unconscious state became deeper. There was nothing more that Doctor Miller could do. Before very long they could both see that he had slipped right away.

John Henry wept for the waste of it.

Poor wee Artie, who always wanted to copy the older boys he admired. He had tried to enlist but had been turned down for the army on the same day that John Henry himself had been accepted. He had escaped the fighting in the battlefields of Flanders, only to meet death instead in the fighting in his own home country, here in County Down.

Chapter Fifty-Seven

John Henry and Rose had a small wedding in his local parish church: the group of brothers whom they met with on a Sunday weren't licensed to conduct marriages. John Henry wasn't too happy that they were being married by the Reverend William Thornton. But since Douglas McClintock's funeral Mr Thornton had been more friendly, even voting him into his job as schoolmaster, and there was no other option. Father Donnelly in St. Martin's, where Rose had gone previously, had refused to marry them unless John Henry converted to Catholicism, which he was unwilling to do.

It was a small wedding by choice. Their families came, and a few friends. Rose was surprised how happy she felt to see that Annie Reilly had put aside their differences and turned up on the day.

They married on a Saturday afternoon, each granted a half-day holiday for the purpose. There was no question of a honeymoon. Money was too tight. But they would have the Sunday to themselves before John Henry needed to return to work.

Rose would not be going back to the Reillys' farm. It was too far from her new home. Instead, she would work part-time for a farmer within easier reach, until the babies started coming and she would have to leave.

Neither John Henry nor Rose had made love to anyone before their wedding night.

It would have been considered a strange and disgraceful thing if Rose had come to her wedding bed as anything but a virgin. Custom and attitudes were laxer for a man, but as it happened John Henry hadn't slept with a woman before the night of his conversion at the tent mission, and since then had managed to resist temptation. There had been opportunities and to spare in the army – Marie Louise had not been the only one to find the tall young Irishman attractive – but he had continued to remember Rose, waiting patiently for him, and his hatred of the idea of deceiving her had helped him to hold back.

They came to this first night together excited, but perhaps equally nervous. They had in their separate ways been looking forward to the physical closeness, the sensual experience. Rose was perhaps a little more nervous than John Henry. Like many of her generation, she knew little of what to expect. There had been whispered reports from girls she'd known at school, passed on to them by older sisters and relayed in turn by the younger girls.

'It hurts a lot at first,' Mary McCartney had told them, 'but it isn't so bad the next time.'

'My sister said she was able to keep her nightie on the whole time,' Maggie Kilmore contributed. 'She says that makes it less embarrassing. Her husband wanted her to take it off, but she was firm.'

Then there had been what she had picked up by simply living in the country and working on a farm, of the breeding and birthing of animals; but she had been given to understand that things were a bit different for human beings.

John Henry, mixing as he had with boys of his own age both at school and at the factory where he had first worked, and later unable to avoid hearing his friends and comrades in the army talking about their experiences with women, knew a lot more in theory. But the responsibility rested on him to make sure that everything went as it should – a heavy weight, he had begun to feel.

Apart from the gossip passed on by their friends, they had both read *The Song of Solomon,* and various other parts of the Bible, which spoke without any reticence of sexual matters.

It wasn't, taken altogether, much to go on.

Rose had managed to get together enough money from her meagre wages to buy some white cotton and sew herself a new nightgown. Anything else she could spare had gone on a few coloured ribbons, to turn her spare dress (the one designated as 'good' and kept for Sundays and special occasions) into something more like her idea of a wedding dress.

John Henry wore his respectable Sunday suit to the wedding, but for his wedding night he had nothing new. But he had seen to it that his nightshirt was freshly washed.

Thus arrayed, they confronted each other across the double bed that had belonged to John Henry's parents.

John Henry had changed and washed downstairs in the kitchen, allowing Rose the privacy of the bedroom, with the warm water carried up in the ewer, and the basin on the washstand. Rose stripped, washed as thoroughly as possible, and dabbed on a few drops from a little bottle of perfume, a present from Peggy McCracken on her last birthday, which she had saved until now. Then she slipped the new nightdress over her head. She heard a soft knock on the door, and called in a voice which she tried to keep from quavering, 'Come in.'

Now John Henry stood, his discarded clothes held in a bundle in one hand. And noticing, as he glanced self-consciously round the small room, that Rose had folded hers carefully and placed them on the room's one chair, at the head of the bed, on the side where she was standing.

'Which side do you like to sleep on, Rosie?' he asked. His voice sounded hoarse, and he coughed to clear it.

'I don't mind,' said Rose in a hurry.

'"For this cause shall a man leave his father and mother,"' John Henry quoted, *'"and he shall cleave to his wife, and they shall be one flesh."* This is a good thing we're doing, Rosie. Nothing to be ashamed about.'

'I know it is, Johnny,' said Rose. She held herself back from giggling. She didn't want to make him feel like a fool. But there was no need for quotations from the Bible right now. 'Johnny,' she said, 'why don't you put those clothes down somewhere, and come round here and kiss me?'

So he did.

And as his hands stroked her soft breasts, and they fell backwards onto the bed, he gave over wondering if everything would be all right, because for him, it definitely was.

Chapter Fifty-Eight

Rose was surprised, and quite a bit upset, at how much their lovemaking had hurt her. John Henry, knowing so little, had entered her long before she was ready for him. In the morning, she found a trace of blood on the sheets, and comforted herself by memories of what friends had said about 'losing your virginity', and supposed that another time, it wouldn't hurt in the same way.

She had also woken in the middle of the night to find herself lying in a puddle of what she thought at first was blood, but later realised was the male input. (Seeds for growing babies, she thought.) She found it surprising, and not really very pleasant. Perhaps she would get used to it. At least it wasn't blood.

These happenings were not what she had hoped for, or known that she should expect, on her wedding night. There wasn't much romance about them. But there was one thing that was all she had hoped of it. Falling asleep, cuddled in her husband's arms, was something she had dreamt of for years, and now that it was happening, she found it made up for the rest.

Things got better, though not all at once. Rose plucked up enough courage to make clear to John Henry that she needed to be ready before he entered her. It wasn't easy. They had never spoken of such things before. But the painful alternative was enough to force her to find the words to explain. John Henry, while saying little, made it clear that he appreciated her courage, and was far from being offended by any reflection on his skills as a lover. He, like Rose, wanted things to go well, and was ready to learn where necessary.

Rose didn't know how unusual John Henry was in this, but if she had known, she would have seen nothing strange in it. She was quite ready to believe, and indeed was sure enough without telling, that her Johnny was a man in a thousand in every way possible.

They made love most nights, and before long it was a pleasure to Rose as well as to her husband.

Before the first year of marriage was up, Rose was pregnant, and in due course bore a fine, healthy, female child. The girl was christened Mary, and both her parents were delighted with her, although Rose knew that John Henry's heart had been set upon a son.

'Time enough for that,' was all he said to her upon the subject, and when Mary was coming two, and Rose was pregnant again, he made his pleasure obvious. Rose hoped for his sake that she would have a boy this time, though, for herself, she didn't mind one way or the other.

When the second girl, Katie, was born, John Henry said little. He still expressed his satisfaction in public, and indeed he loved the child dearly, but to Rose he said, 'It's the Lord's will, Rosie, and when he means me to have a son, He'll give me one.'

The next pregnancy was slower in coming. After a few years, Rose had almost stopped looking for it, until in the end she was taken by surprise.

This time she prayed for a boy, and a boy it was – but not without a long, hard struggle.

Rose woke suddenly in the middle of the night. She turned over in bed, and either heard, or felt – she could never be sure afterwards which it was – a sort of pop. A moment later she was soaked in water.

'Johnny! Johnny!' she exclaimed, pulling at her husband's arm. 'Johnny, I'm starting!'

'Go back to sleep, Rosie, there's a good girl,' said John Henry, sounding quite wide awake. 'It's not morning yet.'

Although the sound of her voice had brought him just awake enough to hear that she was speaking, he was still more than half asleep, and clearly hadn't understood a word of what she had said.

It didn't take Rose long, however, to shake him fully awake. Once he had taken in properly what she was saying, John Henry sprang out of bed. 'We'll have to get the midwife, Rosie!' he said. 'I meant to send wee Mary for her, if it had been a reasonable time of day. But I can't have the wean running out at this time of night on her own in the dark. Will you be all right while I fetch her myself, Rosie?'

'Of course I will, Johnny,' Rose answered firmly. 'You just let Mary and wee Katie sleep on for as long as they will – it'll be a sight easier for us all, that way. You can go for the midwife yourself, and no harm done. But first,' she added, catching at his shirt tails as he started to leap out of the bedroom door, 'you'd need to get some clothes on you and look more like somebody dacent, boyo! And don't be going anywhere till you help me change the soaking wet sheets on this bed.'

The midwife, who was also the district nurse, came promptly enough. She was still a young woman, though older than Rose by some years, and her round, happy face and plump figure told of a nature which for the most part put all worries aside and got on with things cheerfully. She radiated competence and support. Rose knew her well.

By the time she arrived, Rose had put on a clean, dry nightgown which she had kept ready for the occasion and got back into the newly changed bed. The first time she had given birth, she had been very nervous at this stage. But this was the third time, and Rose felt confident enough, though she was certainly not looking forward to it. She just hoped it would be soon over.

The first stage of the labour, which had passed so quickly for Katie's birth, seemed to stretch on and on.

John Henry had stayed home from the village school where he now worked, sorted out his two daughters, and sent Mary off to school, with a message to her teacher Miss Byrne to say that he would not be in, and to ask her to take over both classes, junior and senior, for today.

He was downstairs, keeping an eye on wee Katie and seeing that she didn't try to go upstairs and get in the way, when the nurse came down to speak to him. 'You'd best be getting the doctor round, John Henry,' she said briefly. 'I've written him a note. Will you take it round for me now? Take the child with you – I don't want her left here to get under my feet.' She didn't sound her usual cheerful, friendly self.

Suddenly John Henry was worried. 'Aye. I'll go now,' he said, taking the note. He dumped Katie into her push-chair and went.

Chapter Fifty-Nine

Doctor Miller still lived in the big white house surrounded by gardens at the other end of the village.

Like Rose, John Henry had thought that a third baby would come even more easily than the second. He tried not to panic as he hurried along the wide village street, dodging the hens scratching at the side of the road, with Katie in her push chair, praying as he went.

Presently the quick walk turned into a run. He arrived at the doctor's house out of breath and panting. A small, thin-faced maid answered the door. 'Doctor's out on his rounds,' she told John Henry in a superior voice, which he interpreted as meaning that she thought it was no concern of his.

'Can't you get hold of him?' he asked in despair.

'How would I do that, now, and him in his car and me not knowing where he may be?' she asked. But seeing his desperate expression, she softened slightly. 'Come in and you can wait for him in the surgery,' she suggested, holding the door open. 'Bring the wee girl in with you. He'll not be much longer, for he's been away over an hour already.'

'Couldn't I try to find him, if you've any idea at all which direction he went?'

'What'd be the use of that? And him in the car, don't I tell you, and heading all over the country? Just come in and be at peace for the short time it'll be. I'll make you a cup of tea,' she added, as if, John Henry thought, she expected that tea would solve all his problems.

But in fact the tea, hot and sweet and strong enough to let the spoon stand up in it, calmed him, and as he sipped, and waited for the doctor's return, John Henry went on praying silently while Katie in the push chair slept beside him.

Meanwhile the midwife was growing more and more worried. For some time now, she had been trying to encourage Rose to push. 'Come on, pet, one more try!'

But however hard Rose tried to push, there was no movement. The head was not engaged, and it wasn't any nearer to moving down than it had been hours ago.

Rose was growing more tired by the minute. Soon she would have no strength left to push any more, and then what? The nurse, who had seen the tragic outcome of other such difficult births, was near to despair although, true to her training, she took care not to let her patient see this.

If only the doctor would come!

But, she wondered silently, what could the doctor do that she couldn't do herself?

If it hadn't been for a lingering belief that all doctors could work miracles when it came to the bit, she would have been more than half inclined to answer her own question, 'Nothing.'

At last – was that someone down below opening the door?

The midwife came out to the head of the stairs, and peered over the banister.

It was very dark inside the house, but a burst of sunlight flashed in, making a bright square at the foot of the stairs, as someone pushed the door wide open.

It was John Henry and Katie back and, yes, the doctor with them.

Dr Miller trod up the flight of stairs with no undue haste. 'You stay down there, Johnny, and look after your daughter,' he said. 'You'll only be in the way if you come up.'

Then, pushing the midwife gently out of his way, he went into the bedroom where Rose lay against the pillows, her face white and her eyes closed in exhaustion. For a moment he wondered if she had already gone.

But then the eyelids fluttered, and he knew it was not yet too late.

'Boiling water, Nurse,' he said in the cheerful, brisk voice he kept for times like this. 'I'll need to sterilise this syringe. She'll be the better for an injection. Go and get me some boiling water straightaway.'

And as the midwife faded obediently from the room to fetch the kettle of water she had kept boiling beside the fire in the room below, with a basin to pour it into, Dr Miller made his way over to the bed, and began, with careful hands, to examine Rose, looking for why she could not give birth.

Down below, John Henry could get no more information out of the midwife, except a would-be cheery, 'Don't fret yourself, man, she'll be all right now the doctor's come.' To John Henry, her words held a false note that chilled him to the bone.

If he had not had Katie to look after, John Henry thought he would have gone mad over the next hour. But Katie was there, and in the middle of his prayers he was forced to watch her, keep her from the fire, even sit her on his knee and tell her a story for a while.

When Mary ran in from school, he turned the younger child over to the big sister.

'Go out and get some fresh air, the both of you,' he ordered. 'Play with your ball or your skipping rope.'

But when they had gone outside, he found himself missing the distraction of his children's need for attention. Presently, he sank down on his knees, his head in his arms, resting on the chair where he had been sitting, and stayed there quietly.

Upstairs, the doctor's injection had given Rose some relief from pain. He had examined her thoroughly, and had come to the conclusion that this was a breech presentation. The baby, instead of coming head first, was the other way round. He would need to use forceps to bring it out safely, and even so it would be a chancy business. He was glad to have the help of the sturdy, responsible midwife, with her wide experience of childbirth. She was not likely to panic and let him down.

Gradually things began to improve. He thought he could see his way at last to bringing this baby to safety, without killing the mother. The forceps were doing their job. He hadn't often had to use them before, but he seemed to have managed.

Downstairs, John Henry heard, as if from a great distance, footsteps on the stairs. He sprang to his feet.

The nurse was coming into sight round the twisty bend halfway up. She was carrying some sort of bundle in her arms. 'Aren't you the lucky man, now, John Henry?' she exclaimed, with a broad smile, as she came over to him. 'Here, you can hold him for a moment, if you like. There's another wee John in the family!'

'Thank God!' said John Henry, simply. For a moment he felt unable to move. Then he reached out his hands and took his son in his arms. 'But – Rosie?' he asked. 'How's my wife? I want to see her.'

'You can come up now,' said the nurse. 'But give me that wean first, for I wouldn't trust you to carry him back upstairs without dropping him. Rose is fine, but she'll be needing her rest, mind, so go in and speak to her, just to satisfy yourself she's all right, and then come away again, see?'

John Henry carefully handed over the baby, then went bounding up the stairs, two at a time. But when he came into the bedroom and saw his wife lying there, in the big double bed, looking so faint and pale, his joy dropped from him and he went quietly to bend down beside her. 'Rosie, Rosie, thank the Lord you're all right,' he managed to say. 'And thank you for my wee son, Rosie. But I'd rather have you, if it had come to that.'

'And so I should hope, Johnny McClintock,' Rose said, in a thread of a voice that yet was laughing at him.

'Now you've to get some sleep, Rosie,' John Henry said. 'Nurse and me'll look after the wee one.'

'Mostly Nurse, I expect,' said Rose. She smiled at him again, then her eyelids drooped shut. In another minute she was deeply asleep.

Chapter Sixty

Rose had come back almost from the brink of the grave, and when she was well enough to hear it, she learnt there would be no more children for her.

It was a blow, but not a serious one, for hadn't they got Mary and Katie, and now wee Johnny, too? He was a beautiful baby, plump and fair and always laughing. John Henry was full of joy every time he came into the house and saw him, and Rose loved him as every mother loves her newest baby. In spite, or perhaps because, of the pains she had endured to have him.

As for Mary and Katie, their noses were not put out of joint, for they were delighted to have a new baby to play with, and were the envy of all their friends.

In the evenings, after his day's work, John Henry would sit with the baby on his knee, teaching him his first words. He was younger in spirit himself than Rose had seen him since he came back from the war to find the troubles raging at home. 'What are you teaching the youngster, Johnny?' she asked him on one occasion. 'Sure, he can say "Mama" and "Dada" as right as rain already, and him only ten months!'

'"Amen!"' John Henry told her. 'I'm teaching my boy to say "Amen", Rosie.'

Rose went back into the kitchen laughing, and ten minutes later came running out in a panic at John Henry's roar. But she need not have worried. It was no calamity. 'He said it, Rosie! He said it!'

And, sure enough, the baby was making a sound that was near enough to 'Amen' to pass muster.

John Henry swung the child up into the air, and danced about the room with him. 'That's the quare, fine boyo!' he exulted. 'You'll never go far wrong, wee Johnny, if you can say, "Amen! So be it!" to the Lord's will.'

Rose couldn't help laughing at the pair of them. Wee Johnny was laughing, too, as his father swung him about.

'Will you give over, for dear sakes, and sit down here to your supper while I put the child to bed?' she exhorted him, and presently peace was restored.

Johnny continued to grow and thrive. Rose nursed him through a bad bout of chicken pox, and John Henry sat up at night with her until the worst was over. Johnny was flushed and feverish, and nothing would do for him but to have his daddy read to him aloud or, better still, sing.

John Henry sang the old gospel hymns, 'When he cometh, when he cometh, to make up his jewels,' and 'Shall we gather at the river?' and wee Johnny laughed weakly, or fell asleep smiling, his hand held tightly in his father's.

The fever left him after a few days, and soon he was struggling restlessly to get up, and to be allowed outside to play. Rose carefully followed the nurse's instructions, and kept him in bed with great difficulty until she was sure he was fully recovered. 'I'm not letting you out until I know you're well better, Johnny pet,' she told him firmly.

But in no time Johnny was running about again, his cheeks flushed with health instead of fever, and Rose smiled to herself as she worked about the house and garden and listened to him shouting gleefully with the neighbouring children. Both her girls were at school, now. It would be a couple of years before Johnny followed in their footsteps. She would miss him badly, she knew, when he went.

One of his favourite games was to chase the hens Rose reared for their eggs. He would run madly after them across the ground where they pecked and scratched for food, showing no fear of their beaks. But one day when the cockerel descended with dignity from his roosting perch and advanced towards the child, with his bright scarlet wattles hanging beneath his sharp beak, the comb on his head erect, and his voice raised threateningly, it was all too much for the little boy. Johnny balked, stood for a moment, and then backed hastily away. A moment later, he had tripped backwards over a sheet of iron John Henry had brought in to patch up the hen-house, and gashed his leg.

Rose was alarmed. Her neighbour, Molly Kelly, a plump, motherly woman who had reared a family of her own, came bustling out to see what the racket was about. Molly had had seven children, mostly now grown and gone. Her greying curly hair was tied back carelessly in a headscarf, and as she wiped her hands down the sides of the sacking apron she wore around the house, she left wide dirty streaks.

'Now then, boyo, you'll never die of that!' she said bracingly to Johnny, and to Rose she added, 'Give him a sweetie if you have such a thing about you. No? Well, I tell you what, I'll fetch him one from the wee bag I got for our Kevin, for when he comes down next to see me, with his mammy, our Martha, that's my eldest. Stitches? Not at all, Rose. It's no more than a wee scrape.'

Molly produced the sweetie (Rose was glad to see it had a wrapping to protect it from whatever might be on Molly's fingers) and Johnny cried a bit less once it was in his mouth, but Rose couldn't dismiss the long, deep cut on his leg so blithely.

She put Johnny into his pushchair, and set off to the nurse's cottage.

Nurse was in, and told Rose she had been wise to come. 'Let that get some dirt in it, and it might turn serious,' she said. 'We'll go along to the doctor's and get him to put a stitch or two in it. It's a good time to catch him, for he'll have just finished surgery.'

As they walked through the village street, with Johnny still in his pushchair sucking busily at his sweetie, Nurse told Rose, 'I'd never say a word against that Molly Kelly, for she's a woman with a good heart, but don't you listen to her, Rose, when she tells you how to bring up your youngsters. Molly's own childer mostly survived, but many's the time I was left wondering why, for she was that throughother with them. And it's my belief the two she lost would be with us to this day, if she'd called me or the doctor in sooner.'

Rose shuddered. How dreadful for Molly to lose two of her children. Rose, moving into the village less than ten years ago, on her marriage to John Henry, hadn't known any of this. She was thankful that her own three were so fit and healthy, and resolved there and then never to listen to Molly Kelly's advice, however kindly meant.

Johnny's leg needed seven stitches, and the doctor said she had been very wise in bringing the boy straight to him. If it had been left, the results might have been nasty. He was very pleasant and friendly as he swabbed the jagged cut with disinfectant, making jokes to keep Johnny distracted, for he had a soft spot for the boy whose life he had saved with such difficulty at his birth.

'That's the brave boy,' he said, when the last stitch was in, and Johnny had really cried very little, considering. And he gave Johnny another sweetie, from the bottle he kept for such occasions on the high shelf behind his desk. It was a red-letter day for Johnny. Two sweeties! Normally he didn't see such a thing, except on his birthday or at Christmas.

Rose was careful to say little about all this to John Henry, who doted on the child. He had to hear of the accident, of course, but she tried to play it down.

Johnny hobbled round for a few days with a huge bandage, of which he was very proud, but before long his leg healed and he was none the worse for it.

Chapter Sixty-One

It was just before Johnny's third birthday that scarlet fever broke out in the village. Mary and Katie brought the news home from school. Lizzie Edwards and Jackie Murphy were both off, and said to be very bad. Miss Byrne had said that school would have to be closed because of the risk of infection – 'What's that, Mammy?' – and the Nurse would be coming round to check up on all the children over the next few days.

Rose, while sorry for the Edwards and Murphy families, wasn't unduly concerned about her own three children. She had seen them all safely through various childhood diseases, by now, and didn't expect that this would be any worse. Nurse, when she came to look at the girls, was cheerful and reassuring. 'No trouble there, any road,' she said with a wide beam. 'Two healthy weans as any I've seen the day. Now, just let me have a wee skelly at the child before I go, and that'll be us all set up.'

Wee Johnny was coughing and didn't seem just his usual self. Nurse frowned when she heard him, and looked serious. Then she smiled again, and spoke heartily. 'Well, probably nothing much wrong there either. Still, put him to bed and keep him warm, Rose, and give him a spoonful of the bottle I'm going to leave you. And I'll mention to the doctor to maybe call by and have a wee look at him.'

Something cold settled on Rose's heart.

Johnny was put to bed, and began to get worse.

Rose battled in vain with her fears, and dreaded telling John Henry when he got home from the village school, which had closed early.

To her relief, he took it well, and indeed became a source of strength to her over the next days, as they nursed their son together. He was confident that Johnny would get better. 'The Lord took me safely through a war where my friends were dying all around me, Rosie, and He gave me a job I love in these days when two men out of three have to manage without any sort of one. And He gave me a son when I had almost despaired of having one, and kept you alive when I had nearly given you up. I won't stop trusting Him now, at the first thing that goes wrong. Johnny'll be all right, you just see.'

But Johnny continued to get worse.

Eventually Rose gathered up her courage to say to her husband, 'Johnny, it may be that we're not to keep him ...'

But she got no further. John Henry turned to her with a look on his face she had not seen since their first quarrel, years ago, when she had tried to persuade him not to enlist. 'Where's your faith, woman?' was all he said. Then he went out of the room, and for some time after she could hear him tramping about overhead.

Then there was silence.

John Henry had been praying as he walked about the room. Now he was sitting beside the big double bed, reading by the faint light of a candle, from the sixth chapter of Matthew.

> *Do not be anxious about your life, what you shall eat or what you shall drink, or about your body, what you shall put on. Is not life more than food, and the body more than raiment? Look at the birds of the air: they sow not, neither do they reap nor gather into barns, and yet your Heavenly Father feeds them. Are you not of more value than they? – Consider the lilies of the field, how they grow; they toil not, neither do they spin; yet Solomon in all his glory was not arrayed like one of these.*

It was a passage he had always loved, and come back to time and again. Now it brought him relief, comfort. Johnny would be looked after. He was as sure of that as he was sure of God's love for him, and of his own love for his little son.

But Johnny continued to get worse. The doctor and the nurse came often, and looked grave.

Rose knew that there was little hope.

But John Henry battled on in his stubborn refusal to be defeated. Johnny would recover. He would accept no other possibility.

Johnny lived for another week. The nurse was with him when he died, and she held Rose in her arms.

Rose felt her heart wrenched within her. She could say nothing. It was not until much later that she came to the relief of tears. But John Henry found no such relief. All he knew was that this could not be happening. How could wee Johnny be dead? He could say nothing to the nurse or even to Rose.

Instead, after one low moan that seemed to force itself from his mouth against his will, he walked out of the house. Then he began to run, he didn't know why. He knew only that he had to get away.

Chapter Sixty-Two

John Henry ran until his strength failed.

Ran until his breath came in ragged gasps, and his head was bowed, and his face was white with exhaustion.

He had no idea where he was going. He had left the village road almost at once, striking out across the fields and plunging through the small woods.

Branches whipped his face and arms, almost without his knowledge. He welcomed the pain.

He was torn and bruised and bloody before the first half-hour.

Once he fell on his knees into a wide, deep pool, a hollow recently filled with rain by the thunderstorms of the last weeks; it was surrounded by thorn bushes, with a tangle of reeds and stinging nettles at its brim. He would have stayed there if it had not been for the pain in his heart that drove him on, searching for some further, final pain that was all that could bring him relief. He yearned hopelessly for a sharp knife to cut the lump of agony out of his guts.

He rose to his feet, waded his way across the pool to its edge, and forced his way, regardless of the thorns, and the nettles, up the banks and on further into the wood.

Vague memories of the wood in which he had wandered, lost, during the battle of Passchendaele came to him. There were moments when he thought himself back there, and lived all the misery of that day over again, and the final escape from the wood, only to stumble over the almost dead body of Micky.

He had found relief there, in the end.

But the aching grief of the present returned, and he knew at once there were worse things to suffer than the deaths of his friends and comrades. So many of them. So many dead.

He began a mental roll call of the people who had died. A roll call of death.

The first to matter to him had been the young German soldier, Johan, whom he had met and become friends with on that first Christmas Day when the troops from both sides had eaten, talked and played football together. He had had nightmares about killing Johan; and although that had not happened, Johan had been killed because he had saved John Henry's life, killed by Ian Stewart while he was standing in front of John Henry smiling instead of moving on.

The next had been Mustard Colman, the corporal. John Henry hadn't liked Mustard particularly, But his death had been a shock. He was the first of the comrades John Henry had known since he signed up to die.

Then the deaths had started to come thick and fast. Pootsy, who had written the sign saying *Merry Christmas* which John Henry and Paddy had carried on Christmas Day. Ian Stewart, who had tried to rape Marie Louise, whose dark and twisted urges John Henry had come to understand a little, and who had become if not a friend then someone he spent time with and hoped to help. Marty, who dreamt of his girl Mary Ann who was back at home, and who feared that she would take up with someone else in his absence. But who nevertheless went regularly to the nearby brothel in his free time.

There had been only one survivor from John Henry's original unit apart from John Henry himself. Then that survivor had gone, too. Paddy O'Connor, the young fisherman from Ardglass who had been John Henry's first friend in the army. Paddy, who had been killed by a random shell while sleeping in John Henry's place, and whose loss had been worse than all the rest.

The list went on. There was young Geordie. Later on John Henry had found him alive and fighting with the UVF. But who knew if he had survived in the end?

Then Major Fitzpatrick who had helped John Henry in many ways and who had seemed invincible, shot during an advance.

Micky, the boy who had hidden John Henry's bible for a few days and then returned it, whom he had found dying in the muddy wastes after that same advance.

Major Warren, shot by John Henry's friend Kevin.

Kevin himself, shot by a German soldier only minutes later.

Brian Murphy, tragically shot by his own side as a traitor a month before the Armistice was signed.

Finally Wee Artie Baird, who had missed the fighting in Flanders and had been shot by the Fenian Brotherhood here at home; and who had died on John Henry's kitchen floor.

John Henry groaned aloud at the misery of it. Was it not enough?

Chapter 62

But none of these mattered to him in the same way as Johnny. To lose your friends and comrades was bad. But to lose your own son was different.

There came a time when he found himself walking along a main road. It was dark, his eyes could tell him nothing about his surroundings, but underfoot the hard surface told its own tale. He had already covered many miles, it seemed. He made his way on, along the centre of the road. In the distance he could see the headlights of a car approaching.

John Henry, oblivious to everything around him, continued to walk.

Suddenly there was a screech of brakes, and a car shrieked to a halt a few yards in front of him. Someone hurled open the driver's door and leapt out, cursing angrily. He was a young man, about John Henry's own age, but dressed in a flashy linen jacket and white trousers, with a silk scarf tied cravat fashion at the collar of his open-necked shirt. His plump face was red with rage.

'Are you mad, man? Walking along the middle of the road like that! Do you want to get killed? You came as near to it as you'll ever do, you crazy lunatic!'

John Henry shouted back at the driver. He used language he had never used before, even in his early days in the linen factory, scatological words he had heard on the lips of his companions in the army and had never thought would be on his own. He approached the driver, swinging his fists, still shouting, blaspheming. Bringing up out of his pain every curse he could think of. He stood so near that the driver could feel his hot breath, could feel the spittle hitting him on both cheeks as John Henry mouthed obscenities at him.

The man backed away, frightened for his own sake now. He made a dash for the car, got in, and drove quickly away, taking a wide breadth around John Henry that brought him over the verge of the road, and luckily onto nothing worse than rough grass and some low whin bushes.

John Henry strode on. After a while, he turned off the main road and struck out again across the open fields. The ground here was softer, easier to walk on, with grass underfoot. His outburst, which for a few moments had brought him some relief, had left him empty and very tired.

He had little or no idea where he was going. But as he walked on slowly now, he began to smell the first faint hint of the sea, and as he came nearer, the scent grew until it was almost tangible. There was the smell of seaweed, and of salt, and mixed with it an invigorating something he couldn't identify; maybe it was what they called ozone. He had covered more miles than he would have thought possible. He knew now, at least in outline, where he must be – nearly up to the lough, Strangford Lough, he thought. He didn't really care.

He came at last, still in thick, moonless darkness, to the edge of the shore.

The tide was coming in, and water lapped at his feet.

It seemed to him that it might be some relief to wade in until the waters covered him forever.

He sat on an outcrop of rock at the shore's edge, and there were no words in his mind.

The stars came out, the moon appeared, and the night grew cold, and he felt nothing.

He asked no questions, for it seemed to him there was no one to question.

And since half of his life had been built on the presence of One who occupied the universe, this emptiness overwhelmed him. The pain of his loss was swallowed now in that of a yet greater loss.

Chapter Sixty-Three

And so he sat there, and soon he found himself looking upwards, at the stars that now studded the night sky, bright and distant. They danced before his eyes, an eternal dance of beauty. Huge masses of gas, millions of miles distant. Or night-lights put there for man's pleasure, to lift his heart and thrill him with the mystery and excitement of the created universe.

John Henry had always believed that both these ideas were true. Now, in his returning anger, he hurled away the second.

What beauty could there be in these objects which reflected only an uncaring universe where pain was meaningless to anyone but the sufferer? What did the stars care about him, about what he felt? What relation had the stars to him, except as centres of scientific curiosity, in which he had little interest at the best of times, and tonight, none?

The night wore on, and John Henry sat and looked at the sea.

The moon shone on the water. He had watched it before, and always loved to see it. Now he felt no stirring of pleasure at the sight.

He could smell the fresh tang of the water, the salt and the sea-weed, more strongly now. The tide was still creeping gently in. John Henry was immune from its intrusion. He knew that it would not come further than the foot of the rock, for the seaweed clung only to the very low edges, and where he sat was free of any growth.

Further out, he watched the swirls and eddies of currents. He could identify depths and shallows, patches of rock, seaweed and sand, by the changing colours. By day these would be light green then dark, almost purple, and greeny-blue, with all the shades in between. But now they showed only as different degrees of light and darkness, moving and gleaming. Enticing him to become part of the moving ocean, the immense depths, of which this was only a fraction.

The power of the sea had always spoken to him of mystery. Of strength as yet not experienced. Of depths of love unknown, beautiful and embracing.

On this dark night it spoke only of escape. Of a body floating free, far out. Never again forced to feel such anguish. Never again hurled from the security of years. Never again compelled to realise the built in malevolence of things and events. Life had steamrollered over him, breaking and crushing him, like the huge road-making machines he had watched long ago. The machine had no concern for the stones it destroyed. Only an unthinking, uncaring ability to keep going without ever stopping along its callous route.

To escape from the machine. To hurl himself bodily into the indifferent depths. To feel nothing ever again.

That would be worth doing.

He had made no movement for so long that presently a dark shape heaved itself out of the water, with immense effort, onto the rocks where he sat, and flopped down close beside him. It was a seal.

He sat motionless, and the seal rested there quietly.

It was not quite fully grown, a young seal that had yet passed the cub stage. The moonlight gleamed on its silvery grey body, smooth as silk or leather. John Henry, fearing to move in case he frightened it away, watched it with occasional sideways glances out of the corner of his eye. It lay there so unmoving that he almost wondered if it was alive. But the breath from its nostrils touched the back of his hand lightly from time to time and reassured him.

Its body was thick and solid. There was a strong animal smell, yet there was something also which was like the smell of fish or of any sea creature. This was no seal woman from the Irish legends of his childhood, the safe time when Douglas had read the legends of Ireland to him in a children's version. Cocooned in the soft heavy warmth of his children John Henry had read the stories to his own little Mary at bedtime, she leaning on him while Katie, half asleep, pressed in against his other side. He had been happy then.

John Henry watched the seal for a long time. He could not remember having been so close to any wild creature before. He wished he could reach out and touch its soft slippery coat but he knew that at the slightest movement of his hand, the seal would be gone. Instead, he remained still, and the seal stayed beside him for what seemed a long time.

Then it slid from the rock back into the deep water.

At last the sky began to change. Streaks of light crept in, pink and pale yellow and white, slowly at first, then spreading ever wider.

John Henry stirred. He was stiff and sore.

Chapter Sixty-Four

All round him came the faint sounds of a new day.

First one, then another, the birds awoke, lifted up their voices, tried out their first cautious notes.

The first he heard was a blackbird, a jet black male with a bright yellow beak, his sweet cry sounding like the clear notes of a flute. Then came a chaffinch, with the two irregular notes that gave him his name – 'chiff-chaff.' Hidden somewhere, perhaps in one of the low bushes set not too far back from the shoreline, a tiny wren, his voice too loud for his size, sang his long, excited verse, interspersed with occasional trills and metallic ringing tones.

Then the dawn chorus broke out on all sides.

The speckled thrush repeated his loud, sweet musical phrases. The robin gave out a rich, cheerful note in keeping with the warmth of the new season. The starling, his black back shot with purple and green light, joined in chattering and whistling.

John Henry knew them all. He lifted his head to listen.

Something pulled at his heart.

He remembered listening to the birdsong with Rose early one morning when they were first married.

He felt a sharp pressure, as if his heart was about to burst, and he cried aloud, 'Why? Why?'

Then he buried his face in his hands, and wept as he had not wept since childhood, even in the now far-off days when he had lived through the sufferings of war. And as he cried out, and throughout his weeping, he knew at last that there was someone to question. As he wept, he heard a voice speaking to him, inside his own head; and it seemed that there was help and comfort in the words. 'My son died, too, Johnny. I share your pain.'

Listening, he felt again the Presence, the peace, which had been the most important things in his life until he had lost them both that night.

He lifted his head and continued to listen.

Presently John Henry stood up. It was time, now, for him to set off, to walk the many miles back.

The glow of dawn lit the road and the fields and bushes around him with a numinous light. As he walked, words came to him from a poem read long ago.

> *Earth's crammed with heaven,*
> *And every common bush afire with God.*
> *But only those who see take off their shoes.*

John Henry still had nothing to say. But now it was not because of the numbing pain that had held him throughout the night, but because there was no longer any need of words.

He walked through fields where the young barley sprouted green and silken around him, keeping, now, to the paths made round the edges by other travellers. He walked beside hedges thick with creamy white hawthorn blossom, past low banks where purple vetch grew alongside bright yellow dandelions and white puffs of cow parsley.

He saw clover, white and mauve, a faint speckling of the pale blue flowers he knew as cats' eyes, and the occasional tall red poppy, so rare in his home county, though so common in the Flanders fields that their colour, the colour of blood, had made them an emblem of bloody death. He passed hedges where pink and white columbine, the lesser and the greater, grew in wild profusion, new blossoms every morning replacing those of yesterday, which were dead by nightfall.

Before he had been walking for long, his feet and ankles were damp with the morning dew on the grass which sprang up on the edges of the paths. Each separate drop reflected brightness, as the sun began to move slowly up the sky.

He smelt the creamy vanilla of the great masses of whin bush, covered in their yellow blossoms. He bent from time to time to sniff an early wild rose for its perfect scent. He could still hear birdsong. It was separated now from the joyful chorus of early dawn and dispersed into the individual notes which he heard from one or other of the birds flying or nesting around him. And as he opened his ears to listen he could pick up the chirp of the cricket and the murmur of the bees visiting flowers. Sometimes he would slow down, to see or smell or touch some element of the world he was walking through. But mostly he walked as quickly as he could, for he had a long journey to complete.

As he came nearer to his home he heard a lark soaring into the blue, its song sweet and growing sweeter as it almost vanished into the heights. He stopped for a moment and his mind went back to the first year of the war, when he had been rescued by the song of a lark from the despair that had weighed on him in the mud and ugliness all round him. Rose had always loved lark song. He wished that he had not left her to suffer alone.

He was very tired, but that was not the feeling uppermost in his mind.

He came at last, staggering with exhaustion, to his own village street, and walked slowly along it in the direction of his house. As he came within sight of it, a figure emerged, unidentifiable from this distance except for the familiar faded blue dress with the rough white apron.

The sun came up in its full strength, and he could see now, clearly, what he had already been sure of, that the distant figure was Rose, coming in search of the husband who had been gone all night.

As he came nearer, and she in her turn became sure that it was him, she began to run.

John Henry stood where he was, but as she reached his side he stretched his arms out and held her to him.

For many minutes they stood, fastened together by something more than the strength of John Henry's arms.

And as they stood there together, he knew that, although his pain was still heavy, the peace he felt was also real.

John Henry smiled down at his wife. 'Let's go on home, Rosie,' he said. 'I could do with a cup of tea.'

About the author

Gerry McCullough has been writing poems and stories since childhood. Brought up in north Belfast, she graduated in English and Philo-sophy from Queen's University, Belfast, then went on to gain an MA in English.

She lives just outside Belfast, in Northern Ireland, has four grown up children and is married to author, media producer and broadcaster, Raymond McCullough, with whom she co-edited the Irish magazine, *Bread*, (published by *Kingdom Come Trust*), from 1990-96. In 1995 they published a non-fiction book called, *Ireland – now the good news!*

Over the past few years Gerry has had more than sixty short stories published in UK, Irish and American magazines, anthologies and annuals – as well as broadcast on *BBC Radio Ulster* – plus poems and articles published in several Northern Ireland and UK magazines. She has read from her novels, poems and short stories at several Irish literary events.

Gerry won the *Cúirt International Literary Award* for 2005 (Galway); was shortlisted for the 2008 *Brian Moore Award* (Belfast); shortlisted for the 2009 *Cúirt Award*; and commended in the 2009 *Seán O'Faolain Short Story Competition*, (Cork).

Belfast Girls, her first full-length Irish novel, was first published (by *Night Publishing*, UK) in November 2010 (re-issued July 2012 by *Precious Oil*). *Danger Danger* was published by *Precious Oil Publications* in October 2011; followed by *The Seanachie: Tales of Old Seamus* in January 2012 (a first collection of humorous Irish short stories, previously published in a weekly Irish magazine); *Angel in Flight* (the first Angel Murphy thriller) in June 2012; *Lady Molly and the Snapper –* a young adult novel time travel adventure set in Dublin (August 2012) and *Angel in Belfast* (the 2nd Angel Murphy thriller) in June 2013.

The *Cúirt Award*-winning story, *Primroses*, and the *Seán O'Faolain* commended story, *Giving Up*, will be included in *Dreams, Visions, Nightmares* – a new collection of twelve Irish short stories written by Gerry, to be published shortly. Also in the pipeline are another *Seamus* collection and *Not the End of the World* – a humorous, futuristic, adult fantasy novel.

Belfast Girls

The story of three girls – Sheila, Phil and Mary – growing up into the new emerging post-conflict Belfast of money, drugs, high fashion and crime; and of their lives and loves.

Sheila, a supermodel, is kidnapped.

Phil is sent to prison.

Mary, surviving a drug overdose, has a spiritual awakening.

It is also the story of the men who matter to them –

John Branagh, former candidate for the priesthood, a modern Darcy, someone to love or hate. Will he and Sheila ever get together?

Davy Hagan, drug dealer, 'mad, bad and dangerous to know'. Is Phil also mad to have anything to do with him?

Although from different religious backgrounds, starting off as childhood friends, the girls manage to hold on to that friendship in spite of everything.

A book about contemporary Ireland and modern life. A book which both men and women can enjoy – thriller, romance, comedy, drama – and much more …

"fascinating … original … multilayered … expertly travels from one genre to the next"
Kellie Chambers, Ulster Tatler (*Book of the Month*)

"romance at the core … enriched with breathtaking action, mystery, suspense and some tear-jerking moments of tragedy.
Sheila M. Belshaw, author

"What starts out as a crime thriller quickly evolves into a literary festival beyond the boundary of genres"
PD Allen, author

"a masterclass, and a vivid dissection of the human condition in all of its inglorious foibles"
WeeScottishLassie

Belfast
Girls

Gerry McCullough

Published by

Chapter One

Jan 21, 2007

The street lights of Belfast glistened on the dark pavements where, even now, with the troubles officially over, few people cared to walk alone at night. John Branagh drove slowly, carefully, through the icy streets.

In the distance, he could see the lights of the *Magnifico Hotel*, a bright contrasting centre of noise, warmth and colour.

He felt again the excitement of the news he'd heard today.

Hey, he'd actually made the grade at last – full-time reporter for BBC TV, right there on the local news programme, not just a trainee, any longer. Unbelievable.

The back end shifted a little as he turned a corner. He gripped the wheel tighter and slowed down even more. There was black ice on the roads tonight. Gotta be careful.

So, he needed to work hard, show them he was keen. This interview, now, in this hotel? This guy Speers? If it turned out good enough, maybe he could go back to Fat Barney and twist his arm, get him to commission it for local TV, the Hearts and Minds programme maybe? Or even – he let his ambition soar – go national? Or how's about one of those specials everybody seemed to be into right now?

There were other thoughts in his mind but as usual he pushed them down out of sight. Sheila Doherty would be somewhere in the hotel tonight, but he had plenty of other stuff to think about to steer his attention away from past unhappiness. No need to focus on anything right now but his career and its hopeful prospects.

Montgomery Speers, better get the name right, new Member of the Legislative Assembly, wanted to give his personal views on the peace process and how it was working out. Yeah. Wanted some publicity, more like. Anti, of course, or who'd care? But that was just how people were.

John curled his lip. He had to follow it up. It could give his career the kick start it needed.

But he didn't have to like it.

* * *

Inside the *Magnifico Hotel*, in the centre of newly regenerated Belfast, all was bustle and chatter, especially in the crowded space behind the catwalk. The familiar fashion show smell, a mixture of cosmetics and hair dryers, was overwhelming.

Sheila Doherty sat before her mirror, and felt a cold wave of unhappiness surge over her. How ironic it was, that title the papers gave her, today's most super supermodel. She closed her eyes and put her hands to her ears, trying to shut everything out for just one snatched moment of peace and silence.

Every now and then it came again. The pain. The despair. A face hovered before her mind's eye, the white, angry face of John Branagh, dark hair falling forward over his furious grey eyes. She deliberately blocked the thought, opening her eyes again. She needed to slip on the mask, get ready to continue on the surface of things where her life was perfect.

"Comb that curl over more to the side, will you, Chrissie?" she asked, "so it shows in front of my ear. Yeah, that's right – if you just spray it there – thanks, pet."

The hairdresser obediently fixed the curl in place. Sheila's long red-gold hair gleamed in the reflection of three mirrors positioned to show every angle. Everything had to be perfect – as perfect as her life was supposed to be. The occasion was too important to allow for mistakes.

Her fine-boned face with its clear translucent skin, like ivory, and crowned with the startling contrast of her hair, looked back at her from the mirror, green eyes shining between thick black lashes – black only because of the mascara.

She examined herself critically, considering her appearance as if it were an artefact which had to be without flaw to pass a test.

She stood up.

"Brilliant, pet," she said. "Now the dress."

The woman held out the dress for Sheila to step into, then carefully pulled the ivory satin shape up around the slim body and zipped it at the back. The dress flowed round her, taking and emphasising her long fluid lines, her body slight and fragile as a daydream. She walked over to the door, ready to emerge onto the catwalk. She was very aware that this was the most important moment of one of the major fashion shows of her year.

The lights in the body of the hall were dimmed, those focussed on the catwalk went up, and music cut loudly through the sudden silence. Francis Delmara stepped forward and began to introduce his new spring line.

For Sheila, ready now for some minutes and waiting just out of sight, the tension revealed itself as a creeping feeling along her spine. She felt suddenly cold and her stomach fluttered.

It was time and, dead on cue, she stepped lightly out onto the catwalk and stood holding the pose for a long five seconds, as

Chapter 1

instructed, before swirling forward to allow possible buyers a fuller view.

She was greeted by gasps of admiration, then a burst of applause. Ignoring the reaction, she kept her head held high, her face calm and remote, as far above human passion as some elusive, intangible figure of Celtic myth, a Sidhe, a dweller in the hollow hills, distant beyond man's possessing – just as Delmara had taught her.

This was her own individual style, the style which had earned her the nickname 'Ice Maiden' from the American journalist Harrington Smith. She moved forward along the catwalk, turned this way and that, and finally swept a low curtsey to the audience before standing there, poised and motionless.

Delmara was silent at first to allow the sight of Sheila in one of his most beautiful creations its maximum impact. Then he began to draw attention to the various details of the dress.

It was time for Sheila to withdraw. Once out of sight, she began a swift, organised change to her next outfit, while Delmara's other models were in front.

No time yet for her to relax, but the show seemed set for success.

* * *

MLA, Montgomery Speers, sitting in the first row of seats, the celebrity seats, with his latest blonde girlfriend by his side, allowed himself to feel relieved.

Francis Delmara had persuaded him to put money into Delmara Fashions and particularly into financing Delmara's supermodel, Sheila Doherty, and he was present tonight in order to see for himself if his investment was safe. He thought, even so early in the show, that it was.

He was a broad shouldered man in his early forties, medium height, medium build, red-cheeked, and running slightly to fat. There was nothing particularly striking about his appearance except for the piercing dark eyes set beneath heavy, jutting eyebrows. His impressive presence stemmed from his personality, from the aura of power and aggression which surrounded him.

A businessman first and foremost, he had flirted with political involvement for several years. He had stood successfully for election to the local council, feeling the water cautiously with one toe while he made up his mind. Would he take the plunge and throw himself whole-heartedly into politics?

The new Assembly gave him his opportunity, if he wanted to take it. More than one of the constituencies offered him the chance to stand for a seat. He was a financial power in several different towns where his computer hardware companies provided much needed jobs. He was elected to the seat of his choice with no trouble. The next move was to build up his profile, grab an important post once things got going, and progress up the hierarchy.

In an hour or so, when the Fashion Show was over, he would meet this young TV reporter for some preliminary discussion of a possible interview or of an appearance on a discussion panel. He was slightly annoyed that someone so junior had been lined up to talk to him. John Branagh, that was the name, wasn't it? Never heard of him. Should have been someone better known, at least. Still, this was only the preliminary. They would roll out the big guns for him soon enough when he was more firmly established. Meanwhile his thoughts lingered on the beautiful Sheila Doherty.

If he wanted her, he could buy her, he was sure. And more and more as he watched her, he knew that, yes, he wanted her.

* * *

A fifteen minute break, while the audience drank the free wine and ate the free canapés. Behind the scenes again, Sheila checked hair and makeup. A small mascara smear needed to be removed, a touch more blusher applied. In a few minutes she was ready but something held her back.

She stared at herself in the mirror and saw a cool, beautiful woman, the epitome of poise and grace. She knew that famous, rich, important men over two continents would give all their wealth and status to possess her, or so they said. She was an icon according to the papers. That meant, surely, something unreal, something artificial, painted or made of stone.

And what was the good? There was only one man she wanted. John Branagh. And he'd pushed her away. He believed she was a whore – a tart – someone not worth touching. What did she do to deserve that?

It wasn't fair! she told herself passionately. He went by rules that were medieval. No-one nowadays thought the odd kiss mattered that much. Oh, she was wrong. She'd hurt him, she knew she had. But if he'd given her half a chance, she'd have apologised – told him how sorry she was. Instead of that, he'd called her such names – how could she still love him after that? But she knew she did.

How did she get to this place, she wondered, the dream of romantic fiction, the dream of so many girls, a place she hated now, where men thought of her more and more as a thing, an object to be desired, not a person? When did her life go so badly wrong? She thought back to her childhood, to the skinny, ginger-haired girl she once was. Okay, she hated how she looked but otherwise, surely, she was happy. Or was that only a false memory?

"Sheila - where are you?"

Chapter 1

The hairdresser poked her head round the door and saw Sheila with every sign of relief.

"Thank goodness! Come on, love, only got a couple of minutes! Delmara says I've to check your hair. Wants it tied back for this one."

* * *

The evening was almost at its climax. The show began with evening dress, and now it was to end with evening dress – but this time with Delmara's most beautiful and exotic lines. Sheila stood up and shook out her frock, a cloud of short ice-blue chiffon, sewn with glittering silver beads and feathers. She and Chrissie between them swept up her hair, allowing a few loose curls to hang down her back and one side of her face, fixed it swiftly into place with two combs, and clipped on more silver feathers.

She fastened on long white earrings with a pearly sheen and slipped her feet into the stiletto heeled silver shoes left ready and waiting. She moved over to the doorway for her cue. There was no time to think or to feel the usual butterflies. Chloe came off and she counted to three and went on.

There was an immediate burst of applause.

To the loud music of Snow Patrol, Sheila half floated, half danced along the catwalk, her arms raised ballerina fashion. When she had given sufficient time to allow the audience their fill of gasps and appreciation, she moved back and April and Chloe appeared in frocks with a similar effect of chiffon and feathers, but with differences in style and colour. It was Delmara's spring look for evening wear and she could tell at once that the audience loved it.

The three girls danced and circled each other, striking dramatic poses as the music died down sufficiently to allow Delmara to comment on the different features of the frocks.

With one part of her mind Sheila was aware of the audience, warm and relaxed now, full of good food and drink, their minds absorbed in beauty and fashion, ready to spend a lot of money. Dimly in the background she heard the sounds of voices shouting and feet running.

The door to the ballroom burst open.

People began to scream.

It was something Sheila had heard about for years now, the subject of local black humour, but had never before seen.

Three figures, black tights pulled over flattened faces as masks, uniformly terrifying in black leather jackets and jeans, surged into the room.

The three sub-machine guns cradled in their arms sent deafening bursts of gunfire upwards. Falling plaster dust and stifling clouds of gun smoke filled the air.

For one long second they stood just inside the entrance way, crouched over their weapons, looking round. One of them stepped forward and grabbed Montgomery Speers by the arm.

"Move it, mister!" he said. He dragged Speers forcefully to one side, the weapon poking him hard in the chest.

A second man gestured roughly with his gun in the general direction of Sheila.

"You!" he said harshly. "Yes, you with the red hair! Get over here!"

Chapter Two

1993

There were so many things about her life that Sheila Doherty hated, especially her appearance, her skinniness and her hair, which was a very bright red. She was eight, and just beginning to notice boys. She knew how important it was that other people should think she looked good, and how impossible. How awful it was to be called 'Ginger', to be considered too tall, too thin, too ugly. She hated being called after in the streets, and in the school playground.

When church, Sunday dinner and Sunday school were over, Sheila wandered out into the back garden. Boredom attacked her.

The back garden was not very large and there was nothing much to do there. There was a square of grass, a border bright with flowers in spring and summer, but mostly brown or green on this dull October afternoon, and an empty rabbit hutch against the far wall.

Sheila could vaguely remember the rabbit, a furry, cuddly focus of love a few years ago when she was five or six, and her short but violent grief at his unexplained death from some unidentified rabbit disease.

She mooched over the grass, kicking aimlessly at the few still remaining fallen leaves, and leaned against the wizened old apple tree in the corner near the hutch. Although she was not to leave the garden or go out into the street by herself, it was good for her to be out in the fresh air, her mother said. It might give her a bit more colour.

Sheila's pale skin and red hair, from her father Frank's side of the family, were a source of constant irritation to both Sheila and her mother Kathy. Both would have preferred almost any other combination, but particularly the dark hair and blue eyes for which Kathy had been so widely admired in her youth – as she often told Sheila with some complacency.

Sheila kicked a few more leaves and wished something would happen. If only she had a sister, or even a brother. It would be fun to have someone to play with.

Suddenly a large ball thudded at her feet.

Sheila jumped and said, "Sugar!" Then she blushed, for she didn't often use what Kathy would call bad language. She picked up the ball and stood with it in her hands, looking cautiously around.

It seemed to have come over the wall which ran between her family's garden and the house next door.

She watched. Two hands were gripping hard on the top of the wall. Then a head rose slowly above the edge.

Black curly hair, blue eyes wide open in inquiry, a mouth which broke into a friendly grin as its owner saw Sheila.

"Hi. Can I come and get my ball?"

Sheila nodded silently.

The girl scrambled over the wall, leaving muddy smears on her light blue jeans as she did so. She advanced on Sheila and took the ball which Sheila held out to her.

"What's your name?"

"Sheila. What's yours?"

"Philomena Mary Maguire, but I get called Phil."

They looked at each other steadily for a moment. Then Phil again took the initiative.

"We've come to live next door, here. We moved in yesterday. Is this your house?"

"Yes."

"What's it like, here? Mammy said it would be fun to have a garden. Is it? Do you like it?"

Sheila had never thought about it. She had always had a garden. Didn't everybody?

"Let's play with your football," she said.

"Okay." Phil looked back. Another head had risen above the wall. Brown hair, not as dark as Phil's, grey eyes, a round freckled face with a friendly grin.

"This is my brother Gerry," said Phil. "Can he come over, too?"

"Yes, g-great!" stammered Sheila.

A moment later, Gerry, who was obviously a year or so older than Phil but still small for his age, had scrambled over the wall and given the football a vigorous kick, only just missing Kathy's favourite rosebush. Sheila giggled. This was going to be fun.

They played happily together for the rest of the afternoon. Phil and Gerry were inclined to take the lead and to suggest new games.

Sheila didn't mind. It was interesting. Phil was fascinated by the rabbit hutch and the apple tree. She made Sheila see the back garden with new eyes, as an exciting place of endless possibilities.

"We could make a swing from the tree if we had some rope," Gerry suggested enthusiastically. "We could use the clothes line."

"I don't think my mammy would let me –" Sheila began.

But he had already pulled down the line and was starting to tie it to the tree. So Sheila and Phil joined in and helped him. It was great.

Chapter 2

The afternoon whizzed by, and there was Sheila's mother, woken up from her Sunday afternoon nap, calling Sheila already for her tea.

"I won't be allowed out after tea," Sheila said. "It'll be too dark. Maybe I'll see you at school tomorrow?"

"St Columba's, mine's called," said Phil. "I won't know anybody yet, so it'd be nice if you were there."

Sheila was disappointed. "I go to Alexander Primary, so I won't see you. But we could play after school?" she suggested hopefully.

"Okay," said Phil. "See you, then."

She and Gerry scrambled back over the wall and Sheila went in. St Columba's was the nearby Catholic primary school, she knew. Alexander Primary was Protestant. She thought maybe she wouldn't mention her new friends to her mother, just yet, though Kathy would have to know sometime that the new neighbours were Catholic.

From then on Sheila and Phil were inseparable.

Gerry was a good friend too, but he had his own mates to hang around with usually and, as they all got older, it was only occasionally that he would join in with Phil and Sheila's games. After all, they were only girls.

It was Phil who stood up for Sheila now when people called her 'Ginger,' or 'Carrots', and made fun of her.

"You leave her alone or I'll twist your elephant ears off!" she ordered Chrissie Murphy when she tried to pull Sheila's hair.

And, "Leave off my mate or I'll get my big brother to give you such a hidin'!" when Sandy Bell was teasing Sheila more than usual.

Occasionally Sheila would turn to Gerry to help her and the 'big brother' would soon deal with any persistent trouble makers, going so far as to punch big Geordie Patterson in the eye on one memorable occasion.

When they moved on to secondary school, although they were still separated during the school day, their friendship remained strong.

It was against all the rules, they knew, vaguely, for a Catholic and a Protestant to be best friends but, thought Sheila and Phil, who cared?

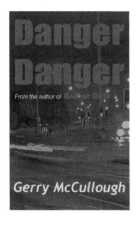

Danger Danger

Two lives in parallel – twin sisters separated at birth, but their lives take strangely similar and dangerous roads until the final collision which hurls each of them to the edge of disaster.

Katie and her gambling boyfriend Dec find themselves threatened with peril from the people Dec has cheated.

Jo-Anne (Annie) through her boyfriend Steven finds herself in the hands of much more dangerous crooks.

Can they survive and achieve safety and happiness?

"starts with a bang and never quite lets up on the tension ... it will hook you from the beginning and keep you spell bound until the very last sentence."
Ellen Fritz, Books 4 Tomorrow

"The emotional intensity of the characters is beautifully drawn ...
You care for these people."
Stacey Danson, *author*

an amazing, page turning, stunning novel ... equal to Belfast Girls *in every respect. I can't wait for her next novel to be published.*
Teresa Geering, *author*

an attention-grabbing plot, strong writing, and vivid characterization,
... fast-paced and highly addictive
L. Anne Carrington, *author*

Angel in Flight:

the first Angel Murphy thriller

Gerry McCullough

Is it a bird? Is it a plane? No, it's a low-flying Angel!

You've heard of Lara Croft. You've heard of Modesty Blaise. Well, here comes Angel Murphy!

Angel, a *'feisty wee Belfast girl'* on holiday in Greece, sorts out a villain who wants to make millions for his pharmaceutical company by preventing the use of a newly discovered malaria vaccine.

Angel has a broken marriage behind her and is wary of men, but perhaps her meeting with Josh Smith, who tells her he's with Interpol, may change her mind?

Fun, action, thrills, romance in a beautiful setting – so much to enjoy!

"it's a fast-paced read, ... exciting, and you can not put this book down"

Thomas Baker, Santiago, Chile

"I could not stop reading! ... a gripping thriller from beginning to the end"
SanMarie Lamprecht

"a fast-paced, exciting read. From the moment I read the first line, I was hooked"

Cheryl Bradshaw, author, Wyoming, USA

"a sassy bigger then life heroine in an action packed adventure thriller in Greece"

Book Review Buzz

Angel in Belfast:

the 2nd Angel Murphy thriller

Gerry McCullough

Angel Murphy is back, in true kick boxing form!

Alone in his cottage near a remote Irish village, Fitz, lead singer of the popular band *Raving*, hears the cries of the paparazzi outside and likens them in his own mind to wolves in a feeding frenzy. Next morning Fitz is found unconscious, seeming unlikely to survive, and is rushed to hospital. Has he been driven to OD? Or is someone else behind this?

His friends call in Angeline Murphy, 'Angel to her friends, devil to her enemies,' to find out the truth. But it takes all Angel's courage and skills to survive the many dangers she faces and to discover the real villain and deal with him.

"brings the city and its people ... to life with evocative description and scintillating dialogue"

Elinor Carlisle, Berkshire,UK

"I could not stop reading! ... a gripping thriller from beginning to the end"
SanMarie Lamprecht

"makes the troubled city of Belfast vibrant and appealing"

P A Lanstone, UK

"I felt like I had been transported to Belfast's often tough, gritty streets"
Bobbi Lerman, USA

"love the fact that we are reintroduced to characters from Belfast Girls"
Michele Young, UK

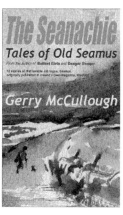

The Seanachie:
Tales of Old Seamus

Gerry McCullough

A humorous series of Irish stories, set in the fictional Donegal village of Ardnakil and featuring that lovable rogue, *'Old Seamus'* – the Séanachie.

All of these stories have previously been published in the popular Irish weekly magazine, *Ireland's Own*, based in Wexford, Ireland.

"heart warming tales ... beautifully told with subtle Irish humour"

Babs Morton (author)

"an irresistible old rogue, but he's the kind people love to sit and listen to for hours on end whenever the opportunity presents itself"

G. Polley (author and blogger – Sapporo, Japan)

"This magnificent storyteller has done it again. Each individual story has it's own Gaelic charm"

Teresa Geering (author – UK)

"evocative characterisation brings these stories to life in a delightful, absorbing way"

Elinor Carlisle (author – Reading, UK)

Lady Molly & The Snapper

**A young adult time travel adventure,
set in Ireland and on the high seas**

Gerry McCullough

Brother and sister Jik and Nora are bored and angry. Why does their Dad spend so much time since their mother's death drinking and ignoring them? Why must he come home at all hours and fall downstairs like a fool?

Nora goes to church and lights a candle. The cross-looking sailor saint she particularly likes seems to grow enormous and come to life. Nora is too frightened to stay.

Nora and Jik go down secretly to their father's boat, the *Lady Molly*, at Howth Marina. There they meet The Snapper, the same cross-looking saint in a sailor's cap, who takes them back in time on the yacht, *Lady Molly,* to meet Cuchulain, the legendary Irish warrior, and others.

Jik and Nora plan to use their travels to find some way of stopping their father from drinking – but it's fun, too! Or is it? When they meet the Druid priest who follows them into modern times, teams up with school bully Marty Flanagan, and threatens them, things start getting out of hand.

Meanwhile, Nora is more than interested in Sean, the boy they keep bumping into in the past ...

Other (non-fiction) books from

A Wee Taste a' Craic:

All the Irish craic from the popular
***Celtic Roots Radio** shows, 2-25*

Raymond McCullough

*I absolutely loved this! I found it to be very informative
about Irish life culture, language and traditions.*
Elinor Carlisle (author, Reading, UK)

*a unique insight into the Northern Irish people
& their self deprecating sense of humour*
Strawberry

Ireland – now the **good** news!

The best of *'Bread'* Vols. 1 & 2 –

personal testimonies and church/fellowship
profiles from around Ireland

Edited by: Raymond & Gerry McCullough

"...fresh Bread – deals with the real issues facing the church in Ireland today"
Ken Newell, minister of Fitzroy Presbyterian Church, Belfast

The Whore and her Mother:

9/11, Babylon and the Return of the King

Raymond McCullough

Could the writings of the ancient Hebrew prophets be relevant to events taking place in the world today?

These Hebrew prophets – Isaiah, Jeremiah, Habbakuk and the apostle John, in *The Revelation* – wrote extensively about a latter day city and empire which would dominate, exploit and corrupt all the nations of the world. They referred to it as Babylon the Great, or Mega-Babylon, and they foretold that its fall – 'in one day' – would devastate the economies of the whole world. Have these prophecies been fulfilled already?

Is Mega-Babylon the Roman Catholic Church?
A world super-church?
Rebuilt ancient Babylon?
Brussels, Jerusalem, or somewhere entirely different?
Should this city/nation have a large Jewish population?
Why all the talk about merchants, cargoes, commodities, trade?

Can we rely on the words of these ancient prophets?
If so, what else did they foretell that is still to be fulfilled?
Do they refer to other major nations – USA, Russia, China, Europe?
What about militant Islam?

"AMAZED when I read this book ... in awe of your extensive knowledge on so many levels: Christian, Jewish, and Muslim culture; the Jewish diaspora ... Greek & Hebrew; ... thought-provoking and troublesome ... many will be offended, but you consistently build your case instead of being sensationalistic."
James Revoir, author of *Priceless Stones*

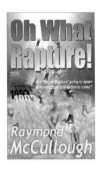

Oh What Rapture!

Is a *'Secret Rapture'* going to spare believers from the tribulation to come?

Raymond McCullough

Many are convinced that very soon an event known as *'The Rapture'* will take place, where bible believers all over the world will suddenly disappear, leaving society at a loss to explain the disappearance of so many. Many non-fiction books, fiction thrillers and movies have capitalised on this theme, earning a fat revenue for their authors/producers.

But is this really what the bible teaches?
Is *'The Rapture'* genuine, or a false hope?
Are those who trust in it being duped, so that they do not get ready for what is coming?
And are they being disobedient to the clear command of the Lord?

Written by the author of Amazon best-selling book, *The Whore and her Mother*, also on the topic of bible prophecy, this volume focusses on the false teaching of a *'secret and separate Rapture'* – an event which is NOT supported by scripture!

This book investigates the scriptures used to back up the *'secret Rapture'* theory and clearly compares them to the other scriptures concerning the return of the Messiah, Jesus (Yeshua). The evident truth is revealed and the origins of the false *'secret Rapture'* doctrine are exposed.

Believers around the world are taught to expect persecution, sometimes even death, for their faith. More have been killed in the past century than in previous centuries combined – in China, Cambodia, Nigeria, Iran, Egypt, Indonesia, Vietnam, etc. Yet many believers in the west confidently expect to avoid any persecution and be *'beamed up'* out of any coming tribulation!

If you thought believers were soon going to be lifted out of a worsening world situation, be prepared to meet the exciting challenge of scripture head on!

Made in the USA
Charleston, SC
23 August 2014